SHORT STORY COLLECTIONS

Beyond the Great Snow Mountains

Bowdrie

Bowdrie's Law

Buckskin Run

The Collected Short Stories of
Louis L'Amour (vols. 1–7)

Dutchman's Flat

End of the Drive

From the Listening Hills

The Hills of Homicide

Law of the Desert Born

Long Ride Home

Lonigan

May There Be a Road

Monument Rock

Night over the Solomons

Off the Mangrove Coast

The Outlaws of Mesquite

The Rider of the Ruby Hills

Riding for the Brand

The Strong Shall Live

The Trail to Crazy Man

Valley of the Sun

War Party

West from Singapore

West of Dodge

With These Hands

Yondering

SACKETT TITLES

Sackett's Land

To the Far Blue Mountains

The Warrior's Path

Jubal Sackett

Ride the River

The Daybreakers

Sackett

Lando

Mojave Crossing

Mustang Man

The Lonely Men

Galloway

Treasure Mountain

Lonely on the Mountain

Ride the Dark Trail

The Sackett Brand

The Sky-Liners

THE HOPALONG CASSIDY NOVELS

The Riders of High Rock

The Rustlers of West Fork

The Trail to Seven Pines

Trouble Shooter

NONFICTION

Education of a Wandering Man

Frontier

The Sackett Companion: A Personal
Guide to the Sackett Novels

A Trail of Memories: The Quotations
of Louis L'Amour, compiled
by Angelique L'Amour

POETRY

Smoke from This Altar

LOST TREASURES

Louis L'Amour's Lost Treasures:
Volume 1 (with Beau L'Amour)

No Traveller Returns (with
Beau L'Amour)

NO
TRAVELLER
RETURNS

NO TRAVELLER RETURNS

A Novel

Louis L'Amour
and
Beau L'Amour

BANTAM BOOKS

New York

Published in the United States by Bantam Books, an imprint of Random House, a division of Penguin Random House LLC, New York.

BANTAM BOOKS and the HOUSE colophon are registered trademarks of Penguin Random House LLC.

LIBRARY OF CONGRESS CATALOGING-IN-PUBLICATION DATA
Names: L'Amour, Louis, 1908–1988, author. | L'Amour, Beau, contributor.
Title: No traveller returns : a novel / Louis L'Amour with Beau L'Amour.
Description: First edition. | New York : Bantam Books, [2018] |
Series: Louis L'Amour's lost treasures
Identifiers: LCCN 2018018973 (print) | LCCN 2018019262 (ebook) |
ISBN 9780425284902 (Ebook) | ISBN 9780425284445 (hardback : acid-free paper)
Subjects: LCSH: World War, 1939–1945—Naval operations, American—Fiction. |
World War, 1939–1945—Campaigns--Pacific Area—Fiction. | Sea stories. |
Historical fiction. | BISAC: FICTION / Action & Adventure. |
FICTION / Sea Stories. | FICTION / Historical.
Classification: LCC PS3523.A446 (ebook) | LCC PS3523.A446 N6 2018 (print) |
DDC 813/.52—dc23
LC record available at https://lccn.loc.gov/2018018973

Printed in the United States of America on acid-free paper

randomhousebooks.com

2 4 6 8 9 7 5 3 1

First Edition

Book design by Caroline Cunningham

Tanker silhouette illustration by David Lindroth Inc.

For my father . . . finally.

Fate is a ship. A steel gray lovely barque—

or a tanker, westbound.

Lichenfield

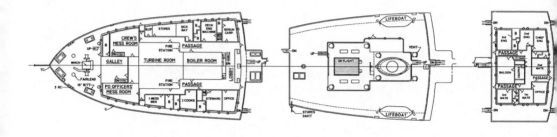

POOP DECK

BOAT DECK

BRIDGE
DECK

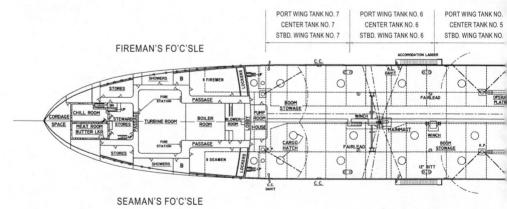

PORT WING TANK NO. 7	PORT WING TANK NO. 6	PORT WING TANK NO.
CENTER TANK NO. 7	CENTER TANK NO. 6	CENTER TANK NO. 5
STBD. WING TANK NO. 7	STBD. WING TANK NO. 6	STBD. WING TANK NO.

FIREMAN'S FO'C'SLE

SEAMAN'S FO'C'SLE

UPPER DECK

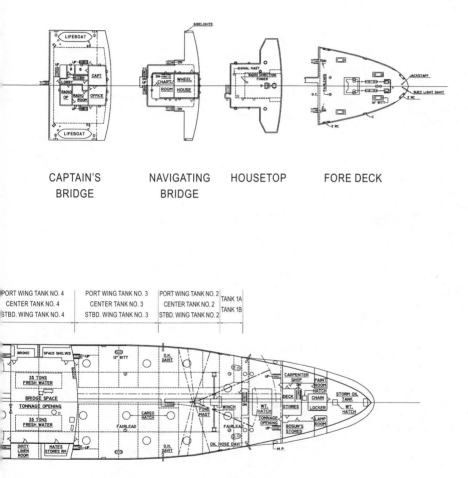

CAPTAIN'S
BRIDGE

NAVIGATING
BRIDGE

HOUSETOP

FORE DECK

Lichenfield

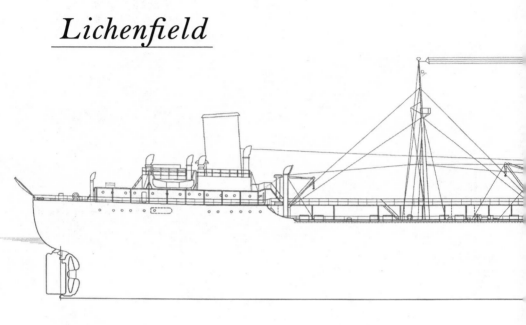

OUTBOARD PROFILE

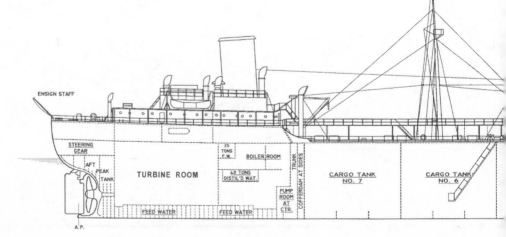

INBOARD PROFILE

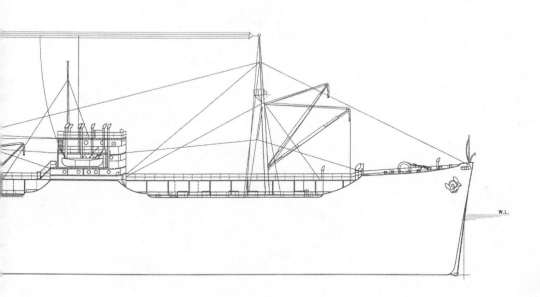

W.L.

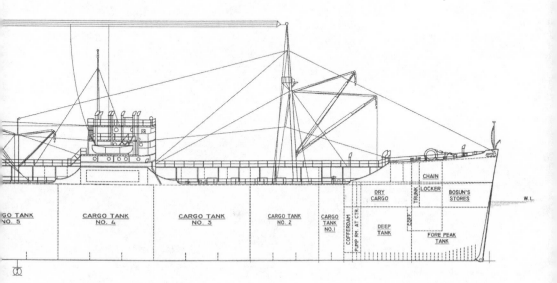

DRY
CARGO

TRUNK

BOSUN'S
STORES

W.L.

CARGO TANK
NO. 5

CARGO TANK
NO. 4

CARGO TANK
NO. 3

CARGO TANK
NO. 2

CARGO
TANK
NO. 1

COFFERDAM

PUMP RM. AT CTR.

DEEP
TANK

COFF.

FORE PEAK
TANK

CONTENTS

WHAT IS LOUIS L'AMOUR'S LOST TREASURES?

L ouis L'Amour's Lost Treasures is a project created to release some of the author's more unconventional manuscripts from the family archives.

Currently included in the series are *Louis L'Amour's Lost Treasures: Volume 1*, published in the fall of 2017, and *Volume 2*, due out in 2019. These books contain both finished and unfinished short stories, unfinished novels, literary and motion picture treatments, notes, and outlines. They are a wide selection of the many works Louis was never able to publish during his lifetime.

In 2018 we will release *No Traveller Returns*, L'Amour's never-before-seen first novel, which was written between 1938 and 1942. In the future, there may be a selection of even more L'Amour titles.

Additionally, many notes and alternate drafts to Louis's well-known and previously published novels and short stories will now be included as "bonus feature" postscripts within the books that they relate to. For example, the Lost Treasures postscript to *Last of the Breed* will contain early notes on the story, the short story that was discovered to be a missing piece of the novel, the history of the novel's inspiration and creation, and information about unproduced motion picture and comic book versions.

An even more complete description of the Lost Treasures project, along with a number of examples of what is in the books, can be found at louislamourslosttreasures.com. The website also contains a good deal of exclusive material, such as even more pieces of unknown stories that were too short or too incomplete to include in the Lost Treasures books, plus personal photos, and scans of original documents.

All of the works that contain Lost Treasures project materials will display the Louis L'Amour's Lost Treasures banner and logo.

LOUIS L'AMOUR'S LOST TREASURES

PREFACE

By Beau L'Amour

O ver the years I have come to realize that it is impossible to com-
prehend my father's life without understanding the brief time
he spent as a merchant sailor. Though he was born in North Dakota,
and wrote this novel while living on a small farm in Oklahoma, his
adulthood was formed and his character was determined by the
sea—an environment that must have been exciting, threatening, and
wonderful to a kid from the upper Midwest.

The sea gave him access to the world. It allowed him to visit England, Japan, China, Malaysia, Indonesia, Arabia, Egypt, and Pan-
ama ... all at a time when few people from the United States ever
made it to either Mexico or Canada. He traveled in the roughest of
conditions and with the roughest of men, yet their world was quite a
cosmopolitan place, full of different races, religions, languages, philosophies, histories, and governments. It was a far cry from the narrow confines of the small-town America where Louis grew up. The
least educated of his siblings, the sea and the places it took him became his university.

By the 1930s, having settled in a spot that was about as far as one
could get from any ocean or foreign country, he began to write of the

times, people, and places he had once known. Many of these stories are included in the collection *Yondering*. Some of them, like "Thicker Than Blood," were lifted directly from Louis's life and experience. Others, like "Glorious! Glorious!," are, almost certainly, pure fiction, but they captured the times in a more realistic manner than the "high adventure" style of his pulp stories.

Beyond simply attempting to entertain and connect a reader to the life he had once known, *No Traveller Returns* might also have been my father's way of dealing with certain issues that had been on his mind in the few years prior to beginning this manuscript.

First and foremost, *No Traveller Returns* is, in a sense, an homage to a time gone by, and perhaps a wistful acceptance that he was no longer the young man who had gone to sea a decade before. He *had* considered going back. After he had helped his parents move to Oklahoma, Louis discussed returning to the sea full-time, and seriously considered the possibility of becoming a ship's officer. He fantasized about being like Joseph Conrad, a ship's mate and a writer at the same time. However, he put off making a choice, and as he connected more and more with life in Oklahoma, it became less of a possibility. But the sea still called to him; you can feel it in many parts of this story.

There was also another, darker question on his mind . . . a question about a moment when the fickle finger of fate passed him over, touching him lightly before moving on.

The story goes like this: While waiting to ship out in the mid-1920s, Louis got a job working standby on a large, modern freighter in the port of San Pedro. A "standby seaman" does routine jobs like chipping rust and rough painting on a ship while it is in port. In Dad's case it was a desperately needed job, and one he hoped would turn into something more permanent: a position with the crew on the ship's next voyage, possibly even a career on what seemed like a good ship . . . a career that could have supported him for years. To his dismay, he did not get the job and the ship sailed without him.

It was never heard from again.

According to Louis, only one life ring was eventually discovered. The ship had vanished, almost without a trace.

As with many aspects of my father's life, there are several versions of that story. In some, the ship is poetically named *The Eclipse*. In others, the mate, who could have hired Louis, seems struck by a premonition of some sort, and mysteriously dismisses him in an abrupt and callous manner, possibly saving his life. The oddest variation is one where Louis sees a strange man, almost a ghost or apparition, in the ship's galley, and takes this presence as a warning not to sail with the crew.

I can't say I completely believe any of these tales, but I definitely get the feeling from this manuscript that Dad was dealing with something personal that had to do with the dangers that could be found at sea. As history tells us, it wasn't too many years after he started this book that the merchant marine, by then part of the war effort, became the service with the highest rate of casualties in America's contribution to World War II.

No Traveller Returns has the distinction of being the first novel-length work by Louis L'Amour. There are vague suggestions of other, earlier projects, but there is no way to know if they were completed or what became of them. Whether these were references to "magazine novels," or novellas, which were essentially just long short stories, is unclear, and what eventually happened to them is a complete mystery. In the days before Xerox machines and in the career of a writer for whom return postage and carbon paper to make duplicates were a financial challenge, the only copy of a manuscript could go missing very easily.

The first indication that Dad was working on this book is in a journal entry from June 9, 1938. He mentions that he intends to "finish 'No Traveller Returns' tomorrow." Though typically optimistic, he almost certainly was not talking about actually finishing the *entire* novel; more likely, he meant he was wrapping up the first several chapters to submit to publishers in hopes of getting an advance. Those chapters were quickly rejected by several different companies, but he continued to make more progress, documenting that he had completed further chapters as the months wore on. He continued to juggle his time between this novel and other short story projects, projects which might earn him money much more quickly.

It was a time when several different aspects of Louis's professional

and creative life were colliding. He was writing the semiautobio-
graphical *Yondering*-style stories, of which *No Traveller Returns* is one,
and he was promoting himself as a character similar to the protagonists found within those pages: a self-educated yet blue-collar adventurer and world traveller. He was making a name for himself on the
Oklahoma poetry scene and in other local literary circles. And, much
more important, he had just begun selling material to the pulps—
high adventure and crime stories—that were more visceral and melo-
dramatic than his other work.

   The important word here, however, is "selling." The personal ad-
ventures and slice-of-life stories earned him little or nothing. Though
a number of them received critical acclaim, they were published in
literary periodicals with a very limited audience. A few of these periodicals might generously be called prestigious; most, however, just
wanted to seem that way.

The pulp sales made Louis actual money, a rare thing in Depression-era Oklahoma, but there were also the issues of pride and self-identity. They might have had lax editorial standards, but pulps were popular and had massive circulation. Louis was thirty years old. He was living with his parents in a house owned by his eldest brother, a successful newspaperman. If he was going to call himself a writer and be taken seriously by the people who were putting a roof over his head, he was going to have to stop talking about it and actually earn some money.

So pride, cash, and the pleasure of finally being valued by well-known editors and magazines drove him to write more and more for the pulps, even though he was hoping they would be only a temporary stop on the road to becoming a respected novelist. He rationed his time between one style and another, hoping that both would take off.

Louis had a vision for his *Yondering* material similar to the one he had for his later Sackett, Talon, and Chantry series. He intended to create a cycle of stories documenting the life he had witnessed in different cities around the world: San Pedro in the 1920s ("Old Doc Yak," "It's Your Move," "And Proudly Die," "Survival," "Show Me the Way to Go Home"); Shanghai in the 1930s ("The Admiral," "The Man Who Stole Shakespeare," "Shanghai, Not Without Gestures"), and Paris in the 1940s ("The Cross and the Candle," "A Friend of the General"). Other stories ("Death Westbound," "Thicker Than Blood," *No Traveller Returns*) would examine the ships and crews, the roads and rails that connected these locations. Through these and other stories he had planned, Louis intended to loosely chronicle an era that was vanishing, even as he was experiencing it: a different sort of frontier, one where a man could travel without a passport and see a world that had yet to close its last borders or map its final unexplored places.

That era's hoboes, itinerant workers, and ship's crewmen lived lives that were, in many ways, clandestine. They were beneath the notice of those who remained at home and struggled to hold down regular jobs, beneath the notice of both captains of industry and labor leaders. Then, as now, many who did hard and dangerously physical work lived what was nearly an outlaw existence. They had their own rules, and their own language, one which I have endeavored to decipher as clearly as possible in the glossary at the end of this book. This jargon of sailors and railroad men and soldiers, cowboys and miners is a vocabulary I grew up with, but it is a version of English certainly not taught in any college classroom.

Louis did not visit this underworld as a dilettante to gain life experience or to discover subjects for his writing (though that was ultimately the result); he was there because of a lack of skills and education, and because he had no family that could support him. He was a participant in, as one of the young protagonists of this book will observe, "a world where men without money lived, searched for work, and traveled by night," a member of the secret society of poet Robert Service's "Men That Don't Fit In."

Typical of a young writer, *No Traveller Returns* attempts to be more ambitious, complex, and intellectual than a great deal of Louis's later work. Such ambition, complexity, and intellectualism are not always the easiest of mixtures. But those elements, and the book's emotional connection to its characters, are what set this work apart, making it unique in nearly every way.

It is worth mentioning that the *Yondering*-style stories, different as they were, had a direct bearing on Louis's later writing style. In December of 1938 he noted in his journal:

> The consensus of editorial opinion at present seems to be that my stories are weak on plot. The atmosphere, characterization, and writing are receiving constant compliments, and most of my rejects are on the basis of weak plot.

Dad quickly corrected this oversight in his pulp writings. However, he also continued on for a few more years, working to try and improve his original quiet and insightful style, hoping that it would lead him to a more "literary" career.

If the war hadn't interrupted Louis's development of this book and then dropped him into even more extreme financial straits once it was over, he might have finished perfecting *No Traveller Returns* and found a publisher. At the time, it was indeed likely that any small success outside the realm of short stories would have altered his career considerably. Later in his life, Dad often wondered if such circumstances might have turned him into an entirely different sort of writer. One can hardly believe he would have been more popular, but who he would have become, and where his talent would have taken him, is something we can never know.

NO
TRAVELLER
RETURNS

A SIMPLE EXPLANATION OF SHIP'S PERSONNEL

DECK CREW

ORDINARY SEAMAN (OS): the lowest rank on the deck crew. After one has put in a certain amount of time and passed a series of examinations, he can attain the rank of "able," or **Able-bodied Seaman (AB)**. Responsibilities include standing watch at the wheel and on lookout, handling lines while mooring the ship, stowing or unloading cargo, and general maintenance, including rust removal, painting, and the repair and servicing of the cargo loading gear.

FIRST MATE: The first, or "chief," mate is head of the deck crew and generally in charge of the ship's operations. Like all of the mates, he also supervises two four-hour work periods, or "watches," a day, one in the A.M. and one in the P.M.

SECOND MATE: In addition to standing his daytime and nighttime watch, the second mate is also the ship's navigation officer.

THIRD MATE: Besides standing the remaining watches, he is an apprentice to the second mate's position. The third mate is often responsible for the ship's lifesaving and firefighting equipment.

ENGINE CREW

WIPER: The wiper is the lowest rank on the engine crew, responsible for the cleaning and less technical maintenance of the ship's mechanical areas. A **Fireman** is the next rung up the ladder of seniority; they maintain and operate the water supply and heating system for the boilers. Finally, an **Oiler** cares for the critical lubrication and maintenance of the engines and other systems.

FIRST ASSISTANT ENGINEER: Under the command of the chief engineer, the "first engineer" stands an A.M. and P.M. watch, supervising an oiler, fireman, and, possibly, a wiper or two. He is often responsible for the maintenance of machinery in the fire room and boiler room.

SECOND ASSISTANT ENGINEER: Besides standing a watch overseeing members of the engine crew, he is usually in charge of the fuel and fresh water supply as well as the boilers.

THIRD ASSISTANT ENGINEER: Along with supervising the engine crew on his watch, his duties may include being responsible for the auxiliary and electrical equipment.

STEWARD'S CREW

The **MESSMEN** serve as waiters, dishwashers, and janitors, and do many other jobs around the ship's living quarters. The **Cooks** prepare food and generally look after the galley area. The **Pantryman** maintains an inventory of kitchen and housekeeping stores and generally assists the Steward.

STEWARD: head of the ship's kitchen, supplies, and housekeeping department.

There are a number of other shipboard jobs, some of them very important, like the **Captain** and the **Radio Operator**, or "Sparks," but they are either fairly self-explanatory or not mentioned in *No Traveller Returns*.

SAN PEDRO

February 1939 . . .

The shipfitter was a big man, hard-muscled from work, yet fat from age and too much drink. His nose was a spiderweb of red veins and his eyes were bloodshot. He stood in the dim and echoing vastness of the tank, braced on a plank supported by sandbags and scaffolding. Above his head were line after line of rivets. His aching arms held an air hammer, its supply line an awkward weight impairing the accuracy of his work.

Alone in Portside Wing Tank Number Seven, he lowered the heavy tool, choking back a groan of frustration and effort. Beneath a dirty wool shirt his ribs were bruised yellow and black, and his head pounded. The ship was a Grosset & Tate tanker, bound out for the Far East as quickly as the yard could get her back in the water. Of the lengthy list of repairs and improvements, this was the last. The work went on late, as late as it had to, in order to be completed.

Though the tanks were carefully vented and scoured before any work was done, the shipfitter still felt delirious. Was it petroleum fumes, the hangover, or the beating he had received? Did it matter? He leaned on the wall of the tank. He shouldn't be here. He wasn't up to it. But chances to work came rarely now. He got the pickup jobs when other, more senior, more reliable men, were out.

Rain dripped through the hatch, and the caged bulb that lit his work glared and swung as the wind outside blustered against its cable.

He tried to clear his head, but every breath hurt him under the arms and over the heart. He cursed, cursed as vilely as he knew how. It had been that damn pretty boy, the one who had attracted the crowd in the Beacon Street Pool Room. A bigmouth acting like he was better than all the other men on the beach.

The 'fitter had ignored him at first. The guy had been telling stories and reciting poetry to a group of young men and girls who looked like they were college students out for a night of slumming in the waterfront bars. But if you listened close, it seemed he'd been everywhere and done everything. And, if anyone spoke up, well . . . the guy would say he'd been there first and done it better.

No one seemed to mind but the shipfitter, who, though he refused to admit it, was already in a foul mood. He had taken over a two-room shack where some of the more unsavory elements that gathered at the Port of Los Angeles could go to get out of the rain. By offering shelter and an occasional alibi, and through sheer physical intimidation, the 'fitter had managed to cut himself in on a good many robberies of drunken seamen and the stealing of tools from Bethlehem and the other shipyards.

But one of his cronies, an oiler from a ship's engine crew who worked strong-arm for him when in port, owed the 'fitter money. The oiler hadn't been honoring their arrangement, and now the 'fitter was searching the streets of San Pedro with retribution, or at least collection, on his mind.

"The Café Olympic or the Astor Bar in Shanghai, just mention my name." Pretty Boy was a pinch hitter for an actor well known for playing brooding, rebellious young men. "They set up a boxing match, you see. I was to fight this great big Russian wrestler."

The 'fitter could stand no more, "You? Pah! Why, I could break you in two!"

"Perhaps you could, friend. Join us, why don't you? Have a drink and let me finish my—"

The 'fitter swung.

He swung right at the smug young man's perfectly etched chin. Pretty Boy went down like he'd dropped through a hole in the floor—but the 'fitter's fist connected with nothing but air! The students scattered in a confusion of shrieks and angry yells, and the shipfitter stumbled forward into a pool table.

Then the young man bobbed back up behind him, having ducked completely under the 'fitter's haymaker. The 'fitter felt two gunshot-fast concussions over his right kidney and turned straight into a jab that split his lips. He struck out but the younger man took the punches on his forearms and shoulders, ducking and dodging, firing blow after blow at the 'fitter's body.

A boxer. The 'fitter wouldn't have guessed it from the look of him, but there it was. He shook his head, and the pain told him he'd been hit harder and more often than he realized. The kid was fast, damn fast. But he knew what to do with boxers!

The big man lunged forward, his legs uncoiling, arms out, trying to get inside, to grapple and break this boy with his weight and strength. But the young man—the boxer—calmly grasped the 'fitter's jacket. One hand closing on the fabric at the elbow and the other at the lapel, the boxer spun the big man around and down, his stylish loafer smashing the side of the 'fitter's knee.

He crashed backward into a chair, the arm of it cracking against the side of his head, splitting his ear. The 'fitter scrambled to his feet to see the boxer dancing lightly forward and back, his right hand brushing dark curls out of his eyes. They were in a ring of wide-eyed patrons, dungarees and overalls mixed with letter jackets and brightly colored skirts.

The shipfitter had rushed again, a wounded bull, enraged as much by the gasping crowd as by the matador he charged. Even before he found himself on the floor again—ribs broken, ears ringing, and a shoulder dislocated—he heard the motherless son, the bloody fop, claiming that *this* . . . and then *this* . . . was what he had done to the Russian wrestler in Shanghai.

In the echoing shadows of the great steel tank, the shipfitter growled. He would have his revenge, somehow. He lifted the barrel of the air hammer. Breathing carefully, shallowly. He could live without the wages, but without the job itself, he had no access to the yards. That meant no access to the stolen tools he pawned or sold. It meant no access to all those things that would never be missed on the ships themselves, items that could be dropped by a lonely stretch of fence to be retrieved later from the outside. When times were bad, a tool or two was the difference between cheap whiskey and canned heat. He had to finish.

The rivets on tanks intended for volatile petroleum products had to be "caulked" like a boiler, a process of burring down the edge to create an airtight seal. The 'fitter placed the head of the hammer against the next rivet and clamped down on the trigger. The noise in the enclosed space was shocking. Even with the cotton the 'fitter had stuffed in his ears, it seemed like it would rip his head apart. He moved the caulking edge around the rivet and moved on.

After four more rivets, he dropped the air hammer and leaned on the wall of the tank, pressure hissing from the fitting on the hose. He'd been on the job four hours and needed a drink, or several. Everything hurt. The fight had been two days ago, and still everything hurt.

Three more feet to go. A couple dozen rivets. He looked at the hammer with dread. To hell with it, the shipfitter thought. To hell with it.

He crawled out of the access hatch into the rain. He pulled up his tools and coiled the hose. At the dimly lit window to the shipyard office he stopped and clocked out.

"Wing Tank Number Seven," the 'fitter said. "All finished."

"A good thing too," replied the little man with the pencil behind his ear. "We're behind schedule. Can't get 'em in lest you get 'em out." He peered at the 'fitter's bandaged forehead and bruised cheekbone.

"What happened to you?"

"Ahh, shut up!" The 'fitter waved him off as he shuffled toward the road, the lights of the yard making halos in the damp air between him and the gate.

Two hours later the shipfitter was dead to the world in his shack with rain dripping from the eves. Beside his dirty mattress was a nearly empty bottle. He was dreaming of revenge, dreaming of that boxer with his skull crushed by a homemade blackjack.

SS *LICHENFIELD*

Three Weeks Later . . .

There was no sound but the low pulse of engines down below, an occasional clatter of pots from the galley, and the hissing of the coffee urn.

The man sat silently, sipping his black coffee over the rim of an enameled cup, holding it in both hands and staring blankly across the room, his lids still heavy with sleep. His face was strong and square, and the hands that held the cup were callused and powerful. He was blond, Nordic. His worn dungarees, faded from many washings, were neatly patched on one hip. His elbows rested on the mess table. His arms were tattooed, a blue and white ship sinking in a blue and white sea on one arm, and a slender girl in a dancer's pose but without a ballet dress on the other. His hair was rumpled, his jaw covered with a stubble of beard. His name was Pete Brouwer, he was a sailor. He could have been nothing else.

Another man stumbled sleepily into the mess room and stood glaring at its one occupant. Then he picked up a thick white cup and drew it full of coffee, adding tinned milk and sugar. He slumped into a seat at the opposite end of the table.

He was short and thick-bodied. Although clean-shaven, his jowls were blue with beard. His eyes were small and deeply set, his big hands covered with coarse, black hair. Mahoney was an oiler, a member of the "black gang," or engine crew. Like many Liverpool Irishmen, he cared for little but whiskey and beef stew.

Though he had never laid eyes on Pete, the blond seaman, before two weeks ago, he hated him. He hated him for reasons he would admit to no one aboard this ship, hated him because he had never wanted to see the man again, yet here they were trapped on the same boat, sharing the same watch, all the way to the Far East and back. Pete wasn't the only man aboard Mahoney hated, but in Pete's case he had to keep his enmity a secret; if he let it show, there'd be hell to pay.

Two others came in, a seaman and a fireman. The seaman, a slender fellow with buck teeth, was humming a popular ballad. The fireman, known as Slug, a top-heavy, lumbering fellow, lurched across to a bench and leaned against the bulkhead. In a minute he was dozing.

There were thirty-three men aboard ship, and each had a name, a life, and a dream. The steward, crew's messman, and pantryman were Filipinos, the officers' messman was an Atlanta Negro, the two cooks were Chinese, and the remainder of the crew were various shades of what is loosely termed "white."

The ship was a tanker bound out from San Pedro for Manila, carrying eighty thousand barrels of naphtha. In two of the after tanks there was a space of several feet between the liquid and the tank top. A slight shortage resulted in the failure to fill the tanks. This was of no particular importance, except that eighty thousand barrels of naphtha is eighty thousand barrels of potential destruction, made somewhat more dangerous anytime the fumes mixed with oxygen in the air. A combination of seals and ventilation minimized the danger, but as the ship moved westward it rolled slightly, and there was a soft whisper as the naphtha shifted inside its tanks.

It lacked five minutes of midnight. At midnight the Man at the Wheel would hear the chronometer sound eight bells. He would relay them again with the bell-cord overhead, and the Man on Lookout would reply by bell from the bow. Then they would be relieved by the twelve-to-four watch and retire to the petty officers' mess, where they had no business to be, to drink coffee and talk. The coffee would be a bitter brown wash and the talk mostly lies. Later, they would go to their quarters in what tankermen called the fo'c'stle, even though it was aft. They would roll into their bunks, and sleep.

The second mate would be on the bridge thinking of his wife, and the third mate would be below in his bunk thinking of his fiancée in Los Angeles. The third mate was just twenty-six and still had confidence in women and romance. The second mate was thirty-seven with a wife and three children, two of whom he was reasonably sure were his. The second mate had little confidence in either women or romance.

As the tanker steamed through peaceful seas, the water parted, rolling back in phosphorescent waves that rippled away into the glassy darkness. Myriads of stars sparkled along the Milky Way like harbor lights along the shore of night. Dennis McGuire, the sailor on lookout, leaned on the rail and watched the slow dip of the bow and the slow, measured lift that followed. He frowned into the vastness of the night and wondered about Faustine back in Los Angeles.

When had he truly decided to leave? Was it when he had signed the Articles of Shipping days earlier or when he had woken up in her bungalow that last morning? At the time, he had felt uneasy and assumed he was confused by his feelings and the obligations that might come if he stayed. Now he was not so sure.

He liked to tell people he had an infallible sense of when to escape any particular situation. For the first time, though, he found he was unsure about the result. There was a strange sense that something was amiss. That should have cleared up when he left Faustine and Hollywood behind, however it had not.

Well, perhaps she had been right. Perhaps he was a fool. There probably was a future for him back there. But this . . . this was real.

What was it made a man go to sea? What made a man leave everything behind and drift away across the world, bound for nowhere or anywhere?

He remembered a night . . . soft and clear and beautiful as nights can be only in the tropics. He stood by the tail of a schooner becalmed off the coast of Celebes. Far up-country he could hear the low throb-bing of drums. A strange and primitive emotion had surged up within him. The line of jungle beyond the thin streamer of beach was an ominous blackness. The air was vibrant with something that touched his nerves and made them tingle, surf and a rush of hot blood beating against the night.

McGuire stirred restlessly, remembering. There had been a yearn-ing to slip over the side and swim for shore, while around the hull the water lapped lazily, whispering to him. The sea. The sea from which all life springs and to which all life returns.

His eyes searched the horizon, then the water nearby. Nothing, al-ways nothing. It had been three days since they had sighted another ship.

He glanced aft and could see the dim outline of the third mate on the bridge wing. A conceited egg, that Wesley. Wesley had a lot of ideas about how a superior officer should act toward seamen. The trouble was too many superior officers weren't all that superior.

Still watching the bridge, McGuire walked from starboard to port, checking the running lights. Of all the time at sea, this was best. The two hours of lookout in the bow. In a few minutes his watch would be up. Just about time to sound eight bells and wander aft to turn in and sleep the sleep of the just or the damned . . . or, well, who really cared anyway?

He wished he'd sight a ship. He liked passing ships at sea, especially at night. It was a melancholy feeling, but he liked it nonetheless. He remembered the night they passed the *Europa* during a gale in the Atlantic. He had gone forward with the Swede to batten down a cor-ner of hatch canvas that had come loose, and it was blowing like the Bull of Barney. He'd looked up, his face streaming with salt water, his oilskins glistening with rain and driving spray, to see the palatial liner passing them, homeward-bound. Through the wind came a vagrant wisp of melody, and he'd stood, leaning to the roll of the ship, watch-ing the lights. It was a lot different standing on the deck of a battered tramp steamer than looking down on one from the port of a liner. Up there they had been dancing, no doubt, and there were men in dinner suits and women in lovely gowns.

Let them have it. The freighter was best. He liked the feel of doing things, the straining muscles, the knowledge that it was just the ship stood between you and the sea, a trip to Davy Jones's locker, or if one was lucky, maybe to Fiddler's Green.

Dennis McGuire let the liner fade out in his memory just as it had on the sea. He'd take his the hard way. Cocktails were okay, and women too, but he wanted neither liners nor pearly gates. This was the life for a man.

Twenty men were in their bunks. Nineteen of them were asleep. In the fo'c'sle, the crew was separated, port and starboard into firemen's and seamen's quarters. The bunks were framed of pipe, painted battleship gray, and a low railing extended along half the length of each bunk to prevent the occupant from falling out. As the ship moved, each of the sleepers made a slight roll to port, and then a slight roll back. On the deck above, just up the passage from the galley, a Filipino pantryman stirred restlessly in his bunk; he was remembering Mindanou, a childhood of fishing with his father.

In the wheelhouse, the light from the compass binnacle threw a soft, mysterious glow over the saturnine features of Tex Worden. The scarred wood of the wheel was gripped in his work-hardened hands. He stared into the darkness toward the chronometer, trying to see the time. He rolled his quid in his jaws and spat with careless accuracy into the sawdust box near the wheel.

The third mate walked into the wheelhouse and stood watching the forestay for a minute.

"How is she?" the third asked.

"Right on course, Mr. Mate, sir."

The mate glanced at Tex Worden's face. There was no hint of a smile. Mr. Wesley turned away, feeling irritated. He always felt Worden was laughing at him. Mr. Wesley didn't like to feel that he was amusing. In fact, Mr. Wesley took himself quite seriously.

Worden moved the wheel a couple of spokes to starboard, an adjustment that turned gears and opened valves. Aft, the steam steering gear hissed and grumbled and the rudder moved. The noise woke a sleepy fireman, who rolled out of his bunk and shuffled toward the head, muttering to himself.

The third engineer, on watch below, glanced toward the oiler sitting beneath the ventilator, and then back at the gauges. The engineer was thin, dark, and nervous. Thin because he was never in the best of health; dark because his father had been a Southern Italian; and nervous because he was the father of the second mate's third child and feared that the second mate knew.

Aft, in the mess room, Shorty Conrad, the buck-toothed seaman, listened to the conversations around him. He was thirty-two, but looked scarcely twenty. He had been born in Australia, orphaned in Texas, and drifted down to the sea. He liked to drink, gamble, and fight and was a failure at them all. He did not have to strain to overhear Mahoney, the twelve-to-four oiler, telling whoever would listen that he was going to "get" Denny McGuire. Shorty smiled to himself. Mahoney had tried before . . . and McGuire could look after himself.

The night was a symphony of velvet darkness in which millions of stars swung their tiny lanterns overhead. Not a gleam was in sight that might have been another ship, but miles behind and to the north a Matson passenger liner was bound away from San Francisco to Tahiti. Her route intersected that of the tanker at a long narrow angle. It would be days before her greater speed would cause the ships to pass, and more days still that they would be just over the horizon from each other, invisible companions in a nearly empty ocean.

Her radio officer was tapping out a story to the Sparks on a Sydney-bound freighter. Jerry, the Matson radio operator, was headed home. He was from the southern islands, though he let few know it. Blue eyes, courtesy of a German father, and a sure hand had cinched the deal with the Radio Service. His dark complexion went unremarked upon among the naturally tanned community of ship's officers. He would leave the ship in Tahiti and find passage to his tiny island. A brother and mother were waiting for him, waiting for him to come home from the sea.

In his bunk on the *Lichenfield,* Ordinary Seaman David Jones stirred restlessly. Beyond the iron hull next to his ear, the sea sounded terribly close. Tears welled slowly to his eyes and trickled down his cheeks.

He lay, staring upward in the darkness. A month ago he had been working on a farm, earning what he could to pay the doctors who looked after his mother and visiting her and his sweetheart on weekends. Now his mother was dead, his sweetheart far away, and he was a fugitive from the law, sailing off to the Far East.

Forward, in his cabin, the second mate arose and put aside his book. John Harlan loved fine books. He liked them not only for their contents, but for their luxurious bindings and paper. He liked the finely wrought illustrations, too.

He smiled at these small pleasures, and then picked up his coat. It would be a quiet watch and there would be a moon. A night for thinking, for dreaming, for making love. It had been such a night when he and Helen—his face darkened but softened again as he remembered. After all, who was he to condemn anyone? There was too much condemnation in the world and too little understanding.

He walked out on deck and stared up at the sky. No, he had been mistaken. No moon tonight, only the stars and the sea. A wraith of wind touched his cheek as he started up the ladder to the bridge.

THE PRIVATE LOG OF
JOHN HARLAN, SECOND MATE

March 20th: It is quiet, and there is no sound but the scratching of my pen and that distant throb of engines that is the constant accompaniment to all our days and nights. There is only the tiny microcosm of the ship, and all about the eternal sea. It often surprises me how little we notice the sea. Always, we are aware of it, but only during periods of storm or emergency does it impress itself definitely upon the consciousness. Our lives are narrowed to the small island of the ship itself, to our association with one another, our day-to-day work, and the expectation of ports to come.

There might be no other world than this. We are, strangely, alone. A tiny bundle of lives thrown helter-skelter into the steel hull of a ship. The end of all the cities might come, all civilizations might be reduced to dust, and we would know nothing of it. There is the intangible connection of the wireless. Sometimes we look up at the slender cables of the antennae and wonder at it, but no more. It is too new, too ephemeral a connection.

Thirty-three strangers live huddled together for a few passing weeks. Some will move on, and a new crew will form from the human driftwood, the shiftless wanderers, the men in dungarees who go down to the sea. Thirty-three men, thirty-three hearts beating against time, thirty-three unknown longings, thirty-three dreams.

Who are these men who share this ship with me? Who exist side by side for a time, and then vanish again? They seem as alike as motes in a beam—blue dungarees, white singlets, and the eternal talk of whiskey and women.

Five years now as second officer of the SS *Lichenfield* I have watched them come and go. Are they like me? Do they wish to write? Paint? Or compose? Did they want a chicken farm? A beer parlor? A dance hall? Do they want to pimp for a woman or preach the gospel? I watch them curiously, and I never cease to wonder. I have known seamen who attended the Sorbonne, Heidelberg, and Harvard. I have known seamen who knew Sing Sing and Devil's Island. And once I saw a drunken wiper with a bloated, booze-sodden face fall into a chair before a shaky old piano and play Wagner and Brahms. One never knows.

The motives of men are a continual puzzle. Why was I, I wonder, cursed with this desire to write, to catch the whimsy of the moment in indelible words? What impulse started me believing there was worth in these transient thoughts and transient men? And that I, at all costs, must record them? Should I write of these men? I know no more of them than any one of us may know of another, for we are all strangers yearning across an abyss that none can bridge. Still, I wonder who they are, where they are going, what they are thinking.

Are they like me, escaping from a dream that has blasted itself? Are they leaving behind a wife they loved, children that meant so much? Are they leaving behind hope, honor, and pride? Are their lives as grotesquely tangled as mine?

Back there is a girl I loved and who became mother of my children. My children? Well, two of them at least. The father of the third I do not know, but he is no less deserving, no less worthy. And perhaps his father is as lonely as I, another helpless man searching for happiness or love.

For almost two weeks I have lived with this crew. Of Slug Jacobs, Mahoney, or Sam Harrell, I know little. I have seen Denny McGuire batter Mahoney into insensibility on the docks, yet I have also seen

McGuire reading the sonnets of Edna Millay. I have seen Tex Worden stagger out of a waterfront brothel and flip his last half-dollar into a beggar's hat. I have seen Shorty Conrad bending over a bit of paper, the tip of his tongue on his lip, his fingers cramped, writing a letter. To whom was he writing? Why?

Somewhere in the lives of these men there must be stories that I could write. They come on watch, they speak respectfully, and occasionally they venture a comment. I have Shorty Conrad and Pete Brouwer on my watch. Pete is a big fellow but very quiet. He is the most capable seaman aboard, a genuine sailing ship man. That much I know, but who is he? Where is he going? What is his life?

PETE BROUWER

Able Seaman

He put his cup down and lit his pipe after carefully filling it from a woven leather tobacco pouch. His initials were worked into the leather with white strips. The whole thing was an intricate, painstaking piece of art. He had done it himself. He drew on the match. The crew's mess and the entire aft house was inside the open-flame line, a red border painted on the deck that cut across the ship's stern from rail to rail. Here it was safe to smoke. Two more such lines bracketed the superstructure amidships. The fires of the galley burned within those lines, and the officers and engineers could also smoke in safety.

Pete had served on tankers before, and it had never felt safe. He could see the plumbing that ran across the decks, knew the systems that were in place: caulked rivets, vents, and careful inspections. But it never felt safe. He was glad he was finally going home.

He stared across the room, looking out the open port at the quiet sea. Soon they would be in Manila. After that, it would be on to Asia proper, back to San Pedro, and then, finally, through the canal and home to Amsterdam.

He would take his sister to the Vijzelstraat. He had never been there, but a seaman had told him it was a good place for music and dancing, with the best of food—good Dutch food, not the slum he had been eating all these years. She would like that, he thought; young girls like to go places. Then he would get a good job on a coastwise run where he could be home often. No more would he go out to the far waters.

So many times he had tried to return and always there was something to prevent it. Sometimes it was a good ship to somewhere else; sometimes he had spent his money. This last time, in San Pedro, he was robbed. His watch, the one his father gave him twenty years ago . . . they had taken that too.

It seemed so good, coming into San Pedro. He had liked that ship, the *Johnson City*, and he had liked the crew. They were all such good fellows, and had been looking forward to a place they could call home, even if it was only for a few days. Pete leaned against the bulkhead at the end of the bench, and his eyes closed.

Behind them the sun, red from its exertions, had been sliding wearily into the sea. To the north was a lighthouse and the long roll of tawny hills on the peninsula were taking on the colors of sea and sky. To the south was Long Beach then a thick forest of oil derricks. Here and there over the town a thin finger of smoke pointed inquiringly at the heavens. A water taxi sputtered by, and farther up the channel was the stack of a Luckenbach boat.

"She hasn't changed a hell of a lot, Pete," Shorty remarked. "She never does. Just the same old oil and lumber docks. Probably the same women up on The Line, too."

"Ya, 'Pedro a good town. I have been here on a vind-ship, fifteen year ago, maybe. Then there vas not so much as now."

"Man, I can hardly wait to get ashore." Deek slapped Shorty on the shoulder with a heavy palm. "I got a swell dame up on Beacon Street!"

"Yeah," Doc laughed, "an' about a thousand other guys got her too!" He looked at Deek and shook his head. "Get wise to yourself, friend. All these dames are after is your dough."

"Nuts t' you, sailor. You're just sore because that gal in Hong Kong gave you the gate!"

"Hell, that was nothing to what she gave *you!*"

Shorty picked up a heaving line and stepped over to the rail. He swung the monkey's fist to get the feel of it, examining the men on the dock.

"A dollar says you can't do it," Doc said, stepping up and measuring the distance with his eye.

"Okay, bud, you just stand by and watch!"

The ship was edging in to the dock, and the mate walked out onto the wing of the bridge, gauging the distance.

"On the dock there!" he shouted. "Stand by to take a line!"

Shorty tossed the coil of rope with more force than one would have thought possible. The hard monkey's fist shot through the dockman's hands and struck him a resounding blow on the chest. The man swore and scrambled to retrieve the line.

"All right, you chisel-bum, give me my money! I hit him! I hit them all, to Singapore an' back!"

Quickly, they paid out the line while Pete took a turn around the drum of the winch. Deek stood by with a cork fender. Leaning on the rail and chewing a cut plug, he swore at the men on the dock with good-natured fluency.

Pete said nothing, watching the gray warehouses, Terminal Island, and the town across the channel. Shorty had taken the line at the winch, and Pete walked forward and with the ease of long practice threw a stopper knot on the line while they took it to the bitts. He worked quietly, surely.

"Hayes!" The mate pointed from the bridge. "Help Chips fix the rat guards. The rest of you see the gangway is down and then you can knock off."

The gangway was hurriedly lowered into place and the longshoremen swarmed aboard and began throwing off the hatch covers. Pete stopped for a minute, wiping his hands on a bit of waste, and watched the scene along the dock. It was as familiar to him as it had been so long ago in Amsterdam when he had first gone to sea with his father. He never tired of watching the endless process of loading and discharging cargo. The thought that cotton and steel were transported to Japan, wheat and lumber to England, more steel to China, rubber, tin, and foodstuffs to the States, just for the happiness and comfort of men, was a marvel to him. So much fuss, when so little is needed to be content!

"Come on, Pete! Let's get ashore! What do you say we see what the town's got. Then we can ship out for Rio in a couple of weeks?"

"No, Shorty, I have saved my moneys, unt now I go home. Tventy year ago I sail away, unt never have I been back. My mama, she write, 'Peter, you come home now. You are all ve have. There is no money.' My sister, she is young girl, unt she all the time work with the fish. It is no good for young girl. My mama, she is old now."

"Sure, Pete, an' I don't blame you. Hell, if I had a home to go to I'd sure be on my way in a rush. But you told me about your brothers, can't they help out?"

"No, no. I am only vun now. Papa he go down in the Baltic, many year ago. Hans unt Karl vent mit a German ship, mit munitions, unt t'ey not come back. Vun, two, t'ree, like that they go. Now all are gone but me."

"You been gone twenty years, Pete? You must've been a little nipper then."

"Ya, I am but ten. My papa, he give me a place mit his ship. I am cabin boy then, unt we go to Pagoda Anchorage, for tea. But I am vashed over side ven I am twelve. A vind-ship in a storm, you know, it can not come 'round. They t'row me a buoy, unt I float t'ree days, unt t'en I am picked up. T'ey take me to Australia. T'ere I am living two year, unt t'en I go in a bark to Cape Town. T'en to Calcutta, unt to Bombay. I write many times home, but do not go."

Doc was shaving his lean neck when they walked into the fo'c'stle, his head back and tilted to one side. The straight razor sounded like sandpaper on his face.

"Hey, you bums," Deek yelled when they came in. "Better get your ears washed. We're going ashore an' throw a wingding! I'm going to paint Beacon Street seven colors t'night!"

Pete walked over to his bunk and sat. He dug into his tobacco pouch and stoked his pipe, watching the others shake out their shore clothes. Then he lit up and inhaled deeply.

"Pete, ain't you comin'? The first drink's on me tonight!" Deek said, straightening his tie in the reflection over Doc's shoulder. "But I'll buy another for the guy that'll shove this monkey away from the mirror!"

Shorty slipped on his blue serge coat. Dressed up, he looked like a high-school boy playing hooky. "You don't have to spend anything. Let me foot the bill."

"No, Shorty, I stay aboard tonight. You fellows go—you drink for me. I like t'e drinking too vell when I am with shipmates!"

"Aw hell, Pete, be a sport. You ain't going to blow your pile in one night! Come on, join the gang!"

"Let him alone, Deek," Shorty said. "He knows what he's doin'. Hell, if I had a home to go to no spree would keep me away."

"Aw, he don't have to spend nothin'! We'll make it a going-away party! The drinks will be on us. Hell, t'night I'd even treat Doc . . . an' I'll see that he buys a round or I'll shake him till he needs one of his own adjustments!"

"Here's an idea, Pete. You leave your dough with the Old Man an' come on ashore. We'll have a swell time."

"Sure, come along!" Deek growled, shoving Doc with his shoulder as Doc coolly began dusting powder over his face. "I'd give a party to get rid of any mug that thinks he's goin' to leave us to go off and be a chiropractor. Hell!"

"Okay, okay, but when you're bumming along the beach for coffee, I'll be playing tunes on the spine of some hot Hollywood blonde."

"Let's go, Pete! Leave your money with the skipper an' we'll shove off. We can't have a sailin' ship man parked in his bunk while all his steamer-bum pals go ashore!"

The moon was suspended low in the sky, and the dark arrows of the masts stabbed a night misted with stars. The dock echoed as they hurried along. The great lumber piles rose above them, and the alleyways between appeared and then were swallowed by the darkness behind. Once, they avoided an open trapdoor in the dock, and Deek swore as he almost stepped into it. There was a glimpse of oily water down below, and Shorty shivered a bit, hurrying to catch up with Pete.

"Don't worry about carrying your money, Pete. The Old Man must have gone up to L.A. You just forget you got it an' we'll foot the bill."

"It is all right, Shorty. I shall spend nothing. I must go home now. Just to t'ink, I have never seen my sister. She was born after I go avay."

They walked along in silence, watching the lurching back of Deek Hayes ahead of them, the straighter, easier carriage of Doc, and Duck Stevens, hustling to keep up. The harbor lights cast flickering streaks along the surface of the water. Farther uptown a police siren wailed in the night, a warning cry that faded away into the distance.

"Ya know, I got a sister, too." Shorty Conrad clapped Pete on the back. "She's around somewheres. We were just kids when my father went off to South America on some wild-goose chase. Then Mom died, and when Dad didn't come back, we were adopted. Sis was taken by some people in show business, people who knew my dad. I'm gonna find her someday. You mark my words."

"Come on, you guys, get a move on. Somebody give us a song."

> As I was a-walking down Liverpool Street,
> With a way, hey, blow the man down!
> A pretty young maiden I happened to meet,
> Oh, give us some time to blow the man down!

. . . The lights were bright along Beacon Street, and many doors were wide. There was music and laughter, the movement of many people, and the glitter of glass along the bars. When one is long upon the sea, one craves joy and laughter. Even the faded joy and laughter of the waterfronts. Even the love that is bought and the liquor that is diluted. The relationship of workingmen to money is ever the same, and now that the exhaustion of labor was gone good fellowship surged to the fore.

Slowly the cautious squint in the eyes of big Pete Brouwer relaxed, like the ebbing of the dark tides under the wharf.

There was a love of old shipmates within him, for he was a believer in the gospel of the sea, the old gospel that a shipmate is a brother no matter who or what else he may be. There was the memory of many men he had served with to make it ring true, but there was also a dark, squat man, an oiler, out of work and at loose ends, who joined them and stayed with them through the night, his eyes careful and alert even while he sang and told stories and slapped them on their backs.

Already the group had begun to break up. Doc was gone—from the station the Pacific Electric had drawn him swiftly away, to Los Angeles and an office where he would begin to practice his profession. The song of the sea would fade from his ears, as would the memory of the trade winds brushing over his skin. The hands that were accustomed to the feel of the wheel would grow more delicate and tender, and the voice that snarled at his comrades in good-natured harshness would become diplomatic and gentle.

Somewhere back in the line of bars and brothels Jack and Bert had fallen by the wayside. The bo'sun and Chips met an old shipmate, a pal from the *Catherine G. Sudden*. But Pete, Shorty, Deek, and Duck Stevens, three sheets to the wind and all decks awash, kept going. Tony's Wine Joint was not crowded, but there were a few men there . . . at least one of them known to the short man with dark stubbled cheeks and squinting eyes, the man who had followed them, perhaps even steered the happy group to the poorly lit building with an alley alongside.

"Ya, vun hundred unt fifty-six days I am at sea, unt we sight no land; the vater in the tanks, she turn green, unt the biscuits filled vit vorms, unt nothing to do but vatch the days go by. Vun hundred unt fifty-six days!"

Deek was leaning against the bar, his big shoulders spreading tightly under the coat. He grinned at the bartender and pointed at Pete.

"Look, you landlubbers! Take a look at a real deepwater sailin' ship man! They don't make 'em anymore, an' he's the genuine article. Five times around Cape Stiff, an' sailed ever' ocean they got!"

Deek glared around the room. It was a good-natured challenge, but he was drunkenly ready to fight or scuffle at the drop of a hat, and ready to do his own dropping. He stared at the liquor in his glass, having no idea that the last three drinks had been the worst sort of rotgut. Deek emptied his glass and, stirred by windjammer talk, broke into a hoarse song:

To larboard an' starboard on deck you will sprawl,
With a way, hey, blow the man down!
For Kicking Jack Williams commands the Black Ball,
Oh, give us some time to blow the man down!

"Shut up, wouldja?"

Deek turned. The big Slav at his elbow stepped back, his feet spread wide, his fists ready.

"I don't want no damned landlubber singing chanteys an' makin' so damn much noise."

"Well, put 'em up, jus' put 'em up, nobody calls me a—!"

The man's fist smashed into Deek's mouth, spattering blood. Scarcely staggered, Hayes swung a powerful right, and a split second later the two men were standing toe to toe, fighting desperately, clumsily. Shorty shoved his way to the edge of the fight, cheering for Deek. The crowd pushed and surged around him.

Pete stood up, bleary and puzzled.

"Hey, Dutchie." A hand caught Pete's arm. "Don't get in that. The police'll be comin', an' you don't want to end up in the gaol. You come wit' me. Sure an' its two old sailor men shall stick together!"

Pete looked down at the shorter man.

"Is bad for shipmates to fight. It makes bad luck for the ship."

The dark-jawed man tugged at Pete's elbow, tried to turn him away from the brawl. "They're not shipmates. That's Russian Fred—he hasn't been to sea in years. It's not bad luck, jus' a fight ... jus' a fight."

"Deek, he—if my shipmates fight, I fight too."

"He'll not be needin' you, Dutchie! Look, could the likes of that whup a shipmate of yours? Nah! Come along wit' me. Somebody might rob you, an' you want to save that dough to go home on. I'm your pal, Dutchie, and I'll be a-takin' you back to the ship. Come along!"

"Ya, I have long voyage to make. My mama, she say, 'Peter, you come home now. You is all ve have.'"

"Sure, Dutchie, right y' are, you'll be rollin' home afore y' know it. Come on!"

Deek had the Russian back against the bar and was pounding him with both hands. Shorty was beside him, yelling. Then someone hit Shorty, and the tight knot of men split instantly into a series of separate brawls. It was a tangle of struggling, cursing men. But Pete was already gone, walking through the back door with the shorter man. And it was very dark in the alley.

The moan of a distant siren sliced into the brains of the fighting men. The fly-specked windows went up and spilled bodies into the darkness. There was the brief scrape and sputter of running feet, heavy breathing, and a curse as someone stumbled. The front door banged open and the remaining patrons used the back, stumbling down the alley without noticing what it held.

Deek ran heavily for a block, then he stopped. He grabbed Shorty's arm.

"Hell, let's walk. I'd sooner do a stretch in the can than run another step! Chees, that mug could sock!"

Shorty's jaw ached, he touched it gingerly. "What the hell happened to Pete?"

"Damned if I know. But hell, he can get along."

"No, listen, he was half-swacked an' had a roll on him that would choke your uncle! I'm goin' back!"

"An' get throwed in the jug?"

"They'll never know I was in that tangle. Maybe I can help."

"Ha! You better take a look at yourself. Listen, either the cops got him or they don't. Come on, let's get out of here!"

Three blocks behind them a Black Maria skidded to a halt and belched a stream of blue-coated officers, who quickly surrounded the shack. Three of them rushed inside, led by a plainclothesman. The room was a shambles of broken chairs, bottles, shattered window glass, and spilled liquor. Tony was almost in tears.

"What's goin' on here?" the detective snapped. "This is the fifth time in two weeks. Once more an' we close you down! Now what happened?"

"You t'ink I breaka da glass? I breaka da chair? You t'ink I poosha the window out? Two beeg man, they fight, pretty soon another fella, he hit a little one in the nose, then they all fight!"

A head thrust in through the back door and called to the detective. "Hey, Mac! There's a guy out here in the alley! Looks like somebody slugged him!"

In the circle of the flashlight's glow, Pete's face was strangely white. Mac felt his heart.

"He ain't croaked, thank God! Call an ambulance."

Mac stood up, pointing at the pockets, turned inside out. "He wasn't in any scrap. They rolled him. Started the fight for cover, looks like. What do you want to bet it was someone in that Happy Valley crowd?" The detective thought for a moment. "Jerry, take three men, get down there, and roust those guys, if you can find them!"

The morning sun warmed the dock and crowned each ripple on the channel with a little halo of gold. The venerable chug-chug of the fat-bottomed ferry set the pace for the morning as it warmed up after the night's chill.

Shorty walked out on the dock. His head felt like a bulging gas drum, and his tongue seemed to have sprouted feathers. Deek swaggered, wearing his split lip and the long gash on his cheekbone like badges of honor.

Duck Stevens, who had left just before the battle, noticed Shorty's eye.

"Hey, Short-stuff, who gave you the black eye?"

"Nobody *gave* it to me! I fought for it!"

"And the mighty Deek. How's the other guy look?"

"Like you're goin' to look in about a minute if you don't shut up," Deek mumbled.

"What d' you want?" Duck said. "I walk out of Tony's last night leaving you birds blooming like a couple of roses, and this morning Pete's in the hospital, and you guys look like you'd been tryin' to shave with a file!"

Shorty stopped still.

"Pete? In the hospital?"

"Yeah? Didn't you know? Somebody robbed him last night down behind Tony's. I already been over there but they won't let anyone in till the cops talk to him."

"A hell of a pal I turn out t' be!" Shorty said. "Hell, I'd rob a bank to help that guy! Who the devil d' you think could have done it?"

Deek shrugged. "Damned if I know. I didn't see nothing after the fight started."

"Damn it! Pete's missed his chance again, an' it's my fault. I was for him comin' along when I could have talked him out of it."

"Hell, it ain't your fault. An' us moanin' about it ain't goin' to help much. Say"—Deek turned to Shorty—"Do you an' Pete know Borly Shannon?"

"The second mate on the *City of Birmingham*? Why?"

"Well, he's not on the *Birmingham* anymore. He's chief mate on the *Lichenfield* now. He was tellin' me that after a trip to the Far East they'd be running to Amsterdam an' Rotterdam!"

"The devil! But where is he now?"

"That's just it—they're just out of dry dock on Smith's Island and hiring a crew. That means one trip out East, an' then Amsterdam! Why don't you guys see him?"

"Boy, you're a lifesaver! The *Lichenfield*!"

"Not for me," Duck said, shaking his head. "I'm not sailin' on any tankers! I'll die soon enough anyway, without getting blown up on one of those wagons!"

"What of it?" Shorty shrugged. "If it was that dangerous they'd never turn a profit. A . . . ship is a ship."

THE PRIVATE LOG OF
JOHN HARLAN, SECOND MATE

March 21st: I don't know when I have ever seen a sea so still. The ship glides along through an almost breathless hush, and even the crew has become infected by it. The men move about quietly, putting things down carefully instead of dropping them. As though the slightest tinkle of sound would shatter the universe like a thin globe of glass. Safety is always an issue at sea. But in most cases, the ship is the protection from danger, not the cause of it. On tankers one lives in a rather unreal world, always aware, careful, suspended in a purgatory between life and death.

The ship is like the Earth. The Earth rolls along through space, and the ship steams along over the ocean. A collision with another such body, or the wrong combination of chemicals, and both become cosmic dust. A big "boom" that nobody hears. Suns, planets, meteors collide, leaving only dust and fragments. Ships sink, resulting only in a little oil and debris. Lives vanish from the face of the waters.

Oddly enough, one so often becomes interested in the parade, so intent in watching others and speculating upon their ways and lives, that one forgets that he is part of it all. Being what McGuire, one of our seamen, would call the "not-so-innocent bystander" has its drawbacks. It is a grand show in the end, and futile or not, I'd not want to miss it, so safety and life are precious.

Funny people in a funny world. It was twenty years ago that I first met Helen, so frail and blond and beautiful. I first heard my mother speaking of how lovely she was, this girl that had moved in to the neighborhood. Then I saw her, and she was like every princess that I had ever dreamed of rescuing from any number of dragons or giants. I think I was in love from the start, and she said that she was too.

And there is the question. Is one ever in love with a woman? Or is it only one's imagination of that woman, that girl? One reads into a certain personality, even a face and figure, a lot of illusions, a lot of qualities that are not really there. But I didn't philosophize then. It was love.

Why should I complain? I had that, and nothing can take it from me, although the memory of these later years has left a bitter taste. I wonder what happened to that girl. I married her and lost her. Oh, she was with me for a while, but time and distance change many things, and neither of us was quite what the other expected.

I doubt if I have changed so much. I was always quiet. Helen was gay and bright, tender and gentle too. She realizes as much as I what we have lost. Neither blames the other now. All that is over and past.

Looking back, I can see many things that might have been different—words that could have been recalled, things that might have remained unsaid—but most of all our mistakes lay in trying to live what at best was no more than a dream. We were two fortunate people—we had an idyllic moment—and then proved ourselves all too human by trying to make a lifetime of it.

There goes the bell. In a minute now Worden will be along to call me, and then another watch on the bridge. It is pleasant up there, gives a man time to think. No sea running, either, and just a light breeze somewhere on our quarter.

Worden is a Texan. Born on a cattle ranch, he tells me. Wonder how he got to sea. A phlegmatic, hard-boiled sort of chap, but a fine seaman, and very conscientious. Drinks like a fish, they tell me, when he's ashore; never at sea, however. He and McGuire would certainly make a pair in a street brawl. I like the man, although Wesley does not. But I can understand that. Our Mr. Wesley is quite conscious of his newly won mate's ticket, and feels quite pleased with himself. A nice enough fellow, but still—all things considered, Worden is nine times the seaman. Give me Worden in a pinch. Wesley is like a lot of these nice boys— smart enough, but they can't stand the gaff.

And there are the bells, eight of them in a row. McGuire always rings them in that snappy, professional manner. I wonder how many more times I'll hear eight bells strung together like that. Well, after this crossing they will all be heard in Asiatic waters—I am not going back.

TEX WORDEN

Able Seaman

Tex Worden shoved his way through the crowd in the Slave Market and pushed his book through the wicket.

The clerk looked up, taking in the blistered face and swollen hands. "What'll you have, buddy? Want to register?"

"Nah, I'm here to play a piano solo. What'd you think?"

"A wisecracker, eh? You guys all get smart when you get to port. I'm used to it, but one of these days I'm coming around from behind here and kicking the hell out of one of you!"

"Well, you don't see me runnin' away, do you? You just come out from behind that counter, and I'll lay you in the scuppers."

At a signal from the man behind the wicket a big man pushed his way through the crowd and tapped Tex Worden on the shoulder.

"All right, buddy, take it easy. Take care of business or move along."

Tex turned away from the officer, waiting for his book. The clerk opened it grudgingly, and then looked up, startled.

"You were on the *Rarotonga*!"

"So what?"

"Why, I heard only one of the crew was saved!"

"Yeah? So who the hell do you think *I* am? And that 'saved' business is the bunk. I saved myself. Now, come on, get my book fixed. I want to get out of here!"

The plainclothesman spoke more affably.

"No kiddin', are you Tex Worden?"

"Yeah."

"Hell, that must've been some wreck. The papers say if it wasn't for you none of the passengers would have got back. Dorgan was on that ship, too!"

"What do you mean, Dorgan?"

"Hank Dorgan, the detective from L.A. He was one of the toughest coppers in this part of the country!"

Tex had nothing to say about that. He picked up his book and turned toward the door, looking the crowd over for a familiar face. Everything he owned had gone down with the *Rarotonga*. There was money coming to him, but how long it would be before he saw any of it was a question.

Near the door he glimpsed a slight, buck-toothed seaman in a blue pea jacket who looked familiar. He edged through the crowd toward him. "Hi, Jack, how about stakin' a guy to some chow?"

"Hey? Don't I know you? Tex, isn't it?"

"That's right. Weren't you on the *West Ivis* when I was?"

"I'm Conrad ... Shorty Conrad. Come on, there's a greasy spoon right down the street." Once they were outside, Shorty looked at Worden, noticing the sunburn and bandaged hands. "What happened to you?"

"I was on the *Rarotonga*."

The sailor shook his head in awe. "*Jee-sus!* You were the only one who came back!"

"Some passengers made it. Not many, but some."

"I heard about that! You're a hero. And with Hazel Ryan yet. And Thornton Price! The actress and the millionaire! You brought them back alive."

"Yeah. Me an' Frank Buck. If this is how it feels to be a hero, you can have it. I'm broke. There's a hearing today—maybe I can hit up the commissioner for a few bucks."

They took stools at the counter and the burly Greek wiped his hands on his apron and stared at them. "You boys got the money? I don't like to ask, but we get stiffed a lot."

"I got it." Shorty showed him a handful of silver dollars.

They ordered coffee and hamburger steaks. Tex leaned his elbows against the counter. He was tired, very tired. He felt he would fall off his stool if he wasn't careful, and he didn't even have the price of a bed. His shoulders ached and his hands were sore. They hurt when he used them and they hurt almost as much when he didn't.

"That gang still down in the valley?" If he could rustle up two bits, Tex knew he could rent a bed in one of the decaying shacks on the hillside. But if he had any more than that the local roughnecks might try to roll him for the rest. Even after a week in the hospital of the ship that picked them up, he wasn't in any shape to defend himself.

"Happy Valley? The same old gang, an' just as tough as ever. It depends on who's in port. Mahoney, Fitzpatrick, the McFee brothers, Russian Fred, Black Pete, and the Swedes. You ain't got a beef with them, do ya?"

"No."

"Jees, but that Fitz could sure scrap! I saw him whip 'Frisco' Grady one night in the damnedest brawl you ever saw! There's a guy around here who beat him, though."

"Who's that?"

"McGuire. Denny McGuire. He don't look like a tough guy, but they say he used to be a prizefighter."

"Ha! I'd like to have seen Fitz get it. That guy's had it comin' for a good long time!" Tex Worden took a long breath. "It was a nasty storm, Shorty. You never saw wind like that."

"She went down quick, eh? I heard it was like fifteen minutes."

"Maybe. Starb'rd half door gave way, then the engine room bulkhead. The water put the fires out. No power, no pumps—it was a madhouse."

They were silent, sipping their coffee and eating their greasy steaks. Finally Shorty asked, "How long were you out there?"

"Fifteen days, just a few miles off the equator. It rained once—just in time."

Familiar faces drifted by the door. He knew some of them but could not recall their names. They were faces he'd seen from Hong Kong to Hoboken, from Limehouse to Malay Street in Singapore or Grant Road in Bombay, from Gomar Street in Suez to the old American Bar in Liverpool. They were pimps and prostitutes, seamen, fishermen, and bums, but they were all walking around on solid ground. He was glad to be back. Hell, he was glad to be alive.

Tex Worden looked down at his hands. Under the bandages they were swollen, with angry red flesh where the blisters were starting to heal. His face was burned so badly he could not touch it to shave. He looked frightening and felt worse.

He did not want to think of those bitter, brutal days when he had rowed the boat, hour after hour, day after day, all sense of time, all sense of motion forgotten. After the storm there had been no wind, just a dead calm, the only movement being the ripples in the wake of the lifeboat.

He blinked and sat up suddenly. "I got to stop by the commissioner's office. They want to ask me some questions about this mess. Sort of a preliminary inquiry, I guess."

There were several men in business suits in the conference room when they entered. They all looked at Tex, and Shorty quickly took a seat near the door, pushing back against the dark paneling, holding his hat in his hands.

"Thank you, son," the commissioner began. "That was a good job you did out there."

"There ain't much I can tell you, sir," Tex said. "But I'll do my best."

The commissioner dropped into a swivel chair behind the table. "Good. We will not keep you any longer than we must, but naturally we have to arrive at some conclusions as to what took place and what caused the disaster. If there is anything you can tell us, we'd be glad to hear it."

Shorty stole a glance at the big man with the red face. A company man, here to protect its interests. He knew the type.

"Well, I had come off watch about a half hour before it all happened, and when I went below everything seemed neat and shipshape. It was a rough night, hard on the passengers but nothing we sailors weren't used to. The ship settled into the trough of a wave and I was sitting on my bunk in the fo'c'sle taking off my shoes.

"Except this time when she settled she didn't rise again, not so quick an' light, at least. Stu, he was lyin' in the top bunk, he sat up an' stared at me. He said, 'What the hell happened?' And I said I didn't know. Then it happened again, worse. This time we took a wave clear over the fo'c'sle.

"He jumped down, and I was pulling my shoes back on. So was he, an' we ran up on deck. We were riding real low and starting to list. Between seas we ran aft, looking for the mate. People were milling around and there was a lot of confusion. Before we found anyone, the signal came for boat stations, so I went up on the boat deck. Last I saw of Stu he was trying to break open a jammed door; I could hear people behind it.

"She was starting to settle fast, going down with a heavy list to starb'rd. I was mighty scared because I remembered that starb'rd half door, and—"

"What about the half door, Worden? What was wrong with it?"

"Nothing at all, Commissioner," the company man interrupted. "The company inspector—"

"Just a minute, Mr. Winstead." The commissioner spoke sharply. "Who is conducting this inquiry?"

"Well, I—"

"Proceed with your story, Worden."

"The half door was badly sprung, sir. Somebody said the ship had been bumped a while back, and I guess they paid no mind to repairs. Anyway, it wasn't no bother unless they was loaded too heavy, and—"

"What do you mean, Worden? Was the ship overloaded?"

Winstead scowled at Worden, his lips drawing to a thin, angry line.

"Well, sir, I guess I ain't got no call to speak, but—"

"You just tell what happened at the time of the wreck, Worden. That will be sufficient!" Winstead interrupted.

"Mr. Winstead! I will thank you not to interrupt this man's story again. I am conducting this inquiry, and Mr. Worden is the sole remaining member of the crew. As a seafaring man of many years' experience, he understands ships, and he was there when it happened. I intend to hear *all*—let me repeat, *all*—he has to say. We certainly are not going to arrive at any conclusions by concealing anything. If your vessel was in proper condition, you have nothing to worry about— but I must say your attitude gives rise to suspicion." He paused, glancing up at the reporters, who were writing hurriedly. "Now, Worden, if you please. Continue your story."

"Well, sir, before we left I was standin' by number three hatch waiting for the last loads to swing aboard so's I could batten her down, an' I heard Mr. Jorgenson—he was the mate—say that he didn't like it at all. The *Rarotonga* usually carried just passengers and mail, but this trip we also had some construction equipment for the Canal Zone. Anyway, the mate said loading so heavy with that bad door was asking for trouble, and he went on to mention the bulkhead amidships.

"I don't know much about it, sir, except the talk in the fo'c'sle about the bulkhead between the hold and engine room. One of the men who'd been chipping rust down there said you didn't dare chip very hard or you'd drive your hammer right through, it was that thin.

"When I was ashore clearing the gangway, I saw she was loaded down below the Plimsoll marks."

"Weren't you worried, Worden? I should think that knowing the conditions you would have been."

"No, sir. Generally speaking, men working aboard ship don't worry too much. I've been going to sea quite a while now, an' it's always the other ships that sink, never the one a fellow's on. At least that's the way it is until somethin' happens. If she sinks, then she sinks, an' that's all there is to it."

"I see."

"Yes, sir. An' there was trouble before we were three days out. Me an' a couple of others were called to help Chips caulk that half door. You know, it's a door in the ship's side they load cargo through. Not all ships have 'em. That door, it didn't fit right. Normal times, with a normal load, it was all right.

"But three days out we had a spot of bad weather, some of that cargo shifted a mite, and she began to make water, so we had to re-caulk the door.

"To get back to that night, sir. When I got to my boat station, I saw one of the officers down on the deck with his head all stove in. I don't know whether he got hit with something or whether it was done by a bunch of passengers fightin' over the boat. Ever'body was yellin' an' clawin', so I waded in an' socked a few of them and got them straight-ened out.

"I told them they'd damn well better do what they were told be-cause I was the only one who knew how to get that lifeboat into the water. After that they quieted down some. A bunch of them ran off aft, because there was another boat already in the water, but I got busy with the lifeboat cover.

"All of a sudden it was still, so quiet it scared you. The wind still blowing and big waves all around but ghostly still. You could hear a body speak just like I'm speakin' now. It was like everything quieted down to let us die in peace.

"All those people who'd been yellin' an' fightin' stood there lookin' at me, and one little fellow in a gray suit—he had a tie on an' every-thing. He was Jewish, I think. He asked me what he could do, and I told him to get to the other end of the boat, to loose the falls and lower away when I did.

"I got the boat cover off, and we got the boat into the water, and the ship was down so far and canted over that it was no problem gettin' those few folks into the lifeboat.

"I took a quick look around. The other boat was already away, and there were two ABs with it, Fulton an' Jaworski. They had maybe thirty people in that boat, and I saw one of the stewards there, too. There was nobody else in sight, but I could hear some yellin' forward.

"I jumped into the boat and told the Jew to cast off. I got oars into the water, and we started looking for others. When we got out a ways, I could see Sparks was still in the radio shack.

"Then the ship gave a kind of lunge and went down by the head. She just dipped down and then slid right away, going into the water on her beam ends with all the portside boats just danglin' there, useless, as they couldn't be got into the water. At the last minute, as she went under, I saw a man with an ax running from boat to boat cutting the falls. He was hoping they'd come up floating, and a couple of them did.

"All of a sudden I see a man in the water. He was a pleasant-looking man with gray hair, and he was swimmin'. He looked so calm I almost laughed. 'Cold, isn't it?' he says, and then he just turns and swims off, cool as you please. You'd have thought the beach wasn't fifty feet away.

"It's things like that fairly take your wind, sir, and there I was, trying to pull the lifeboat away from the ship and hopin' for the best.

"I turned my head once and looked back. Mostly I was trying to guide the boat through wreckage that was already afloat. When I looked back—this was just before she went under—I glimpsed somebody standin' on the bridge, one arm through the pilothouse window to hang on, and he was lighting his pipe with his free hand.

"It just didn't seem like it could be happenin'. There I was just minutes before, a-comin' off watch, all set for a little shut-eye, and now here I was in a lifeboat, and the ship was goin' down.

"There must have been nearly a hundred people in the water, and not a whisper out of any of them. Like they was all in shock or somethin' of the kind. Once a guy did yell to somebody else. Then something exploded underwater—maybe the boilers busted; I wouldn't know. Anyway, when it was over, a lot of those folks who'd been in the water were gone. I fetched the bow of my boat around and rowed toward something white floating in the water. It was a woman, and I got her into the boat."

"Was that Hazel Ryan?" a reporter asked.

"No, it was Lila, a stewardess. Then I held the boat steady whilst another man climbed in. He pointed out three people clingin' to a barrel. I started for them.

"The sea was rough, and folks would disappear behind a wave, and sometimes when you looked, they weren't there anymore. Those people were havin' a time of it, tryin' to hang on to that barrel, so I got to them fast, and folks helped them aboard. The Ryan woman was one of them.

"I'll give her this. First moment she could speak, she asked if there was anything she could do, and I said just to set quiet and try to get warm, if I needed help I'd ask for it.

"It was funny how black everything was, yet you could see pretty well for all of that. You'd see a white face against the black water, but by the time you got there, it was gone.

"One time I just saw an arm. Woman's, I think it was. She was right alongside the boat, and I let go an oar an' grabbed for her, but her arm slipped right through my fingers.

"Some of those we'd picked up were in panic and some in shock. That Jewish fellow with the necktie and all, Schwartz, he didn't know a thing about the sea, but he was cool enough. We moved people around, got the boat trimmed, and I got her bow turned to meet the sea and started to try to ride her out."

"Did you think about the radio? Ships might have been headed for your position."

"Sparks was in there, and he was sending. I am sure of that, but he hadn't any orders, and most shipmasters don't want any Mayday or SOS goin' out unless they say. If he sent it, he sent it on his own, because the old man never made the bridge. Later—well, after the storm we had no idea where the wreck had happened."

"The man you saw lighting his pipe?"

"Jorgenson, I think. He was watch officer, but they were changin' watch, so I don't know. He wasn't heavy enough for the old man.

"Anyway, I'd no time to think of them. The sea was makin' up, and I was havin' the devil's own time with that boat. She'd have handled a lot easier if we'd had a few more people aboard.

"Lila, she was hurtin'. Seemed like she was all stove up inside, and the shock was wearin' off. She was feelin' pain, turnin' and twisting like, and the Ryan woman was trying to help. She and that little Jew, they worked over her, coverin' her with coats, trying to tuck them under so she'd ride easier. The rest just sat and stared."

"No other boats got off?"

"I don't know—except that boat with Fulton and Jaworski. They were good men, and they'd do what could be done."

"How was the weather?"

"Gettin' worse, sir. There was nobody to spell me on the oars because nobody knew anythin' about handling a boat in a heavy sea. I shipped the oars and got hold of the tiller, which made it a mite easier.

"Lila had passed out; spray was whippin' over the boat. I was hangin' on to that tiller, scared ever' time a big one came over that it would be the last of us. You just had to live from one sea to the next."

"How long did the storm last?"

"About two days. I don't rightly remember because I was so tired everything was hazy. When the sea calmed down enough, I let Schwartz have the tiller. I'd been grippin' it so hard and so long I could hardly let go."

"You were at the tiller forty-eight hours without relief?"

"Yes, sir. Maybe a bit more. But after that she began to settle down, and the sun came out."

"The boat was provisioned according to regulations?"

"Yes, sir. We'd some trouble about water later but the rations were what they were supposed to be."

"How about the crew and the officers? Were they efficient in your opinion?"

"Sure. Yes, they were okay. I've been going to sea quite a spell, and I never have seen any seaman or officer shirk his job. It ain't bravery nor lack of it, just that he knows his job and has been trained for it.

"Passengers? Well, all of a sudden everything is different. There's turmoil an' confusion; there's folks runnin' back and forth, and the passengers don't know what's going on."

"How long before she sank?"

"Fifteen minutes, give or take a few. It surely wasn't more, though. It might have been no more than five. We'd made quite a bit of water before the cargo shifted and she heeled over. With that half door underwater, then maybe the engine room bulkhead, the water might have put the fires out. No pumps or power—she just filled up and sank."

"Mr. Commissioner?" Winstead asked. "I'd like permission to ask a few questions. There are a few matters I'd like to clear up."

"Go ahead."

"Now, my man, if you'd be so kind. How many were in the boat when you got away from the scene of the wreck?"

"Eight."

"Yet when you were picked up by the SS *Maloaha* there were but three?"

"Yes."

"How do you account for that?"

"Lila—she was the stewardess—she died. Like I said, she'd been hurt inside. She was a mighty good woman, and I hated to see her go. Clarkson—he went kind of screwy. Maybe he didn't have all his buttons to start with. Anyway, he got kind of wild and kept starin' at a big shark who was following us. One night he grabbed up a boat hook and tried to get that shark. It was silly. That shark was just swimmin' along in hopes. No use to bother him. Well, he took a stab at that shark and fell over the side. The shark got what it wanted.

"Handel, he just sat an' stared. Never made no word for anybody, just stared. He must've sat that way for eight or nine days. We all sort of lost track of time, but he wouldn't take water, wouldn't eat a biscuit. He just sat there, hands hangin' down between his knees.

"I'd rigged a sort of mast from a couple of oars and part of the boat cover. Anyway, the little sail I rigged gave us some rest, and it helped. Late one day we were movin' along at a pretty fair rate when I saw a squall coming. She swept down on us so quick that I gave the tiller to Schwartz and stumbled forward to get that sail down before we swamped. With the wind a-screaming and big seas rollin' up, I'd almost reached the sail when this Handel went completely off his course. He jumped up and grabbed me, laughin' and singin', trying to dance with me or somethin'.

"Strugglin' to get free, I fell full length in the boat, scrambled up, and pulled that sail down, and when I looked around, Handel was gone."

"Gone?" Winstead said.

"You mean—over the side?" the commissioner asked.

"That's right. Nearest thing I could figure out was that when I fell, he fell, too. Only when I fell into the bottom, he toppled over the side.

"Rain and blown spray was whippin' the sea, and we couldn't see him. No chance to turn her about. We'd have gone under had we tried.

"For the next ten hours we went through hell, just one squall after another, an' all of us had to bail like crazy just to keep us afloat."

"So," Winstead said, "you killed a passenger?"

"I don't know *what* happened, mister. Whatever it was, it was pure accident. I'd nothin' against the man. He was daffy, but until that moment he'd been harmless. I figure he didn't mean no harm then, only I had to get free of him to save the boat."

"At least, that is your story?"

There was a noise at the door. Shorty half-turned to see two women coming into the room, followed by a man. Then another man entered. One of the ladies was Hazel Ryan; he recognized her despite the lack of makeup and the sunburned face. The second man to enter was Thornton Price. The four sat down on one side of the room. The younger of the men was big, a broad-shouldered fellow. He caught Shorty's eye and waved a hand cheerfully.

"All right," Winstead said briefly. "We will let that rest for the moment. That accounts for three. Now, what became of the other two?"

"Schwartz, he come to me in the night a few days later. We were lyin' in a dead calm, and most of our water was gone. Sky was clear, not a cloud in sight, and we'd a blazin' hot day ahead. He told me he was goin' over the side, and he wanted me to know because he didn't want me to think he was a quitter.

"Hell, that little kike had more guts than the whole outfit. I told him nothing doing. Told him I needed him, which was no lie. It was a comfort just to have him there because what he didn't know he could figger out when I told him. But he wouldn't accept that I needed him.

"It even came to the point where I suggested we toss a coin to see who went over. He wouldn't listen to that, and we both knew I was talkin' nonsense. I was the only seaman. The only one who could handle a boat. It was my job to bring that boat back with as many people as possible. Sure, I wanted to live as much as any man, but I had a job to do. I ain't done nothin' I wouldn't do again."

"I see. And what became of Mr. Dorgan?"

"Were you ever fifteen days in an open boat with damned little water? He died, too!"

Thornton Price's voice cut into the room. "You mean you killed him!"

Winstead turned quickly. "Ah, Mr. Price." He paused, looking at the commissioner. "You say Worden killed this other man?"

"Yes, I certainly did!" Price spoke heatedly. "I had been asleep, and just as I awakened, I heard Worden speaking. He said, 'You row the boat, and when you stop rowing, you die!'"

"Did you say that, Worden?"

"Yes. I did. I—"

"That will be enough!" Winstead snapped. "You have admitted you murdered two men. I think that is all until I can talk to some higher authority!" He glared at the shipping commissioner.

"What were the circumstances, Worden?" the commissioner asked.

"It was Dorgan, sir. After the storm I had no idea where the ship went down, so we had to head east—the closer we got to the coast the more likely it was that we'd be found. Well, he kept arguing. He was a police officer, and he tried to throw his weight around. He said I was crazy, that I was goin' the wrong way. He said I drank water at night when they were all asleep. Twice when I passed water forward for somebody else, he drank it—or he shared it with Mr. Price.

"Most of the others, they tried to take a hand in rowin' the boat. He was a strong man, but he refused. It was life or death for us, sir. It wasn't no talking matter. I was rowin' my heart out, but not for him.

"One night I woke up with him pourin' the last of our water down his damn throat. The Ryan woman, she was tuggin' at his arm to try to stop him, but it was too late.

"I went at him. We had it out, right there. He was some bigger than me and strong, but there was no guts to him. I smashed him up some and put him between the oars. I told him to row, that he'd live as long as he rowed."

"And what happened to Dorgan?"

Tex Worden's face was bleak. "He quit rowin' a day before we got picked up."

Winstead turned to the commissioner. "Sir, this man has just admitted to killing a passenger; perhaps he killed two or three. As to his motives—I think they will appear somewhat different under cross-examination.

"We have evidence as to this man's character. He is known along the waterfronts as a tough. He frequents houses of ill fame. He gets into drunken brawls. He has been arrested several times for fighting. His statements here today have cast blame upon the company. I intend to introduce evidence that this man is not only a scoundrel, but an admitted murderer! He is hardly an unimpeachable authority!"

Tex sat up slowly.

"Yes, I've been arrested for fightin'. Sometimes I've come ashore and had a few too many; after a trip on one of those scows of yours, a man has to get drunk. But I'm a seaman. I do my job. There's never a man I've worked with will deny that. It's easy to sit around on your fat behinds and say what you'd have done or what should have been done. You weren't there.

"Handel now. He wasn't responsible. Somethin' happened to him that he never expected. He could have lived his life through, a nice, respected man, but all of a sudden it wasn't the same anymore. Maybe it affected his mind, or maybe he was always crazy.

"Hazel Ryan? She has moxie. When I told her it was her turn to row, she never hesitated, and I had to make her quit. She wasn't all that strong, but she was game. A boatload like her an' I could have slept halfway back.

"Dorgan was a bad apple. Everyone was on edge because of him. He'd been used to authority and was a born bully. He was used to takin' what he wanted an' lettin' others cry about it. I told him what he had to do, and he did it after we had our little set-to."

"Who did you think you were, Worden? God? With the power of life and death?"

"Listen"—Worden leaned forward—"if I'm the only seaman in the boat, when we have damn little water, an' we're miles off the steamer lanes, when we're sittin' in the middle of a livin' hell, you can just bet I'm *Mister* God as far as that boat's concerned.

"Your company wasn't there to help. You weren't there to help, nor was the commissioner. Sure, Schwartz prayed, an' Mr. Price prayed, prayed with tears streaming down his face. Me, I rowed the boat."

He lifted his hands, still swollen and bandaged. "Fifteen days on and off, tryin' to get back where we might be picked up. We made it."

"We made it," he repeated, "but there was a lot who didn't."

The commissioner rose, and Winstead gathered his papers, his features set and hard. He cast a measuring glance at Worden.

"You'll have a chance to explain all that, my man, at a formal inquiry. And I'll have Thornton Price there as a witness."

"You'll have to call me, too, Mr. Winstead!" Hazel Ryan's voice was throaty, deep.

Winstead turned.

"Why, of course, Miss Ryan. I had planned on that. You will make a most valuable witness!"

Hazel Ryan walked over to the table. In a neat gray suit, she was a picture.

"But my testimony would not be the same as that of Mr. Price. I will tell the story of a man who sat at the tiller and kept that boat afloat during a storm, who fought the waves until his hands were frightfully blistered, and who took off his coat, yes, and his shirt, to help make a pillow for the stewardess. I'll tell the story of a man who fought and killed to keep water for the rest of us, and how he rowed the boat when we were too weak to stand, how he missed serving himself water at least three times so he could give it to me, and to that—to our Mr. Price. Call your inquest, Mr. Winstead, I'm sure everyone would love to hear what I have to say."

Shorty got up and walked over to the window, watching the smoke rising from over Terminal Island. He heard Winstead go by behind him, and a few moments later, the others. Then Tex came up, his eyes hard. They turned to go.

"Oh, by the way, Worden!"

"Yes, sir?"

The commissioner walked up and put his hand on Worden's shoulder.

"Officially, I have to tell you to remain in port. But man to man, I'll say you're in a bad spot. Winstead is going to do whatever he can to discredit your statements about the condition of his ship. That includes criminal charges. The insurer will fight the company's claims, and anyone who gets between them will be eaten alive.

"Miss Ryan would be a big help, but still . . . Well, I don't envy you. Personally—and I never said this—I'd get on the first ship I could find."

They rode a self-service elevator down to the echoing marble and bronze lobby. When they reached the street, Tex hesitated on the curb. Up the block a brand-new convertible was idling, and both the car and the women in it were attracting attention.

"That Ryan lady is all right," Tex commented. "You can never tell about passengers, but she's okay!"

"That guy with her?" Shorty pointed. "That's McGuire, the boxer I was telling you about."

Tex nodded his approval. "Well, he goes around with swell dames. Either one of them could put their shoes under my bed—especially the redhead."

"Uh-huh. She looks familiar. I guess I've seen her on the screen. I heard McGuire did some work in pictures. Fight scenes, stuff like that."

Down on Harbor Boulevard a taxi sped past, the tires whining on the pavement. Shorty looked up at Tex again.

"I gotta connection. There's a tanker that's just out of dry dock. Want to give it a try?"

"Well," Tex shrugged, "I don't make my livin' in no courtroom."

THE PRIVATE LOG OF
JOHN HARLAN, SECOND MATE

March 22nd: Fire and Life Boat Drill today, and it is good to see how the men come alive. Everyone has their task and station and, of course, tanker crews take these drills very seriously. The response must be automatic, and in the chaos of an emergency the crew must react in a rapid but orderly manner. Instilling a pattern of cooperation has additional benefits. Every crew has troublemakers, and there are few worse than Mahoney, one of our oilers. The hope is that constant training and the camaraderie of working together can smooth over unresolved differences. I like to think that our crew, even a newcomer like young David Jones, would be among the best in a crisis. A crisis we pray will never come.

I shall not go back. I made that decision on my return from the last trip. My plans during my short stay were made with that in mind. Helen knew what I was thinking, even though we did not discuss it. However she wishes to live is her business, but I want Steve and Betty to have every possible chance, and they can't have it with her. She knew what I had decided, yet when I suggested taking the children to Tom and Hazel in Oakland she said nothing. They will be happy there, for Tom and Hazel have no children of their own, and have the money to care for them better than either of us could. The other child is not mine, and Helen will know best what should be done with him.

I have said I was not going back. I wonder if anyone ever goes back? What was it Hamlet said, "That undiscovered country, from whose bourn no traveller returns . . ."

He was speaking of death. But is not every goodbye, every leave-taking, a little death? Can a man ever return quite the same as he left? We say goodbye, we leave familiar, well-loved people and places, and the days, weeks, and months pass, perhaps years.

When we take the road back, and finally stand where we stood before, all is strange.

Our very bodies have changed. The dust of many roads, the brine of ancient seas, the air we have breathed, the food we have eaten, the wounds we have received, all these things change us. We have come back, groping in the past for something that is no longer there, a gap that nothing can fill.

Old places are better left behind; old loves better kept as memories, and as the ship steams onward into the days and nights, all that I have known and all that I have loved, I am leaving behind me. Little Steve will become a man without me, Betty will grow tall, will have sweethearts, will marry, raise children perhaps, and die, and I shall not go back.

After this last time at home, Helen and I have come to a parting of the ways, and the fault was neither hers nor mine. She was alone too much, but the only way I knew was the way of the sea. If she changed, who am I to criticize?

Out East where I am going, where this ship is taking me, there are plenty of men who never go back. They work, and live, and die among those romantic islands where the seas go blue, the foliage holds so deep a green, and where the very names sing a melody. Saigon, Semarang, Cebu—Vanua Levu, Baliwan, Sumatra—Hankow, Hong Kong, Shanghai—Well, I have visited some; now I shall know them all.

I can hear some of the fo'c'stle crowd singing back aft. Shorty Conrad, oddly enough, plays a guitar, and sings western cow-trail ballads with a voice that is surprisingly good and would be better if he would avoid that nasal tone that all those fellows persist in using. Jones (and his first name is David, too!) sings very well. He is an ordinary seaman making his first trip, a nice lad of about seventeen. He is singing a song that was popular a few years ago, "I'm Waiting for Ships That Never Come In." Well, aren't we all?

DAVID JONES

Ordinary Seaman

David Jones walked slowly into the morning. Already there were miles behind him, and it was still early. He gazed up to the bright green leaves of the cottonwoods, rustling endlessly, and his eyes filled. He stopped for a moment, looking back. Then he went on, the dust curling up from his steps in little whorls. He wiped his eyes, fearful of meeting someone who would wonder at his tears. He felt very young and very much alone.

The dust climbed his clothes and settled in his nostrils. The heavy air lay thickly about him and slow sweat streaked his face. Ahead, he could see the highway, a ribbon of hope that led away into new lands and all his tomorrows. When he reached it, the hot smell of the asphalt made him feel slightly ill. He walked on and then somehow the morning was gone, and it was afternoon. There were short rides and alternating periods of hiking, but his feet were tired, and in places his clothes stuck to his body with perspiration.

Ahead of him the road forked, the main highway swinging to the left along the railroad, while another road dropped under the track and disappeared in the grove of elm and cottonwood. A small stream flowed lazily between grassy banks and low brush. It looked cool and pleasant under the trees. He left the grade and walked down to the stream. Off to the left the crows were holding a caucus in a green meadow, and several cows dozed, tails switching away flies. The air was cool, and occasionally a stray breeze drifted down among the trees.

He seated himself on the bank and pulled off his shoes and socks, letting his tired feet sink into the cool water. Leaning back, he stirred his feet, liking the swirl of water around his toes. Somewhere downstream a fish leaped, and he idly flipped a stone toward the spot, then watched the ripples slowly widen, lapping against the opposite shore.

Suddenly he heard voices, and sat up quickly, heart pounding. Already he was acquiring the awareness of the casual wayfarer, who, being a stranger, is always uncertain of his reception. He drew back warily.

Three men were coming across the grass from the road. One was a young fellow close to his own age, the others were older. One of them, a big man in his late thirties, had broad, powerful shoulders and a flat nose.

"Hi, kid! Coolin' off the dogs, are you?" he commented. "Hoofin' it don't never pay. Better to grab yourself an armful of boxcars. Ain't that right, boys?"

"That's right. This hitchhiking ain't so hot. I don't mind the hitches, but the hiking gets my goat. It's too hard on shoe leather, and The Sally don't have so many to offer anymore."

"'The Sally'?" Davy was puzzled.

"Yeah, the Salvation Army. The guys and dames that stand on the corners at night singin'. You know, 'Throw a nickel on the drum an' you'll be saved.' Good people usually, but some of their flophouses are so crummy a guy can't sleep for fear the blankets'll walk away."

The third man sat down on the bank and pulled off his brogans and heavy woolen socks. He lowered his big feet into the water. Then, rolling up his trousers, he began washing them with thick work-coarsened hands.

"Going far?" David asked.

"West Coast for me," Flat-Nose answered agreeably. "I keep lookin' for the Rock Candy Mountains, but they sure are hard to find. I been huntin' between jobs for twenty years now.

"Tommy and The Polack," he added, "were talkin' about heading north to Portland. Me, I ain't going a bit farther north than I am right now. A guy's got to have web feet to live up along that coast, it rains so much."

Tommy began collecting sticks for a fire, and slipping on his shoes and socks, David helped him. He felt better, and only when he stopped to look back toward the road did he remember Morningside. The hours since he had seen his mother buried seemed like years.

"Come on, kid," Tommy said. "Might as well string along with us. We'll show you the ropes, an' it'll save you some walkin'.."

The big man returned with four tin cans and a half-gallon pail; they had been stashed back in the trees, Davy realized in amazement. Left behind for the communal use of other men . . . other hoboes. He filled the small pail from water upstream, and Tommy added coffee from a small paper sack. Dusk had settled over the countryside. Somewhere in the distance he could hear a cowbell. David looked up at the stars just appearing through the tops of the trees, and then back at the faces of the men near the fire. The Polack had come up and was tying his shoes. In the flicker of the flame their faces softened, and David moved nearer to the fire, pushing a handful of sticks closer.

"Say, Jack," Tommy said, looking at the big man. "I asked the kid here to string along with us. That okay by you?"

"Sure thing. Glad to have you, kid. The more the merrier."

The hum of talk hung over the fire, friendly, cheerful. The coffee tasted good. Davy's new friends used a slang he could barely understand: "red-ball freights," "shacks," "Gandy Dancers," and "manifests." It was a different world. But he felt somehow that he had always been a part of this, a world where men without money lived, searched for work, and traveled by night. These were the hoboes he had heard of—not toughs, but men with restless feet who had no trade, or only an outmoded one.

He was dozing against a tree when the whistle sounded. The three scrambled to their feet and kicked out the fire, and David got up, alert and ready. The coals hissed as they spilled coffee over them, and a thick, acrid smoke lifted to his nostrils. Then they were racing up the railroad embankment to crouch in the shadows away from the bright glare of the headlight. The huge engine thundered by, the cars rumbling after it. Suddenly he was afraid. The train seemed to be going too fast.

"Stick with me, kid," Jack yelled. "You stick with me!"

Then they were running beside an empty boxcar. Tommy swung in easily, and Jack after him. The Polack suddenly seemed to shed his lumbering awkwardness and heaved himself into the door with ease. Running desperately, David found himself panic-stricken at the thought of climbing into that speeding doorway, of what would happen if he tripped over some obstruction in the dark and took a header under those grinding wheels. But then, with a lunge, he grabbed at the sill and lifted himself up. For an agonizing moment he felt himself slipping, but a couple of strong hands grabbed him, and he was inside.

The train rumbled through the darkness, and the car creaked and groaned as they rounded a curve. Ahead, David could see the bright glow of the firebox as the locomotive pulled up a long curving grade. The wheels bumped monotonously, and once the headlights of a car at a crossing threw the boxcar door into broad relief.

The long freight rushed along into the night, thundering through little villages and past lonely farmhouse lights. Once they passed a farm where someone stood alone in the dark, lantern in hand, watching the train go by.

David sat in the doorway thinking of Morningside and Ruth. In the distance the lights of a town hung a wreath of stars against the dark. Finally, he lay flat on his back and stared up into the rumbling jolting darkness, until his eyelids grew heavy and then closed.

He was startled into wakefulness by a rough hand on his shoulder, and in the dim light of early morning he saw Jack's hard, flat face looming above him. "Come on, kid, make it snappy! We overslept, an' this damned town has a couple of bad bulls. We got to unload toot sweet. Get up, fer Christ's sake!"

David sprang to his feet and was just in time to see the "Yard Limit" sign flash past. The Polack, obviously frightened, leaped from the door and hit the ground rolling. A gunshot bit through the clear air.

But the big Polack was on his feet, and plunged into the brush just as another bullet whipped by him.

Rough hands pulled David away from the door of the car. "What's the matter? Why did they shoot at him?" he exclaimed, his face white.

"We're in a spot, kid. This railroad bull is a bad egg. He's killed twenty 'boes, maybe more. He'd kill you just as quick as look at you. There's two of 'em here. The Diamond-Back an' a big guy who's even worse. The guy's name is Hans Wolfe, but they call him the Big Bad Wolfe."

"But we haven't done anything!" David protested.

Jack shrugged. "We rode the train. Look, nobody gives a damn what happens to a hobo. The Wolfe has killed plenty. When he asks you questions, talk nice, see? No matter what he does. Just talk careful and keep your trap shut unless he asks you something."

They waited silently. There was something in the faces of Jack and Tommy that frightened David. He had heard stories of murderous railroad detectives from a farmhand who worked with him during harvest once, but had thought them just stories.

The train screeched and groaned to a stop, the cars bumped several times, and before they could drop to the ground a big man with a heavy, round face thrust his head into the door.

"All right, bums, on the ground! An' no funny stuff! I'm goin' to blast the first guy that makes a wrong move!"

They crawled out. Tommy's coat got caught on a nail in the door, but when one of the men grabbed him and jerked, he said nothing, although the coat ripped and Tommy almost fell. They stood in a line, waiting. The smaller man, his black eyes glittering, searched them.

The Diamond-Back went over Jack swiftly, while Wolfe loafed against the car. A Bull Durham sack, half-empty, a stubby pocketknife, some matches, a piece of leather string.

Tommy showed little more. A half-pack of tailor-mades, a stub of pencil, an extra pair of socks, and a few odds and ends. Wolfe snorted and turned to David, taking in his quiet face and general neatness.

"What you got on you?"

"Not very much, sir."

"Where you from, an' what's your name?"

"I'm David Jones, from Morningside."

"Jones, huh?" He turned to Diamond-Back. "Here's another Jones! Why the hell don't these punks find another name? That Old Man Jones sure must have got around!" He turned back to David. "Just one of the Jones boys, huh?"

"My name is Jones. I'm from Morningside. You can write there and find out if you want."

"What the devil do I care? You're just a bum, I don't give a damn where you're from!"

Wolfe searched him casually, finding the four dollars and twenty cents left of the five Miss Hazelton had made him take before he left. There was a note from Ruth, sent the day he left, and a snapshot of her: a frail, sweet girl with tranquil eyes.

"We'll keep this dough," Wolfe said. "That'll pay part of the fare for the ride you had."

The Diamond-Back stepped closer, craning his neck for a better look at the picture. "Let's see the dame, Chief," he said. Taking the picture, he studied it a moment in silence. "Hot-looking skirt, ain't she?" He grinned at David. "You should've brought her along, kid, I'd like to have taken her out in the bushes for a while!"

"She's a decent girl!" David said, his face set. Jack wet his lips and swallowed, watching Wolfe warily.

"That's what they all think!" the Diamond-Back laughed. "Bet she's been sleepin' with the butcher all the time!"

David's fist swung, hard. But Wolfe was watching and grabbed the boy's arm, spinning him around. Roughly, he slammed him back against the side of the car. With one hand on Davy's throat, he drove his big fist three times into the boy's face, slowly and methodically. "Smart kind, huh? I'll show you who's smart!" Wolfe whipped a hard right into the boy's groin, and as Davy tumbled forward, kneed him in the face.

Blind with pain, David tried to strike back, but fell forward to the ground, his face a smear of blood. Wolfe drew back his foot to kick, but Jack struck down the Diamond-Back's gun and swung a powerful fist to Wolfe's chin. The big detective fell back against the car, but then as Jack closed in, he pulled him into a clinch.

Tommy grabbed the Diamond-Back and swung him around. Before the shorter detective could raise his gun, the two fell to the ground, grappling desperately.

Tottering, David crawled to his feet. He was just in time to see Jack knocked staggering and Hans Wolfe fumble for his pistol. David caught up a chunk of coal, and stepping in, he smashed it against the base of the big detective's neck. The man dropped to the cinders, his body limp.

Jack regained his balance, and stooped over Wolfe. When he looked up his face was white and strained. "Tom," he said, "leave that guy! The kid's killed Wolfe an' we got to scram."

"I'm getting our stuff back. All right. Let's go!"

Crashing through a fringe of brush, they reached the narrow road, running hard. Then they took a path through a stretch of timber, and not until their breath was coming in gasps did they slow or take time to think. Frightened, scarcely able to realize what had happened, David walked beside the others, his throat tight.

Jack stopped, wiping the sweat from his forehead with a dirty bandanna. "Listen," he said, "those guys will be after us anytime now. It ain't sixty miles to the state line. But—"

"Hold on," Tommy said, "there's a car back there by that farmhouse!"

They waited beside the road, watching Tommy, afraid to talk. David felt sick, and suddenly he was very tired. Jack's big shoulders drooped. "Don't take it too hard, kid. That guy's had it coming for a long time. He's killed a lot of 'boes. It was lousy, him making those cracks. Anybody can see that girl's decent. When you been on the bum as long as I have, you find out there's lots of guys like Wolfe. Some of them get known all over the country, guys like Maricopa Slim and the Gila Monster, Yermo Red, and some others. Sometimes I don't know which is worse, the fat-cat bosses or the murderin' so-and-sos they hire to do their dirty work."

Almost before they realized it the car skidded to a halt. They piled in, Tommy shifted gears quickly, and they were off.

All day they kept to country roads and narrow lanes. Over devious routes they made it to the state line, and some miles beyond. At dark, out of gas, they abandoned the car in a lonely grove.

"We got to watch our step," Tommy said suddenly. "They'll have the word out. The longer we can stay clear of towns and people the better. But we got to eat, somehow. I got three bucks from Wolfe's pocket. Probably some of yours, kid."

Twice they ducked into the brush and hid. Once a truck passed them with three men carrying shotguns. All of them saw it, but they said nothing. It was a moonless, starless night. Lying in the brush waiting for the truck to pass, David thought of Ruth. All of that seemed so far away now. Soon they would have the news back in Morningside, the news that David Jones was a killer and a fugitive. Tears welled in his eyes, and a lump came to his throat. He tried to see Tommy's and Jack's faces in the dark, but could not.

There was a light ahead of them: a filling station where the country road they were walking crossed a paved highway. "Listen," Jack said. "We ain't going to get far without grub. Give me some of the dough. I'll go up to that joint and buy something to eat. Most of these stations have a few groceries. You guys stay out of sight."

Two large signboards made a V at the crossroads, and the two waited, watching the road through the latticework beneath the signs. One view commanded the highway, the other the lane.

"Gee, Tommy, Jack's a swell guy, isn't he?"

"They don't make 'em any better. Used t' be a pug, a long time ago, an he's still pretty good in a fight. I met him back in Chi. We come through together."

"You've both been mighty square with me. I don't know what I'd have done if—"

"Nuts! You wouldn't have been on that freight if we hadn't come along. We're all in it together, kid. If any one of us gets caught, he swings, see? Me an' him just as much as you!"

Suddenly Tommy gripped his shoulder. "Look!"

A big open car was swinging into the filling station from the highway. As it stopped, several men with rifles and shotguns got out. One man, tall and quite fat, walked toward them and stopped, looking down the lane. He carried a double-barreled shotgun in the hollow of his arm.

Inside the filling station there was silence, while they watched, helpless. Somewhere down there was Jack, cornered like a rat in a trap, and they could do nothing.

There was a sudden crash of glass and a shot, several men yelled, and then they saw a dark figure dash from the rear of the station with an armful of groceries. He leaped a ditch and came rushing on, running parallel to their hiding place. An avalanche of men poured from the station, and there was a crash of shots. Jack staggered, and pitched over on his face, spilling cans onto the road. Then he was on his feet again, stumbling forward. Tommy and David ran from behind the signs and dragged him into the brush. The posse spread out and came on, walking fast. Several of the men had flashlights.

"They got me, guys. Beat it, quick!"

"Nuts t' you, sailor! Grab an' arm, kid, an' let's go."

David grabbed Jack's arm, and then a thought struck him. "Say, let's duck around and grab their car!"

For a fleeting instant, Tommy hesitated. Then: "Well, I'll be damned! Let's try!"

Warily, they circled the station. The posse was hunting for them, but carefully because of the darkness. Most of them were family men, brave in numbers but with too much to lose and hesitant when spread out.

Half-dragging, half-carrying Jack, the boys slipped through a vacant garden plot and hunkered down at the edge of the road.

"You wait," David said. "I'll get the car!"

A bewildered station attendant in overalls and a greasy shirt stood staring after the posse, who were stumbling and swearing in the thick brush.

David slipped behind the wheel silently. It wasn't until he pressed on the starter that the attendant whirled about, his face pale. But the big car leaped forward, and the man sprang back, barely escaping its sudden lunge. A hundred yards farther on, David braked hard, stopping for Tommy to heave Jack in behind, then he let out the clutch and accelerated. Several men rushed into the road and fired futile shots after the car.

"We got to make time. They'll be phoning ahead."

"Not from that station they won't!" Tommy said. "I jerked down the wires!"

All night the big car droned on. David crouched over the wheel, listening to Jack's heavy breathing in the rear seat. The big man moaned occasionally, and David's hands gripped the wheel harder.

It was morning when he drove the car into a little clearing near some old straw stacks. The tank was empty.

"Help me with him," Tommy said. "He's all in."

Together they lifted Jack out and stretched him on the ground. He had been shot three times, and when he tried to speak the blood frothed from his mouth.

"I'll find some water," David said.

Taking a bottle from the car, he walked down to a ditch. When he returned it was too late; he knew it even before he got back. Tommy was standing there, swearing softly.

"We got to beat it," Tommy said. "Gosh, but I hate leaving him. He was a grand guy. He never had nothing, but he could do a day's work with any man."

The afternoon was hot and close. The breeze whispered itself away in the trees and vanished, leaving only heavy air, thick with the ominous heat that precedes a storm. Tommy looked up at the sky, where heavy billows of cloud were rolling up, black and threatening.

"Looks like we're in for a gully washer, kid. Wish we could find some shelter. We'll look like drowned rats when that's over. Make us too easily spotted." They plodded on, staying under cover as much as possible. Sometimes they passed fields where farmers were working, and once they crossed a highway to hide in the tall grass beyond.

"Say," Tommy said suddenly, "there's a water tank! Maybe there'll be a freight along pretty soon. We could get under the tank if there isn't." David looked at the clouds. A few spatters of rain fell. "Nobody will look close when there's a storm."

They sat down under the tank. It had been painted red, but the paint was blistered and peeling. A little shower came and went suddenly, leaving the skies still gray. David felt very homesick, very lonely, and very tired. He watched a big beetle crawling over the rocks and gravel, headed in one direction in spite of everything. Several times David pushed it back or put obstacles in its way, but it persisted, heading toward the track.

When a train whistled, they hid in the brush until it swept by—a fast passenger, not bothering with wayside water tanks. Los Angeles–bound, it was carrying people who knew where their next meal was coming from and weren't worried about the police. The train disappeared, and when Davy looked at the track again, the beetle was crushed against the side of the rail.

It was dusk when a freight stopped. They watched from the brush while the train crew moved back and forth, shouting and joking. Then, as the train began moving away, they crawled into an empty and rumbled off into the gathering night.

All over the country men were sitting down to eat. Davy imagined miners coming in from the pit and workers from the mill. They were putting down their black lunch boxes and washing over tin basins while they told their wives the latest yarn. With forks clutched in big, work-hardened hands, they talked of politics, of the price of the gold they broke from the rock but never saw, of the latest joke on the shift boss.

Back in Morningside, hundreds of miles away now, it might not be raining. Girls would be coming out to walk along the streets, arm in arm, talking and laughing or singing popular songs in low, sweet voices. They would drop in at the soda fountain at McKinley's Drug and talk with Oscar, who jerked sodas. The young fellows would sit around making wisecracks, talking football or the latest dance. Ruth and Grace would show up, and Jimmie, who clerked in the grocery store down the street, would ask Ruth if she'd heard from David. Or maybe they would be talking about him, and wondering about the story of the killing. They would speak of David Jones, and how they might have guessed, how trouble always finds trouble in the end.

David and Tommy traveled only by night. Once, they were questioned by a brakeman, but he didn't seem to care if they rode his train or not. Another time Tommy had a fight with a drunk who would have been better to have just slept it off. Soon after, a crowd of transients crawled into the car, and there was talk of riding fast trains, of flophouses, and much bragging. Then a short, tough little man spoke . . .

"What d' ya think—somebody bumped off the Big Bad Wolfe the other day!"

"Yeah," another said, "I heard that, too. The Diamond-Back got hell kicked out of him in the same mess. Three hard guys, it was. I heard one guy killed the Wolfe with one blow of his fist."

"Who's Wolfe?" Tommy asked, and David swallowed dryly.

"Wolfe?" The speaker stared incredulously. "I t'ought ever' guy on the road heard of the Wolfe. He was a dick. A railroad bull back East a ways. He killed a flock of 'boes. Just knocked 'em off to be tough. He beat me up once when I was a little nipper, an' I ain't never forgot it. Whoever did it should have a medal!"

When they left the train in Los Angeles they ate hotcakes and drank black coffee in a greasy spoon with money they'd begged on the street nearby. David was tired and still hungry. Seeing himself in the glass, he saw that his face was dirty, and his clothes dusty. Tommy grinned at him. "You sure changed some, kid! We better find a spot where we can wash up. What you plan on doin'?"

"I don't know," David said slowly. "I'm here, but I don't know what to do. I want to get a job, but that seems to be hard."

"You're damned right it's hard," Tommy said. "I got an uncle down in Oceanside. I'll go down there an' work with him for a while. I wished he had room for two, but he's pretty broke most of the time."

"I always wanted to see the ocean," David said finally. He couldn't fight the feeling he had to hide, but he knew he had to find some way to relax and forget.

In the bright morning the highway was a stream of cars flowing both ways, and David headed south toward the port. The air was crisp, and there was a feeling in it of vast spaciousness; it was a sense of the sea, although he did not yet recognize it.

Big trucks rumbled past, then small, sleek cars sliding in and out of traffic, streaming their way down to the port or back toward the hills, an almost musical rhythm in their comings and goings. David did not wait for a ride; he walked on into the bright sunshine, and the salty wind seemed to wash his doubts away. All was behind him now: Morningside, Wolfe, even his friends and the events of the last few days.

A truck ground to a stop beside him. "Hop in, buddy! If yer going down to 'Pedro!"

David got in. The truck driver was a big man in a grease-stained undershirt and overalls. His rugged face was scarred, but his grin was good-natured. "Kind of tough gettin' a ride, ain't it?" he asked.

"I haven't been trying very hard this morning," Davy said. "I like the sunshine. It feels good after some of the weather I've been through."

"Boy," the driver chuckled, "you should let the Chamber of Commerce quote you. Ever been here before?"

"Nope. Think I could find a job down there?"

The driver shrugged. "Damned if I know. You planning on going to sea?"

"I don't know," David said. "I'll try anything."

"I'll tell you what," the driver said. "You go down to the Harbor Chandlery on Front Street. Tell the boss you want to see Shannon, Borly Shannon. Tell him Mike sent you."

THE PRIVATE LOG OF
JOHN HARLAN, SECOND MATE

March 23rd: A light sea is running this evening, wind about force two; sighted a Standard tanker as I came off watch. She was homeward-bound. That is always a good feeling. The sea is a dangerous place, and ships like ours more dangerous still. On the tankers carrying high-test gasoline, naphtha, or benzene, they make us wear shoes without iron nails, for fear they might strike sparks. None of us pay much attention to it consciously, but at the back of our minds we are always aware of the risk.

My copy of *Standard Seamanship* tells me, "The flashpoint of an oil is the temperature at which it gives off an explosive vapor." The flashpoint of naphtha is only sixty-two degrees Fahrenheit. A dropped hammer might strike a spark that would ignite some fumes, or the spark might come from a bad electrical connection—lots of things. Is it any wonder we become somewhat indifferent to opinion, and live our own lives as we choose? I often think the average person is less understanding than he might be. People are so quickly moved to censure those who do the dangerous work of the world. Miners, lumberjacks, firemen, the police, and lots of others. They risk their lives providing for those who often criticize their ways.

I wonder how many women who wear diamond rings ever thought of how hard it was to get the diamond, the gold or platinum? Often enough, lives are lost in the process. The same is true of all the things that make up our civilization, from sirloin steaks to sponges, orchids, and the fish on a dinner plate.

McGuire claims to, at one time or another, have worked at most of these things, and in conversation with him one does gather a certain disdain of public opinion. He is one of the few, however, who seems given to analysis or to have considered the subject in its social and philosophical implications. An odd chap, McGuire. Full of friendliness and good humor, a fine seaman without taking it too seriously, and reportedly he was once a decent boxer. Yet, for all of that, he is one of the most thoughtful men I have met. One feels that his knowledge of life and of people is far beyond his years. But why should I say that? Age, after all, is only the confirmation of youth. If one is not wise when one is young, age will bring no wisdom. It merely brings a few more years of being a fool. Most of our great men were young men, or were men already great when young. I believe Alexander Hamilton was much the youngest Secretary of the Treasury, yet he is considered the best, and certainly established a financial system for a country scarcely known to the world as a nation.

I watched from the chart room today as Schumann, the old German fellow the men call "Hitler," shuffled aft to the fireman's fo'c'stle. Gray, fat, and stooped, he goes about peering almost blindly from behind those curious glasses. I wonder what such a man thinks of. Possibly nothing. Sometimes I wonder if he is not too far in his dotage for such a job, yet O'Brien says he is a good man, a careful man, and O'Brien has few words of praise for anyone.

The old fellow is one of those men you rarely notice on the street, yet I suspect he was once a fine-looking man. His shoulders are broad, and his hands are well shaped. He has probably lived a lifetime of drudgery that is much like not having lived at all. It is a fate that any of us could face, a lifetime of work and little else. He rarely talks, at least where I can see him, and merely moves to and from his work in the stupor of years.

Strange, how life avoids some people and yet goes out of its way to find others. McGuire, who presents his thoughts and philosophies as the mood strikes him, says it is because some people have an "adventure-type mind." There are those to whom things happen, and McGuire undoubtedly deems himself such a one. The average man travels in the same world in which the adventurer lives; but if he goes to China he carries St. Paul, Waukegan, Macon, or Pawhuska right with him. He lives aboard the boat with those of his own kind; when he goes ashore it is to a hotel where he meets others like himself. He sees the sights, buys a few knickknacks, usually made in England, Germany, Czechoslovakia, or the United States, and then goes home. He is never aware that he has missed an adventure, that aside from the benefits of sea air and the escape from everyday tasks, the experience was wasted on him.

I like the "adventure-type mind" theory. My fault with life is that people too often do the expected thing—it is a boring habit to get into and takes a lot of real joy out of life. Why can't people be more absurd? I'm afraid the world, including myself, takes life too seriously.

I remember seeing a very pompous gentleman on the street in Frisco. I had the devilish idea of walking up and whispering to him that his shirttail was hanging out behind. To panic him for a ghastly few seconds . . . but also to bring him a touch of being alive!

Or to buy a rose for some old newslady, or to give five dollars to some hungry man. If you stayed out of the insane asylum it would be little short of a miracle, but you would have brought some excitement into a few lives.

When you see a man like Schumann, or any who seem trapped in a humdrum existence, you wonder how you could get their attention, reach out and wake them up, show them that every day need not be like the last.

FRITZ SCHUMANN

Fireman

When he reached the top of the ladder he stopped for a minute to catch his breath and looked back down on the metallic beauty of the engine room. He could never grow accustomed to these modern ships. Driven by a steam turbine, boilers automatically fired by oil, no coal dust or grease, no soot or grime anywhere, everything clean and shining. And that was especially true in "Speeder" O'Brien's engine room. O'Brien was only the second assistant, but to everyone aboard, even the chief himself, O'Brien was the spirit incarnate of the ship. Crazy, Fritz reflected, crazy in the head, but he knew machinery and loved to work with it.

Old Fritz plodded out on deck and shuffled slowly aft. Every time he climbed the ladder he remembered he was growing old. He seldom thought of it otherwise, for he lived within his dream. Yet, if he was ever going back it would have to be soon. He stopped now, standing by the starboard rail and staring out over the water, remembering Raiatea. Always, his thoughts turned south toward the shores of Raiatea and Arutua.

Twenty years! It was a long time. His sons would be men now, stalwart men with the blue eyes of their father and the clean brown limbs of their mother. They would have wives and children of their own, they would have forgotten him, or would remember him but vaguely.

"Hey, Hitler!" Shorty said, slapping him on the shoulder as he went by. "How's tricks?"

"Dun't call me Hitler!" Schumann turned to stare after Shorty, frowning. Then he smiled under his gray mustache. Ah, well! Boys must have their little joke. Hitler! He snorted and shuffled inside the fo'c'stle and sat down on his bunk. He had been angry when they first called him that, but now he wasn't bothered. He only imitated anger because he knew that they liked to tease him.

He got up, and taking a large glass, walked into the head, where he drew fresh water. Returning, he watered the flowers in the window box under the port in the for'rd bulkhead. They were geraniums, blooming contentedly miles from land. He studied them carefully, putting his face down near the flowers to see better. Behind the square-cut, steel-rimmed glasses, his old eyes blinked thoughtfully.

Three years he had been on the *Lichenfield*, before that in the engine room of the *Point Lobos*, before that another ship. It didn't matter. He had always had flowers, always geraniums.

He looked up at the sound of footsteps in the passage. Denny McGuire walked in, a small bundle of dirty clothing under his arm.

"How the flowers coming, Pop? I always stop in here to have a look at them. Maybe it's the poet in me, I don't know. First time I ever saw a sailor growing flowers on a ship."

"Vhy not?" Fritz shrugged his heavy shoulders. "They grow any-where. It is taking only care, no more. Flowers is friendly t'ings, it is nice to haff t'em. I look at t'em unt I t'ink all is not cold machine, but somet'ings is flowers, too!"

"Yeah, but you better not let the O'Brien hear you make a crack like that about his engines. He'd throw a fit." Denny leaned over to look at the geraniums. "Why only these flowers, Pop? Why don't you grow something different, something hot and rich like hibiscus? These are like a lot of little old maids."

"I like t'em. Vun time back in the old country t'ere vass a fraulein has flowers like t'is. Down in the islands, too, I haff t'em. T'ey are memories, each vun. Memories of days I haff lived, unt days vhich are no more. T'ey are nature vhere all is machine. Man, he needs nature nearby always. It vill reassure him."

"Sometime I'm going to leave the sea and all this talk of booze and women. I'll chuck the whole works and get me a place on the California coast where I can sit and watch the sea from a distance. Somewhere with mountains close by. There will be lots of flowers, too, and trees. Maybe a few dogs and a couple of riding horses. How's it sound to you, Pop?"

"Ya, I like t'at. It is the best t'ing for a man. Man vas nefer made for the sea."

"Going back to Germany, Pop?"

"Nein. It is t'irty year since I haff been t'ere, unt I nefer go back. I t'ink much of Germany. It is my country. I am always a German. But I do not like t'is Hitler. He is no German.

"Vhy, Denny, you are a boy that readts. You should know. T'ere is no race vhat is pure, novhere in the vorld. All is mixed up. T'ese Aryans, t'ey mix many times mit efery kind of peoples. T'ey come from Caucasus, unt around Sout' Russia, unt about the Danube. T'ey come vest unt mix mit Iberian peoples, unt some mit the Basques. T'ey mix, too, mit peoples of the Ural-Altaic linguistic group."

"Yeah," Denny agreed, "but you never learned that in any engine room. Where did you go to school, Pop?"

"I go to Heidelberg, unt t'en to school in England. Vun time I speak good English. Now sometimes is good, sometimes bad. This race buiness, ach! It giffs me trouble mit the insides. No peoples is pure, unt vhere t'ey mix the most, t'ere is great civilizations. Vhat of the United States? Of England? Unt vhere ve get t'ese great civilizations? Borrowed, most of it! Alphabet, numerals, the foundations of chemistry unt medicine, t'ey come from the Arabs, a Semitic people! Sumerians, Babylonians, Egyptians, Mayas, Aztecs, Chinese—vas t'ey Nordics? Ach, sure! I loff my fatherland, but such nonsense!"

"You're well away from it all, Pop. We've a good ship here, and the sea is wide and there are many ports. I've got to be running along. Be seein' you!" McGuire clapped the old man on the shoulder and headed off.

Old Fritz sat down on the edge of the bunk and took off his glasses. It was part of his pride that he had worn them, unbroken, for thirty years. Now they were almost a part of him. He rubbed his eyes and relaxed, staring across the fo'c'stle. His work tired him now. In his sea chest, a relic of older years upon the water, he carried an engineer's ticket. He hadn't used it in a long time, and probably never would again. He was content with a humble berth and his dreams.

A streak of sunlight fell across the room from the open port, sunlight reflected from the dancing light off the water. As the ship rolled it moved slowly back and forth upon the ceiling, and he watched it, lost in thought.

It had been like that the morning when he had awakened on Arutua with Mahuru in his arms, the first golden light falling across the hard-packed earth floor, and the bright glory of the sea beyond the beach. Lying there he could look across the white sand and hear the roar of the breakers upon the reef. Overhead the trade winds murmured to the palms, and he had felt a vast contentment rise within him.

It was so long ago. He had been thirty-five then, young and strong, with broad shoulders and hair like gold in the sunlight. Already years of fighting and struggle were behind him. Among the most talented students at Heidelberg, and later he had done well in England too. At twenty-two he had won five duels, but then he became entangled in a struggle of local politics, and his life was forever changed when he killed the son of an important official . . . in a duel of the sort where a wound was usually sufficient to end the confrontation.

There had been two years in sail, and two in steam, roaming the far places of the world. A year in the Cameroons, another in India, two in the United States, and one along the South American coast. At thirty-five he had finally come to the islands.

It was his fate. He knew as soon as he sighted Tahiti through a glass, knew it when he went ashore in Rarotonga, in Ahu Ahu. But it was in Arutua where he stopped. That was, for him, the island where the South Seas really became the place of dreams.

The old schooner had skimmed along, only to lose the breeze as they were coming down upon the island. Green clumps of palm against the blue of the sky, and great masses of cumulus towering thousands of feet above. Then a ruffle of white surf around the reef, and he heard that sound, the sea roaring against the coral.

Up would come a slow swell of water, long and unbroken. A great, glistening wall with an emerald cave forming beneath, each swept down upon the reef only to break into splinters of spray and vanish. He watched it as the schooner drew slowly nearer, and tried to find the beginning of each new swell, but there was no beginning. They rolled in as though the turning of the world was behind them.

And then Arutua. White beach and thatched huts, arching palms, and beyond that, the island and more sea. He went ashore in a boat and walked up the shelving beach to shake hands with the native men. He talked with them, smiling down at the wide-eyed children who had gathered about, then he looked to the ship, departing beyond the spray of the barrier reef. When he turned back, he saw her.

She had come out of a hut and walked down the beach toward them, a tall, graceful, golden-skinned girl with flowers in her hair. Their eyes met, held, and she smiled.

Mahuru! The girl was a castaway. The chief told him that as they sat together near his hut. Almost two years before a canoe had drifted ashore, an outrigger. The Polynesian girl had been lying on the bottom, half-dead from thirst.

Two weeks later the schooner that delivered him had come back down from Apataki, sliding through those long green swells to pick him up. "Nein," he had told the captain in his broken English. "I shall not go back. I vill stay here. T'ere is var unt death, t'ere is struggle to livf. Here is peace."

So he had stayed. For three years he lived on Arutua. In those three years he had learned from his wife, learned to handle an outrigger, to fish, to live like a Polynesian. His body became sun-browned and hardened. He would swim, sometimes over a mile a day, and would dive and trade for oysters, selling pearl shell for a few extra coins when trading ships called. They had a child by then, a boy. One day, Fritz decided to leave Arutua and move to Raiatea. It had been Mahuru's home before her canoe had drifted away across the sea.

The schooner *Alden* had called at the island. Old Fritz stirred on the bunk-edge and frowned behind his glasses. He remembered how Captain Wallace Benson had come ashore, a sturdy half-caste with him and a bulky blackfella from Australia.

"To Raiatea?" Benson turned brusquely. "Yeah mate, I'm goin' that way, but there's no room. No room for no damned beachcomber and his woman."

A few minutes later Benson had looked up to see Mahuru walking across the sand toward the thatched hut. Motherhood had brought even more beauty to Mahuru. Slim and amber-limbed, she moved as though to unheard music, and Wally Benson's eyes narrowed.

"Who's that?" he demanded of a native.

"That Mahuru, Matayo's woman. Matayo, big white man."

Benson suddenly realized he had heard of Schumann . . . at least he had heard the name Matayo from other island traders. A man with pearl shell to sell, and rumored to have collected the rare and valuable pearl as well.

After he had spent the morning conducting his business, Benson walked down on the beach and found Fritz Schumann. Benson smiled, the thin line of his mustache stretching upward.

"Hey, mate, I reckon I spoke too hard a while ago," he said. "You're not the usual type of beachcomber. I'll carry you to Raiatea."

"There'll be two more," Schumann had said. "My vife and child."

"Child?" Wally Benson hesitated. "Well, all right. I'm sailing in an hour, so get aboard!"

Fritz Schumann had walked over to the little hut to speak to his wife. He explained briefly, and saw her begin to gather up their belongings. As for himself, he had stood silently by the door staring out over the reef with thoughtful eyes.

Benson walked forward to where Schumann sat in the bow with Mahuru and his son. He smiled at the girl. Then he turned to Schumann.

"You play cards? Two of my men do. Come on down an' let's have a game. You said you have some cash."

Fritz got up. When he stood he was several inches taller than Benson. He turned and spoke swiftly and coolly to his wife in her native tongue; then he followed Benson to the cabin.

Custer, one of the half-castes, was there. So was a thin, hard-faced white man named Martin. In the corner the blackfella sat hunched against the wall. When Schumann took a seat at the table he was careful to see that his back was to the wall, and not too far from the door. Casually, his eyes turned toward the Aborigine.

"He is plenty strong, t'at man! Plenty strong!"

"Yeah, that's right," Wally Benson remarked, "an' the dumb brute knows how to use it too!"

Schumann played coldly, calculatingly. There was no question in his mind as to where he stood. This man wanted his wife. He also wanted the pearls Schumann had gathered in his years of diving at Arutua. How many he actually had, no one knew. How could they? But he was aware that, as with all rumors, imagination played its part.

However, there had been the years before Fritz Schumann had come to Arutua, years before he had become Matayo. Those years had taught him much of men and their ways. The same cool skill, the same careful manner that had won the six duels had won other battles.

He had come aboard that day fully aware of the risk he took. The journey to Raiatea was not long, and somewhere on that journey he had known there would be trouble. Sitting on his bunk in the *Lichenfield*, lost in his dreams of yesterday, he remembered words that Denny McGuire had said: "It's the direct method that wins. If there's trouble, don't wait for it—go right to it!" Denny McGuire, he decided, was a smart boy. Though Fritz Schumann, even the Fritz Schumann of those long-ago days, didn't consider stepping into the path of violence much of a "method," he was no advocate of avoidance once an issue presented itself . . . and he had been afraid there might not be another schooner at Arutua for a year or two.

He had played cards carefully, and he had won steadily . . . even though Wally Benson, Martin, and Custer were cheating. Fritz Schumann was not a stranger to cards, and despite their efforts he had swept most of the money from the table.

Finally, Benson drew back. "You got me, Dutchie! Cleaned me out!" But there had been an ugly light in his eye.

"You got a schooner," Schumann had said. "I vill stake my pearls!" Pearls they had never seen—but that mattered little, for they intended to take whatever he had regardless.

And Schumann played three of a kind to beat two pair. Custer leaned back in his chair, his eyes turning from one to the other. Martin sat very still, watching the cards. Finally Wally Benson pushed his cards away and laughed.

"Well this is a showdown all the way around, innit? You play a flash hand of poker. Better than I do, an' that's sayin' something. You won the hand, but I'm takin' the game. You think you'll ever get to Raiatea?"

Benson lit a cigarette, and flipped the match toward the porthole. "What do ya think, Dutchie? Who's got the best hand now?"

"I t'ink I got it, Captain Benson. I know you take me to get my vife, my money. You t'ink one dumb beachcomber is easy. Vell, now you guess again. I got the best handt. It is under the table, Vally Benson. Under the table, unt pointed right at your belly. Now t'at I get your ship I change the rules. . . . I vill pay shares, fair shares of every voyage." Schumann looked directly at the blackfella, "Unt I vill need a mate . . . Vhat *you* t'ink, huh?"

The *Alden* raised Raiatea shortly before daybreak, and as the sun threw crimson into the sky, it moved down on the island, one of the most lovely on earth. High mountains lifted their crowns above the sea, over the pale green lagoon and the gold of the land beneath. The way into the channel was dotted with tiny islands.

Schumann was at the wheel, and beside him Mahuru held little Jerry. Forward, just abaft the form'st, Martin's body rolled in the scuppers. There was a bullet hole between his eyes. The four men of the native crew stood silent, watching the channel. Wally Benson loitered amidships, and near him the half-caste Custer sat. Watching the two of them was Button, the Aborigine. Schumann held a steady hand on the helm as the yellow fangs of the reef gnawed the blue water, and let the *Alden* slide easily through the channel and into the little cove.

"Let go for'rd!"

He heard the splash of the anchor, and saw the bow swing. The natives worked swiftly, their fingers made surer by the threat of the gun. Watching them work, eyes straying at times to the beach, Schumann never forgot to observe the pair amidships. The crew were Malays, and he could depend on them to go with the winner. His only allies were the two pistols in his waistband and the Aborigine whose loyalty he had bought.

Several natives had come down to the shore. Mahuru was watching them eagerly. Her father and brothers were here, somewhere. The two men in the waist of the ship got to their feet. Schumann made his decision.

"Vally Benson! You unt you man jump over the side, unt svim!"

Benson's mouth opened and closed. "You crazy? We wouldn't get halfway before the sharks got us."

"Vhat you plan to do mit me unt my child?" Schumann lifted a pistol. "Vhat is it but vun shark to another? Ofver you go!"

Even as he spoke, he saw Custer's arm flash up and the silver gleam of the knife as it left its sheath at the back of his neck. But the black-fella moved, and the knife thudded to the deck.

Custer struggled, but he was held in a grip of iron.

"Vhich is it? T'e gun or t'e shark?"

Wally Benson hesitated, then with a curse he turned to the rail.

"Take t'e knife. Natives t'ey kill shark mit knifes!"

Benson hesitated again, and then picked up the knife. He went over the side, and as he struck the water the Abo tossed Custer, his wrist broken, after him. A moment later Schumann saw a dark, muddy-colored shape lance past the stern, and heard Mahuru's whisper.

"Ma'o."

There was a fierce tumult in the water, and Schumann turned away from the rail to find three natives coming aboard. One of them was Mahuru's brother.

The journey from Arutua to Raiatea had been an interval he rarely remembered now. It was a bit of nightmare in the midst of enchantment. In the days that followed they built a palm-thatched hut on the edge of a little cove where he could look down the miles of reef reaching out to the sea beyond the island. In the spray-misted distance the gigantic shoulder of Bora Bora loomed up, while towering masses of cumulus clouds blessed the islands with afternoon rains.

Old Fritz Schumann walked out on the deck and stopped by the rail, staring off toward the horizon. Out there to the south and west was Raiatea, Bora Bora, and his wife and sons. Why had he left? Why had he ever let himself be led away from that paradise for even an instant? A man needed but little on the islands below the line; why dream of more than that?

He hadn't wanted more—for himself. But Jerry was growing older, and young Fritz was nearly two. Fritz Schumann thought of that, and began to remember the world he left behind, began to recall the books, the schools, and the music. There would come a time when these islands would no longer be so free, so primitive, and he wanted his children to be ready. He wanted them to have a future, to understand and to be able to join the world beyond the horizon.

He had started with a larger and better house. He was a seafaring man, and as such had a knack with tools. Then he brought plants down from the hills, laid out a neat orchard, planted cotton and tobacco. Some early explorers had left lemon and orange trees, and pineapples were plentiful, so it hadn't meant much work. Then, after several voyages in trade, he sailed the schooner to Papeete and sold it.

A war of which he knew nothing was on, but they knew him in Papeete, and did not think of him as German. He took passage for San Francisco, and had scarcely landed before he was interned. It had been a year before he was freed, and by then his money was gone, spent in a futile struggle to win his freedom. The worst of it was, Mahuru could neither read nor write, and no one else on Raiatea could either. In spite of that, he had mailed letters and all the children's textbooks he could afford; he hoped that someday his sons would read them. The last book he sent was a boy's book on Morse code, and he dreamed that someday Jerry or Fritz would reach out to him across the deep waters, communicating in a way that was bringing all the people of the world together. But he had no idea if the letters or the books ever reached their destination.

Even after the war there was still feeling against Germans, and he could find no work. Finally, a ship took him aboard as fireman, and he made a trip to Cape Town and then one to South America. But time passed, and somehow he never earned enough money, never got back to Raiatea, to his wife and sons.

Tex Worden stopped behind Schumann, waiting for Denny, who had been hanging some clothes to dry in the heat of the huge fiddly over the boilers. He felt gingerly of his still-peeling nose and touched Fritz on the shoulder.

"Let's shake it up, Hitler," he said. "They're puttin' grub on the table. With this crowd, a guy's got to be on his toes to get himself enough to eat."

When Denny walked into the mess room, he was rattling a pair of dice.

"Come on, you guys, I'll roll anybody for an extra piece of pie!"

"Nuts t' you, sailor!" Shorty said. "Not with those dice of yours. You ate my dessert five times running before I found you had a loaded set of tops!"

"It's the price of education, m' boy! It never pays to trust people. Now take Fritz here—he's a man of experience. Would you trust your future on a bet, Pop?"

"Not anymore, especially Irishmans mit crookedt dice!"

"So, how d' you like *them* onions, McGuire? Pass over that dish of hamburgers an' shut up!"

"Could I interest you in a nice pitcher of milk? One cup of tinned milk, to forty cups of water! It makes young men old and old men older, puts kinks in your back and wrinkles in your voice. Makes you feel like dancing a *haeva*."

"What's that? I thought I'd heard of it all, but the *haeva* is a new one on me!"

"Ask Pop here, he knows. Didn't you say you'd been down in the islands, Pop?"

"Ya, it is vun of t'em native dances, mit lots of viggles."

"Down in the Society and Cook Group," Denny said. "Tell them about the time the chief made you his *tyo*, Pop. That's a good yarn."

"It vas nothing. Vun time the chief he vant to make his *tyo*, his friend, of me. I vas new to the islands t'en, unt did not know my duties. Soon the chief—he seemed mad at me. Finally, vun man who speaking English tell me vhen I become the chief's *tyo* I am supposed to sleep mit his vife. I cound see vas very serious."

"What happened?" Sam Harrell leaned back against the bulkhead. "Sounds like a situation that could go wrong no matter what you did!"

"Nein. I vas t'en vorking for England, unt it vas necessary ve keep a very good feeling among the natives. I had not yet met my vife, I vas a young man mit lots of ent'usiam for my duty. His Majesty's vork must be done, unt so the chief unt I vere soon again friends."

"Now that," Sam said admiringly, "is what I would call a noble spirit of self-sacrifice. His Majesty's Service, eh? My, my!"

THE PRIVATE LOG OF
JOHN HARLAN, SECOND MATE

March 24th: It is one of those enchanted mornings when the air seems effervescent and the sounds of voices and movement forward on the fo'c'stlehead seem almost like music. The mate has several of the men working up there, and the bright clarity of the morning seems to have touched them. They are painting the anchor winch, I believe, and doing other work forward. They laugh and joke. Listening to these sounds from a distance, they almost sound like my children playing in the yard, though if one could truly hear them, I'm sure the men's humor would be sprinkled with the roughest of stories and told in language that would curl an old maid's hair.

Sometimes I wonder if their crass behavior isn't more of an act than anything else. I have seen sailors and longshoremen doing dockside work call out to passing women in the most uncouth manner, yet they seem, if one watches closely, to be vastly more interested in proving something to one another. The same men, if alone, are more likely to be polite, if not actually chivalrous. And, of course, I have seen the hardest, most seemingly evil of men perform the most heroic of feats without pausing for a second thought. In fact, it is often these men who are actually *more* likely to drag a fellow crewman from a deluged deck or wade into live steam to turn a valve.

One never knows what potentialities are contained in a ship's crew. I doubt if the autocratic Mr. Bligh quite realized the stuff of which Fletcher Christian was made, and certainly none of them could have guessed what a chapter in history they were to make. A mutiny on a small ship on a lonely sea, then the astounding voyage of William Bligh, navigating a twenty-foot boat over four thousand miles to safety. Almost every move of both groups has been closely studied and chronicled. The mutineers supposed they were losing themselves to the world, but they were also creating a story for the ages. And not alone the men of the *Bounty,* for what of the *Birkenhead,* slowly sinking while the troops stood in solid ranks as women and children took to the boats? What of the battered old *Kingsway,* surely the most unassuming of four-mast schooners—who could have guessed her voyage would be a nightmare of strife, hatred, and blood? Could any one of the small crew of the *Mary Celeste* have guessed that unassuming brig was to become an eternal mystery? We know these stories, and others, but how many ships just disappear?

Sometimes, it seems, the greatest possibilities for drama are disguised beneath the most unexpected exteriors, and one never knows when circumstance is going to lift some apparently inferior person to almost heroic stature. After all, courage and cowardice are so much a matter of conditions and circumstances, and no man is to be blamed or congratulated because of them. In the last analysis, I suppose humor is the most civilized of all our traits—and sometimes the most barbaric.

I'm glad my children will grow up with Tom and Hazel. Tom has such a grand sense of humor, and so much quiet tolerance. The kids will get from them the one thing I want them to have more than anything else—the quiet satisfaction in seeing a good job well done. Not to think only of the monetary reward, but to do something worthwhile in the best possible manner.

Thinking of jobs well done, there is a curious example aboard ship. With him, however, it has passed the sensible boundary and become an obsession. I refer to Con O'Brien, the second engineer. Unquestionably the man is a fanatic on the subject of his engine room. He is a tall, rawboned man with cold eyes and a jaw like a clamp. His hair is coarse and black, worn in a stiff pompadour, coming to a pronounced widow's peak over his forehead. O'Brien speaks hesitantly and tends to glare intently during his pauses, turning what might be taken as insecurity in another man into something more intimidating ... at least if one is not used to it. I haven't heard the entire story, but his face is a network of faint scars from a horrible motoring accident. He must have been sewn back together by a master, but in the right light you can see them, a jigsaw puzzle, a Frankenstein's monster.

His engine room is spotless. He works over it like a miser counting his gold, and rises to pitches of fury over carelessness or unnecessary dirt. I suspect all the men below of being secretly afraid of him as he prowls about, wiping brightwork, or listening for a single flaw in the sound of any of that purring machinery he loves so much. Off-duty, he is a surly, uncommunicative man, yet occasionally he will let down his guard.

A week ago I stopped at his cabin with a message from the Old Man, and found a worn and stained copy of Butler's *Erewhon* on his bunk. I suspect the chief engineer would have rid himself of O'Brien long ago but for his genius in the engine room. He can make anything work, and in a breakdown he is amazing, accomplishing the work of three men, moving about among the grease and metal like an enchanter working a spell.

The other day we came off watch and were eating lunch in the saloon. It was just the two of us, and we drifted into talking of the future of The Machine. For once he was in a conversational mood. In all my life I never learned so much of science and of mechanical developments. Finally, we got around to Butler, and *Erewhon*.

"I like it," I told him. "I like novels of fantasy, or prophetic novels. But as for a time coming when machines rule the world, well, that's preposterous!"

He looked up, a queer light in his eyes. Then he smiled, and his face was almost pleasant. "Preposterous?" he said. "It took m-millions of years for Man to reach his present state. Consider the development of The Machine in comparison."

"But a machine doesn't have consciousness!" I protested.

"Consciousness—it's just a name for something we w-wish to have. Think of a potato in a dark cellar. We think vegetables, they don't have consciousness. But the sprouts will grow over and under all obstructions to find the light. Call it what you want but I w-wonder if what we have isn't the same thing, just a million cells growing toward different kinds of light.

"You could say that The M-Machine is dependent on Man. But Man, in many cases, is dependent on machines. How long would our civilization function without them? We now have machines that make other machines, and we have machines that have created unemployment. If war comes it will be guns and bombs and aircraft that do most of the killing. Machines!" As he became more adamant, his hesitancy disappeared and the intensity shone in his eyes.

"Machines guided by men," I suggested.

He shrugged. "For how long? A generation while humans grow softer? A century? Then a time will come when all machines are created by machines and fueled by machines. They will not have to contend with passion or sentiment. Think of what we already have—machines that speak and hear, read and write, machines that calculate, machines that match colors. What of the photoelectric cell? Who can guess all its possibilities?

"Even in the time when Butler wrote *Erewhon* there were machines that could store and reconfigure information, like a Jacquard loom. There were men who designed mechanical engines that could do complex calculations. Every machine has its own nature, its own personality. This ship we are on is an example. If it was designed well and treated well it performs accordingly. Abused, it is like a man—it may heal, but it carries the memory of its wounds or abuse to the grave."

We talked on and on, and after a bit, I left him. Insane? Not so much, perhaps. His ideas are thought-provoking, to say the least. And we must remember: The Machine is new, with at best a half-century of real development. What will another hundred years bring? Or two or three?

Yesterday afternoon I was talking a little with Davy Jones, one of our ordinary seamen. He is a nice lad, quiet-mannered and friendly. He was showing me a picture of his girlfriend, and she reminded me of Helen when I first met her, the same eyes and hair. I asked Jones if he was going back and he looked odd, and finally said no, he was not. McGuire has sort of taken him in hand, and the boy is developing well. Pete Brouwer had him helping on a splicing job, too, and there couldn't be a better place to learn. Those two will protect him, if they can, from the sort of bullying that so often goes on. It's an unfortunate part of the world in which we must live.

There is some difficulty back aft (the crew's quarters are aft on this ship). We aren't sure what the trouble is, but it seems to have started back in San Pedro. Seamen are closemouthed about such things. There has been no open strife so far, but there will be if I know that bunch. Mahoney, I suspect, is at the bottom of it. There was trouble just before we left between him and McGuire.

Mahoney is a surly, brooding sort. Both violent and manipulative, he is the perfect example of the bad apple that can spoil the whole lot. Unfortunately Jacobs is a fit second for anything he might start. Neither of them are the type you'd want to meet in an alley. Jacobs is a brute, not quite a moron but easily influenced.

A light breeze is picking up, and eight bells draws near. So far the voyage has been a marvel of smooth seas and easy watches. I hope it lasts.

Until tomorrow, then . . .

CONNOR O'BRIEN

Second Engineer

When he was safely away from the dock he paused long enough to light a cigarette. It was a relief to strike a match without fear. Even in dry dock a tanker was dangerous; until the ship was thoroughly cleaned it remained a giant tin can full of fumes. The properties of chemistry and metallurgy, form and function demanded respect. A ship allowed men to sail her for a time, but only if they returned the proper amount of care.

All across the globe tankers sailed, sliding in and out of ports, their tanks brimful of explosive power. That power could feed a mechanical world, but it also held the potential for death. So many things could happen. The flow of the salt water through a hose could generate static. A flash. The end of it all. Strange, how one became accustomed even to that. Nothing remained fearsome or thrilling for long. Man is so constituted that anything becomes a bore after enough time. Con O'Brien shrugged. He'd seen that sort of fire and twisted metal first-hand. He'd had a powerful machine torn from under him. What did it matter, after all? A few years more or less?

At the Wilmington–San Pedro Road, O'Brien paused again. It was a long hike to the Pacific Electric station, or he could wait and take a bus. He started off, walking rapidly. His blue serge suit was rumpled, and his shoes were worn and down-at-the-heel. He still wore his white-topped officer's cap, emblazoned with his insignia as second engineer.

A car streaked past, doing an easy sixty. O'Brien stared after it. They were fast these days; even cars straight from the showroom were mighty fast. Funny, he'd never cared about driving since the day he'd lost control on the Indianapolis Speedway. Twenty-two then, and racing among the fastest company in the world: Johnny Aitken, Dawson, and DePalma. Now he was almost twenty years older, and hadn't driven a car in all that time. It wasn't a case of losing his nerve—he had simply lost all interest. The car he had lovingly cared for had failed him . . . or had he failed it?

It had been during those three months in the hospital after the crack-up that he had decided to be a marine engineer. He started studying while he was trapped in bed: reading, planning, thinking about it day and night. Mechanical parts so heavy they never failed. A machine so big he could live inside it. An engine where he could see into its hidden depths, reach into it as it turned to take its temperature or oil its bearings.

Doc Weber always joked that a piece of metal must have got into his head in the wreck, and that it had affected him in some way. "You've got cylinder oil on the brain and a crankcase for a heart," Doc used to say. "Next time you crack up they'll need a machinist, not a doctor!" Of course, it was true—there was metal in his head, not embedded during the wreck but placed there afterward. He was a miracle of modern medicine, burned, broken, and torn, but still alive.

Turning from the highway, he followed a path through the lumber-yard along the docks. The passing of the cars bothered him. He liked the quiet machines now, and never went near the roaring dromes of the big auto tracks. He liked the calm efficiency of the engine room on the *Lichenfield*, or the immaculate, metallic beauty of a municipal power station.

He wondered if those big hydroelectric plants impressed others as they did him. It was like walking into a huge cathedral, the organ hum of the dynamos serving as the hymn of his religion. There was no confusion, no hurry. No clangor of tools or roar of escaping steam. Those plants were the most finished products of the machine age, for all was smooth metal and cold cleanliness, guided by a few men doing orderly, quiet work.

A big red interurban was heading into the station, delivering people from Los Angeles or Long Beach. He walked up the path alongside the old trestle, passing a bunch of men gathered around some dice. Once he reached the platform he found a seat in one of the smaller local streetcars and relaxed into it. Even after all this time his back and knee would start to hurt if he walked for too long. On a ship there was never very far to go.

It was the end of his ninth trip on the *Lichenfield*. Before that he had been chief engineer on a steam schooner, and before that on a coastwise run as an oiler. Several times since he had earned his engineer's ticket, he had shipped as an oiler, fireman, or even wiper. Anything to be away and at sea. It was always better to be at sea.

Now, however, they were going to be in dry dock for weeks. The officers would be retained, the rest of the crew paid off. He'd considered looking for a position with another ship, but he liked the *Lichenfield*. He was used to it and it was used to him—it ... *needed* him; no one else cared for it like he did. But that meant time at home, more time than he might be able to stand. Home was one thing when a man was far away; it was another when he had to live there.

Clara was on the divan when he opened the door. She was lying there in a faded negligee, reading a magazine. A box of crackers stood open on the table close by, and there were two cups still mottled with the grounds of coffee. She sat up, a large woman with rust-colored hair and a heavy, sullen face. Con looked at her a moment, looked at the stuffy, untidy room of which she was the living expression.

"Hello, Con," she said. "When did you get in?"

"Last night," he said briefly. "H-How are the kids?"

"Okay," she said, brushing the crumbs to the floor. "Jane is around somewhere. Junior's playing next door."

Con turned and walked into the bedroom, taking off his coat. The room was dark, sunlight glowing around pulled-down curtains. He let them up one by one. The bed was unmade, a heavy tumble of blankets and sheets, and Clara's dress lay across a chair. He opened a drawer and looked at the jumble of clothes. For a moment his eyes narrowed, then he swallowed and carefully felt among them for his shaving kit. When he had found it, he walked to the bathroom. He was wearing a dark brown shirt and a white striped tie, and he removed them carefully, lathered his face, and began to shave. He would have to clean the apartment, and Clara would reproach him for it. She assumed that it was mute criticism for being a bad wife and mother. In fact she wasn't good at either, but he also couldn't stop himself. Things had to be right. Had to be right or, eventually, he couldn't get his breath or think straight.

She came to the door and watched him. "When you leavin'?" she said finally.

"Coup-Couple of weeks," he said.

"Well . . ." she said. He didn't know what she meant and figured she didn't either.

Con shaved methodically.

"I wish they'd make up their minds." Clara leaned against the wall. "Sometimes it's two days, then it's two weeks. You never know what to expect. The kids, they don't know what to expect. I wish you had a job like Carl Winters or Mrs. Hendrick's husband."

His eyes sought hers in the mirror, objections stuttering out of him. "I'm lucky. I'm lucky to—to have any kind of job these days. And . . . I-I make more than either one of those—them."

"A lot of difference that makes! We never know how long you'll be home!"

He took a breath and focused on the neat swath cut by the razor. The ship's schedule wasn't all that erratic, she was just complaining. He began silently compiling a list of everything that would have to be done to prepare the *Lichenfield* for dry dock. That was really the mate's and the chief engineer's job, but he still thought about it. He couldn't stop himself.

Carefully, Con rinsed and dried his razor, working quietly. He wondered why women were constantly marrying men and then wishing they did something else or made more money. Usually, they knew what to expect when they got married, but that didn't seem to help much.

Jane came in, stopping in the doorway. "Hey, Daddy. When'd you get back?"

"Just a short—a little while ago. How's—how are—?"

"All right. School's almost out and I've been up to Ray's house. They always have a lot of fun."

Con straightened up. "Ray's? I told you not to g-go there anymore." The kid was bad enough, but he was also the son of a saloon owner. It was one of the places in 'Pedro that the Navy men still patronized. The family's apartment was on the second floor.

She examined a fingernail. "Well, Mother said it was all right."

Con looked down at Jane gloomily. Ray's father spent his time either serving booze or drinking it. His mother was no better. With a sharp pang he saw Jane as she really was, the boldness of too much knowledge in her eyes. His heart sinking, he recalled the kids who had lived in the alleyway back of the house when he was a boy. Jane looked just like that girl, the girl who had entertained the neighborhood boys.

Slowly, he gathered his things together and walked into the other room. He stared at it, suddenly feeling sick and empty. The slovenly appearance of the place, the memory of Clara's heavy body on the divan. Con sat down slowly, running his hand over his face. He felt like crying. He adjusted the dirty cups on the coffee table, searching for some sort of order.

Jane followed him into the living room, picking up the confession magazine her mother had been reading. She had put on lipstick, and her clothes . . . well, he wasn't sure. They were the sort of clothes a young girl like Jane—only thirteen and without much of a figure— might wear. But she had somehow found a way of wearing the skirt and blouse in a manner that mimicked the provocative styles of older girls. It made him uncomfortable trying to figure it out.

It was easy to talk about staying home, but what could he do? He had tried that, tried it twice. Each time Clara had filled his ears with complaints about money, and sulked when he did the dishes. He had returned night after night to the hot, unkempt apartment, to the half-cooked food, to a daughter who thought of him as a stranger. If he couldn't make friends with the men on his own ship, how in the world could he hope to influence an adolescent girl? He took a deep breath and went to finish dressing.

Junior came in while he was knotting his tie. He was bigger, and his face broke into a wide grin when he saw his father. "Dad! I told Mother you'd be home. I was watching the ship news every day! You goin' back to China?"

"After they fix—fix her up. I'll be here—around home for a while." Con stared into the boy's eyes. "How you getting along, son? How's school?"

"It's okay. I'm learning to play basketball. Mr. Campbell—he's our coach—he said I was big enough. And we could finish that motor, right? The one where you were going to taper the cylinder?"

There were days when Con couldn't talk much, days when his face hurt and the burns on his body seemed to tighten. For those times he had bought Connie Junior a model airplane and they had built it together, silently pinning and gluing wood, stretching the light cloth. Now he was teaching Connie about engines, tiny engines that they could fix and modify on the kitchen table. Each had different qualities, different needs.

Con smiled, the strain going out of his patchwork face. "Go—um, get your coat on, son. We'll go downtown."

Con O'Brien walked a little straighter when he walked with his son. Listening to the boy's rapid-fire talk about school and sports, he kept glancing down at him, a sturdy little fellow who seemed to have the best of both his parents in him. Maybe that was why he was so wholesome and freehearted. There certainly wasn't much that was wholesome about Clara anymore. All she did was eat candy, read confessions, and let the house get dirty.

Con ran his hand over the back of his head. It was bothering him a little today. That meant a change in the weather. Odd thing, that a man should go through life with a silver plate as part of his skull, yet it had done the job for twenty years now.

"When you goin' to take me down to see the ship, Dad? Gee, I'd like to go down in that engine room! Do you have many men working for you, Dad? Many sailors?"

"A few, son. We don't call them—sailors. The engine crew is called the black gang. There's an oiler, a fireman, and a wiper working with me."

"I'll bet they sure like you, Dad. All those fellows. I'll bet they think you're swell!"

Con's face stiffened. "I don't know, son. Maybe."

Why don't you tell him? a dark part of his brain suggested. Why don't you tell your boy the men think you're nuts? That sometimes a whole voyage passes and they never speak to you outside of work? Tell him that you look at them and want to communicate, to say something good-natured and not about work, but you can't.

Maybe all the good stuff in you, all the friendship, drained out back there on that racetrack. Maybe it can't generate around that silver plate, maybe the broken ribs stuck it and it died, died right inside of you so all you can do now is look at them and wish they'd take you in, wish someone else would accept you like this boy who, because you're his dad, simply doesn't know any better.

The sign read "Mile High Cones 10 Cents!" and the brightly lit interior was crowded with adults and children. They placed their order and then found seats. Con felt tired, but it was good to see Junior there, a clean-cut lad, the sort any man would be proud to call his son. How he'd like to take him back to the ship, to show him the engine room.

But he wouldn't dare. He'd never dare let Junior see that his dad wasn't a regular guy, that he didn't fit in. It would hurt the kid, and remembering the untidy house and the cracker crumbs, the coarse, uncaring woman he'd given this boy for a mother, he knew that Junior was going to get hurt enough, more than enough, before it was all over.

He thought of Jane. His fears were hard to have, hard to face about one's own daughter, but Con had the harsh, worldly wisdom of a man who had seen a hundred ports. If he'd been with his daughter every day he might not have noticed or it might not have happened. Con knew enough to realize that orders and restrictions would be little help now. He'd tried, but it was a job for two, and he'd been too long away.

All he could do now was feed them, see they had clothes, try to give them what he could. And the most important thing to give Junior was a man to be proud of, a man to pattern himself after, a regular guy whom everyone liked. The boy needn't know it was all a lie, that his father was an oddball who walked alone, ate alone, and lived a solitary life, cut off from the men he lived with every hour of the day.

How long since he had lain in the arms of a woman? Given himself with all there was in him, and taken as much? It had been years, so long now it was only the memory. Clara had been different before, and he had been a rising star.

What happened in that crash? What happened in those roaring moments when his car had gone screaming into a skid and rolled over and over to have Perroni's powerful racer rip through and over him? What had allowed his body to recover but torn his heart out by the roots, left him helpless and tongue-tied?

Someday it would happen again. Every time he went down the ladder to the floor plates, he felt it coming. There would be a time when a ship would sink in a sea of flaming oil, when he would die with the screams of burning men mingling with his own. It would come; the flames would get him in the end. The only thing that remained was his son; the only thing that mattered was giving his son a memory to cling to, an example of a respected and competent man.

It was hard. Too damned hard. Kids saw things so clearly; they realized so much even when you thought you were fooling them. He looked at the boy again, listened to him talking about football, about boxing, about the racing cars his father had driven, telling him how the coach had read them accounts of "Speeder" O'Brien's races, and told all the boys at school how much nerve that took, and what a fine sportsman Speeder O'Brien had been.

But Speeder O'Brien had died back there on that track. And here he was, a pitiful shell of a man, putting up a front for his son, trying to give him an illusion to cling to.

He knew all Clara wanted now was a meal ticket, a place to live and enough to eat. She was young and pretty when they married, she had come to the races and had gotten what all her friends had wanted: a brave, and possibly reckless, young driver. The center of attention. Then there was the wreck and all that excitement turned to horror . . . but she had stuck with him and borne children. He owed her. He owed her the money he made, if nothing else.

If she'd sunk into a way of living that was without effort, it was partly his fault. The kids came and went much as they wished, and Con O'Brien kept on because it was all he could do, it was all he had left.

Sometimes he found himself wishing for another mother for his children, for some girl who would be to him all that a woman could have been. Vaguely, he felt that he might shake off his sense of tension and isolation if there was only someone who cared, someone who understood and could help him just a little.

"Look, Dad!" Junior said suddenly. "There's Miss Lane!"

"Who?"

"Miss Lane. She's my teacher. She sure is swell, too."

Con O'Brien looked up to see a slender young woman coming toward them. She was pretty—very pretty, in fact. She had the sort of bright, laughing brown eyes that never seem to change as the years pass, and a simple way of dressing and doing her hair. She came up to the table, holding out her hand to Junior.

"Why, Connie! I thought you'd be home studying your history lessons and here I find you eating ice cream!"

Junior grinned. "I got that history, Miss Lane." He made an expressive gesture with his hand. "It's right in the groove! And this is my father."

"Oh!" He felt the quick warmth of her glance and he stood for the introduction.

"How do you do? Connie has been telling us so much about you, about your trips to China and Japan, about the ship when it was in the storm that time off the coast of Chile. So many interesting stories! He keeps a map to show where you are."

"I'm afraid he's been talking too much," Con said, his face flushing as he realized that wasn't quite what he wanted to say or how he wanted to say it. "Um, sit—sit down?"

Another boy had come in and was making motions to Junior. "Dad," Connie said eagerly. "There's Dave. I'll be back in a minute." And then he was gone.

"Well!" Miss Lane said, laughing. "It looks like we've been deserted!" Her quick eyes saw his uncertainty. "But we can wait, can't we?"

They sat down, and Con groped for something to say, but there was nothing. He took his glass and swallowed a mouthful of water, then put it down and stared desperately after Junior. He could talk to his family, but those were subjects . . . subjects already raised. He could give orders to his crew; he knew what they had to do. He could feel every stitch, the pathways of mended flesh in his face. He heard her saying, "Connie tells me you are an engineer, Mr. O'Brien. Have you been going to sea long?"

"Um—twenty years," he said, looking at her. The look wasn't his usual glare; he could feel the difference. It was more like when he talked to Junior about engines. He took a breath. "I don't talk to people very well. I don't—I guess I don't know the trouble—what the trouble is. Ever since the accident—there was a car crash. I don't care to, um—I can't talk much."

"You seem to be doing all right now," Miss Lane said. "Connie is always telling me about how you are such a wonderful engineer and a good officer to your men."

He flushed. Then he looked up, his mouth tight. "I guess . . . I like machines. They—well, you don't have to—they know what they have to do.

"M-Most of that about me being, um—that was lies." He groped painfully, wanting her to understand. "On the ship—I guess they think I'm off my course. I can't talk—so well. The equipment, it has to be—has to be right. Connie, I—I want him to think . . ."

His face was red from effort, and he stopped, glaring down at the table and twisting his glass in his fingers, turning it round and round, wishing it was a ratchet driver. He wet his lips with the tip of his tongue. "You see, things aren't—um, at home. You know, well his mother's pretty busy, and—an' well . . ." There were so many things he wanted to express to his wife and daughter, but the words had deserted him long ago. But now . . . well, it wasn't easy, but he *was* talking.

"Yes, I know." Marcella Lane was remembering the one time she had called on Clara O'Brien: the stuffy, untidy room, and the woman she couldn't quite believe was actually the one she was seeking. "But Connie's a fine boy. He learns so fast; his mind is so quick and eager. It's nice to work with him."

Con O'Brien looked up gratefully. "I wish I could be with him a lot. But—well, I have to work, and it isn't—isn't easy for me to get work."

He stopped. There was something warm and friendly about this girl, something that made it easier to talk. Suddenly, he found himself wishing his suit was pressed, and he was glad he had shaved.

Abruptly, he looked up. "I can't be keeping you like this. Connie will be back in a minute, and . . ."

"That's all right, Mr. O'Brien. I like talking to you. Connie's a lot like you."

He found himself suddenly choked up—he so wanted to be like his happy carefree son. From some strange distance he felt that ecstatic freedom he had once found behind the wheel of a car: throttle wide, heat pouring off the exposed pipes, engine howling. In some poor but effective way, this woman had given him a few words and opened his heart a fraction.

It was over an hour later when he and Connie walked back up the steps to the house. Con O'Brien entered slowly, hating to return, wishing there was somewhere else to go. Jane was there, sitting in a big chair with her legs over the arm. She looked up, and Con tried to talk to her a minute. But it was different than with Junior. He embarrassed her; he could feel it, feel her pull back. These days she was more of a stranger than Clara.

In the morning he would return to the ship, prepare it for the next few weeks. He'd come ashore fearing the time he'd have to spend at home, but even with Jane's distance, even with his problems with Clara, he was happy. Just why, he couldn't say, but somehow it felt different. Was it only because of Junior? Or was it also because of Marcella Lane? But what difference could she make to him? Would he even see her again?

Long after he went to bed, he lay there staring up into the dark. Maybe, after all, there could be something left for him. When he fell asleep at last, it was with the picture of Marcella Lane, and with the sound of her voice, talking to him as if she enjoyed it.

THE PRIVATE LOG OF
JOHN HARLAN, SECOND MATE

March 25th: There is a vague uneasiness about this trip that will not leave. Queer, that such a feeling can affect one so much. It is as though something has been left undone, something we are all forgetting. Is it merely the act of leaving, that sense I have mentioned before about one never returning the same? Well, I will not be returning. Perhaps that is it—this time there are many things left undone . . . a life that is being left behind.

O'Brien, surprisingly enough, seems singularly cheerful this trip. Several times he has talked to me, first about the Samuel Butler novel, and then very rationally about his boy and how he was starting to play basketball. Funny, I'd never imagined him to have a son. Wonder what kind of kid he is.

Some of our restlessness may come from the sea. After all, we cannot help but realize the tremendous power that lies beneath us, that at best we only steam across it by pure good fortune. As for the seas, Man has conquered them, but men have not. That isn't paradoxical, for while men have drowned and their ships sunk, Man continues to follow the ways of the sea. However, I can imagine a time when Man will be no more. To my way of thinking, Man's tenure upon the Earth is coupled with too much uncertainty for one ever to be sure of anything.

For instance, a very slight change in atmospheric conditions or a difference of a few degrees of temperature, and we might no longer exist. A plague resulting from those new conditions, or any one of a multitude of other things, might severely alter our development. Man tries to learn all the rules, tries to build walls about himself to withstand the elements and the forces of his own civilization, and to protect himself from all danger, yet there is so little that can be done.

In the grand scheme of things Man is transitory, but that vast power that is the sea will remain, and from it will spring new life.

Sometimes at night I walk out on the wing of the bridge and stare down as the ship slips through the starlit sea. Here and there down below will be the white eye of a porthole. And always the mutter of the engines. I see the shadow of the man on lookout pacing back and forth across the bow, hear him sound the bells. I look within and see the solemn figure standing at the wheel, his face lighted by the faint halo from the binnacle of the compass. Always the man at the wheel impresses me as a priest officiating at some sacred rite. Why, I wonder, do men always speak softly in the wheelhouse at night? Is it merely the power and eternal nature of the sea?

When the moon is bright one can look back along the wake and see the water boiling from the ship's passing. Yet it is a short trail. What remains to tell of our passing? What remains to tell of the passing of anyone? Our children, perhaps?

Sometimes I think that all that is wrong in the world stems from a belief that this life is only a beginning. I believe Man is wrong to ascribe his nobleness to gods, for in knowledge of his own nobility lies his greatest strength and goodness. Man is only so much as he believes himself to be, and all these things he has created, written, painted, or sung—are they not fine? I believe that when Man comes to believe and trust in himself instead of looking beyond the stars for salvation, when he accepts that his world is no better than he makes it, then I believe Man can at last glimpse strength, greatness, and something of beauty.

Bah! I am serious tonight. Wouldn't it be better to pick up my Voltaire and chuckle with him? We need a new Voltaire now, and I'd like to read what he would say of war, of the gold standard, and American politics. But, in a way, we have our Voltaires—only now they are cartoonists. They will, before this era has passed, have copied the absurdities of our civilization on paper, copied them in almost wordless caricatures that betray all the shameful ridiculousness of our modern world. What will future generations make of our United States, where the two parties viciously attack any idea advanced by their opposite, no matter how good it might be for the nation?

None of it makes much sense. Even our lives on this ship don't make much sense. I am leaving my marriage behind, and Mr. Wesley is planning for his. Pete Brouwer wants to go home to Amsterdam, Davy Jones has left his home behind. Mahoney growls and gets drunk; Carter, another oiler, is a religious fanatic and attacks Mahoney for drunkenness when his own intolerance is just another form of intoxication. O'Brien rarely wants to leave his beloved engine room, but Augie Donato dresses in over-loud clothes and every minute he can he goes ashore—to what?

I think too often of the crew as a unit. I struggle to set down my thoughts about them to keep each separate, to fight the tendency of those of us on the upper decks to see them simply as bodies that arrive and sign the articles, become part of our company, and then pay off or jump ship. Nameless men each moving on their own course.

This morning at four, coming off watch, I remembered a message for Pete Brouwer, and went aft to the seaman's fo'c'stle. I walked down the passageway and stood in the door for a moment, staring inside. A dim light was burning overhead, and the two tiers of bunks, one along each bulkhead, were hung with curtains. There were benches before the bunks, someone had left a locker door open, and it moved slightly with the roll of the ship.

As it moved, the men's bodies rolled slightly, each one a gray-blanketed duplicate of the others, each movement alike, each bunk framed in dull gray pipe. It was dark, and silent. I stepped into the room and could see that Pete was already asleep. Yet, once I was inside the fo'c'stle the similarity in the men vanished, for the expression of each was different. Men are not so alike when they sleep, and there was each man, alone now, and unsuspecting. I felt that I had intruded, and so slipped quietly back up to the deck and the stars, then went forward to give myself to the same helplessness.

I have made no plans for my future. My decision was merely to leave, to go out to the Far East. There I hope to find a place on some boat in those waters. It will be nothing like this, but some tramp, probably, with a native crew. But I'll stay out here. I've lost my stomach for the States since things went bad for Helen and me. Yet when I see some of these homeless men, I wonder. It is not so bad for Tex Worden. He is a hard-boiled, matter-of-fact sort who lives day to day, does his job, and spends his money quickly. Shorty Conrad is different. He is just the sort one would find clerking in a grocery store or running a garage in some jerkwater town, not the type one would expect to find at sea. He has a sister somewhere, he tells me, and is looking for her. They were parted as children.

Most of them are men without women. At least, men without women in the larger sense. Their attachments are casual and women have little influence on their lives. But that is always true of such men. One wonders just how much influence women have upon the lives of explorers, drifters, warriors, and seamen. Many are married, but usually they are far from home. In many cases their lives are intervals of dissipation between long periods that are isolated and monastic. In many cases even those intervals of dissipation are so brief as to mean little.

Pete, who has followed the sea for many years, has no wish to be an officer or even bo'sun. His life is in the fo'c'stle. He is a quiet fellow, of simple tastes, and one who knows more of seamanship than any other man on the boat, not excepting our chief mate, Mr. Shannon. Shorty, I believe, has no great ambitions. His greatest pleasure seems to be just mingling with the crew, playing poker (he rarely wins), singing, and listening to Denny McGuire's endless stories, which I too have found easy, and entertaining, to do.

So I end my journal for another day. We are changing our course on the morrow, which means a little more work for me. But navigation appeals to me. As on many of these ships, the second mate is actually the navigating officer. Man may see his future in the heavens but those same stars are also the key to our more mundane destinations here on earth.

SHORTY CONRAD

Able Seaman

After three bells sounded he kept on painting, taking his time and doing a careful job. Occasionally he straightened up to look at the hull of the lifeboat, and each time the paint showed smooth and even, with not a holiday or a run in sight. He squatted on his haunches and dipped the brush in the white paint, scraped the surplus off on the edge of the can, and began lower down. Then after a few minutes he stood up, laid the brush carefully across the pot, and, turning to the ladder, dropped quickly to the main deck.

Whistling, he walked aft to the washroom next to the seaman's fo'c'stle. When he returned the saltwater soap and towel to his locker, he glanced out the port. A school of flying fish, their bright scales glinting in the sunlight, scudded by. The light reflected off tiny pinnacles of water and ran shimmering along the sea to bubble up in dancing waves. He closed his locker carefully and started forward along the catwalk.

Climbing the ladder to the bridge, he stopped, looking back along the wake. There was not a cloud in the sky; the sea danced with blue and the mingled gold of sunlight. For all one knew the sea went on and on, past all the little islands and the big continents, past the sandy beaches and the jagged reefs, along lonely shores, and around old wrecks . . . forever. His father would tell him that when he was a little boy, going on and on as he drifted off to sleep. He went up the last few steps and came face-to-face with Mr. Harlan. Shorty grinned. "Swell day, ain't it?"

"Beautiful," Mr. Harlan said, glancing back. "Reminds me of spring when I was a kid. The snow melting and running down the gutters in little brooks, and you feel sort of lazy and warm."

Shorty leaned on the rail. "Sis an' me used to go out and sail paper boats or build dams in the water. We'd get our feet wet an' get bawled out plenty by Mrs. Haley!"

Shorty stepped through the door of the wheelhouse, and Pete glanced down at the compass, bringing the wheel up a couple of spokes to put her dead on the course. "Two six-two," Pete said, watching the compass tip slightly, wavering on the course, "two sixty-two, and vee are right on!"

"Two sixty-two it is!" Shorty said, faking a snappy salute. "You'll find a pot of paint an' a brush on the boat deck just abeam of number 3 lifeboat. Shannon says to finish that an' then start on number 4."

Pete disappeared through the starb'rd door, and Shorty could hear his feet descending the ladder to the Old Man's deck. He glanced down at the compass, gave the wheel a spoke, and looked out at the sea. The forestay was a thin black thread against the sky, a thread that moved slowly with the motion of the ship. Following it down with his eye, he could see the point of the bow and the thin pencil of the jackstaff.

Mr. Harlan passed by, walking across the bridge, then pausing to level his glasses toward some distant object, scarcely discernible on the skyline. For a moment, he held still, then he lowered the glasses and walked to the wing of the bridge. Below, in the radio room, Shorty could hear Sparks at work, and tried to pick out the signals, but the code was only a tangled mass of sound to him, jumping and leaping.

Harlan stepped into the wheelhouse and stood looking out the windows over the sea. He was about medium height, slender but with well-set shoulders. He had a quiet, pleasant face, with laughter never far from his grave eyes, but his humor was the sort that usually stayed inside, only visible once you got to know him. Shorty watched the man, liking his efficient manner, always so smooth and faultless, but without any of the priggish pomp of the third mate.

"Say"—Shorty glanced at the compass again, easing the wheel gently—"do we pass anywhere close to Wake Island?"

"No, Wake will be off to the south of us, quite some distance. The closest land before we sight the Philippines will be the Marianas."

"Japanese, aren't they?"

Harlan nodded. "Japanese Mandate. After we pass them we'll be over some of the deepest water in the world."

"Guess it don't make much difference," Shorty said. "A guy can drown just as easy in ten feet as ten miles!"

Harlan went into the chart room, and then after a few minutes returned to the windows looking out over the bridge at the sea. "Ever been to Manila before?" he asked.

"Yeah, I was there on an Isthmian boat, the Steel Engineer. That was about ten years ago. I met Pete out by the Paco cemetery. We got drunk and slept there all night."

"You two been shipping together ever since?"

"No, we made one trip that time. He wanted to go to Amsterdam, so he shipped out of Hoboken for Liverpool, figuring to get a Dutch boat from there. I went back to the West Coast, then down to Antofagasta. Didn't see him again for six years. We ran into each other in the Straits Hotel in Singapore."

"He's been going home a long time."

"Uh-huh. Sometimes I wonder if he'll ever make it. I guess we all want something we don't get."

Harlan nodded, without turning, his eyes on the horizon. "What do *you* want, Shorty?"

"Me? I don't know. To find my sister, I guess. She's the only relative I got, unless my old man's alive somewhere. Then maybe a little place ashore somewhere."

"How'd you lose track of her?"

"She was adopted by some show folks used to know my dad an' mom. She went back East with them, an' later I heard they went to London. A guy who sold patent medicine took me. I ain't never seen nor heard of her since. Maybe she changed her name, got married, I don't know."

John Harlan walked out on deck, and Shorty held the course, watching the numbered degrees on the compass. When he'd started going to sea everyone steered by points, and now they were all beginning to steer by degrees. It didn't make much difference, only going through the old "boxing the compass" routine wasn't so important anymore.

Shorty watched the sunlight on the water and listened to the measured tick of the chronometer. Memories were slippery things. A good deal of what happened vanished somehow, and a guy only remembered so much, odds and ends that didn't seem to have any earthly connection. That was the way it was with his folks. He remembered his father best on that last day, packing his things, eager to be off. Every minute or so he'd stop and start explaining to Marie again, telling her how it was his one chance to strike it rich. And Shorty remembered his mother standing very quietly, watching him. Maybe she guessed she'd never see him again.

Raoul Carmody had been a handsome young man. Said to be brilliant and temperamental, he had very large, magnetic, black eyes. His voice was low, and his black hair curled away from his high forehead in a careful wave. A great actor, some claimed, but erratic. Always committing to some new enthusiasm with which he was carried away. Marie Carmody had married him in Melbourne, where they were both in the cast of an Ibsen play. For a time their star had soared high, and then during a lull while visiting the United States, they had gone out with a road show. But they had spent too freely, and when the show began to play to smaller and smaller crowds the Carmodys didn't have the wherewithal to leave.

The company had been staggering along for several weeks when it reached Merivale, and two nights at the Merivale Opera House failed to solve the anemic state of their finances. The show folded and the manager promptly eloped with the ingénue and the little remaining capital.

Raoul Carmody, despite having sixteen years in dramatic stock behind him, was only in his middle thirties, a handsome, aristocratic-seeming young man whose dark eyes brought a flutter to the pulses of the rotund Mrs. Haley. As Mrs. Haley was the proprietor of the town's best boardinghouse, those soul-searching glances were not without their value. Especially comforting was the fact that she was a romantic, middle-aged lady content merely to bask in the reflected aura of such a presence.

Marie Carmody, the burnished copper of her hair lighting the rooms of the rambling old frame house, was no less welcome. The fact that Marie was an artist at preparing mysteriously tasty foreign dishes, and that she was always ready to make herself useful, probably had as much to do with Mrs. Haley's hesitation in presenting a bill as Raoul Carmody's magnificent voice and eyes. Conrad, who was a matter-of-fact, worldly little fellow, and Faustine, who was two and a picture of round-eyed innocence, also won a place in Mrs. Haley's affections.

As the days passed, the rest of the company drifted away. Marie began selling tickets for the local opera house, and Raoul fell into the company of a tall, harsh-featured man named Tracey. Shortly after, he returned one night to tell his wife he was going to South America. There was a wild and almost unbelievable story about lost treasure and a map, just the sort of story to appeal to Raoul Carmody's romantic nature. Hastily, he packed and was gone. The family never saw him again.

Shorty moved the wheel thoughtfully, remembering those two years in Merivale, two years when they had hoped day after day to see his father coming home. At first there had been letters, one from New Orleans, another from Cartagena, and after that silence, until one day a soiled and worn message arrived postmarked Ushuaia, a place on the extreme southern tip of South America. The message, Raoul said, would be taken by a native to the nearest town. They had been successful. He would soon be home. And that was all.

Then, in the belated backwash of the great flu epidemic, Marie Carmody died. Bon and Dorothy Malloch, old friends of the Carmodys, had taken Faustine, who was already a beautiful child. They had no place for Conrad. But a month later, Doc Dunlap and his medicine show reached town, and Doc, in his smoothest manner, impressed Mrs. Haley with a story of the fine home he could give Conrad; and when he left, the boy went with him. Doc Dunlap had filled the boy with glowing promises for the future, and colorful accounts of life on the road selling Chief Hollowoll's Indian Herb Remedy.

Afterward, Shorty decided the only surprising thing about Doc Dunlap was that the promises lasted a full week. Conrad soon found that neither Doc nor his peroxide-blond wife had any inclination toward work. Setting up the platform for the shows, distributing advertising, and even mixing the Indian Herb Remedy soon fell completely on the boy's shoulders. In the years that followed, he also learned to do a hot "buck and wing" and to play the guitar.

Doc's round red face grew more and more surly, and he drank more and more. Income fell off steadily, and once they were laid up in a tourist park in Plainview, Texas, for two solid weeks while Doc Dunlap stayed drunk. Bella was almost as bad, and she drifted from having secretive affairs with various men into openly flaunting them in Doc's face.

Then one day it all ended. Doc Dunlap and his trailer were camped on the shore of a small lake near Post, Texas. Doc had taken a suitcase of the Indian Herb Remedy, crawled into the car, and driven off downtown, leaving Conrad and Bella to straighten up the trailer and mix some more of his specialty.

It had been a cool, pleasant afternoon, and Shorty recalled every detail of what happened. He had lugged a heavy bucket of water into the trailer and was carefully preparing to mix The Remedy when he heard voices. Bella, in a flaming crimson kimono, had been sitting on the steps, but now she was gone. Glancing out, the boy saw her standing very close to a tall, rawboned man with a thin, hard face. He remembered the man very well indeed. He had first seen him two weeks before, in Lubbock. He had walked away with Bella that night after Doc had passed out. Conrad had seen him again in Slaton, and now he was here. As he watched, they went into the stranger's trailer.

A few minutes later, staggering and drunk, Doc returned. He lurched up the steps, his face swollen and red, his eyes ugly. "Where's Bella?" he snarled.

Without thinking, Conrad pointed. "Over there," he said.

With a curse, Doc Dunlap half-fell, half-stumbled down the steps, and then he started weaving toward the neighboring trailer, mumbling under his breath.

His mouth dry and his throat tight, Conrad crept silently after him, afraid to go for fear of what might happen yet too curious to stay behind.

Eyes wide, he saw Doc lurch up the steps and jerk open the door. Peering past him, Conrad could see Bella lying beside the stranger on the narrow bed. The stranger drew himself to one elbow, his eyes narrow and dangerous. "Get out," he said, his voice emotionless. "Get out, you fatheaded fool, or I'll kill you!"

Doc began to swear. The man suddenly sat up, and Doc, his face white with fear, had stumbled and fallen heavily down the steps. Inside, they heard laughter. Conrad turned and ran blindly for the trailer. He was working over his mixture when Doc came in. The man's eyes were thin with hatred and suspicion.

"What you prowlin' around for?" he snarled. "I'll teach you a thing or two, you filthy good-for-nothing!" He jerked up a broom that sat by the door and crashed the stick down across the boy's shoulders. Conrad staggered and backed away, but Doc Dunlap lurched after him, swinging viciously at the boy's face. He missed, and the stick crashed into the ceiling in the narrow confines of the trailer and snapped. Doc staggered and almost fell. Lunging forward, he grabbed the broken broomstick and struck the boy over the head. Then he began to beat him, pounding Conrad with furious blows, venting all his hatred and cowardice.

It was a long time later that Conrad became conscious. Dimly, he remembered being struck over the head, and then the sensation of falling. Slowly, he crawled to his feet. Doc Dunlap lay across the bed in a drunken stupor, his face red and bloated, his breath hoarse. There was no sign of Bella.

Moving quietly, the boy limped to a built-in cupboard and found a sack needle and some coarse thread. He returned to the bed and picked up Doc's feet, laying them out in line with his body. Then carefully, he drew the sheet tight around the man's body and began to sew. In a few minutes the sheet formed a tight white sheath in which Doc Dunlap could not move a muscle. The man's eyes were just opening when Conrad Carmody stopped and picked up the broken broomstick from the floor where it had fallen. Lifting the stick, he brought it down across Doc's rump with all the force he could muster, and then, with all the beatings he had taken from Doc Dunlap floating through his mind, Conrad gave the man such a whipping as he would never have again.

At the wheel of the SS *Lichenfield,* Shorty Conrad grinned. Served him right, the old devil, he thought. If ever a man had a licking coming, that drunken old beer-belly did. Shorty remembered how he had only stopped when his arms became weary. Then he had picked up his few belongings and left the trailer. He started west and kept going. As far as he knew, Doc Dunlap was still right where he left him.

It was after that affair that Shorty had dropped the surname but retained the Conrad. The "Shorty" had been acquired in the natural course of events; somehow, it had become the custom on labor jobs, in mines, and at sea, to call all the tall men "Slim" and the short ones "Shorty." And often enough they were neither very slim in the one case, nor very short in the other.

Harlan came in from the bridge as Shorty rang seven bells. He walked into the chart room, and glancing over his shoulder Shorty could see him figuring on a slip of paper. Finally, Harlan returned to the wheelhouse and walked back to his station at the windows where he could watch the sea.

"Have you shipped out in the Far East?" Harlan asked. "I mean from Far Eastern ports?"

"Me?" Shorty said. "No. I haven't."

"I was just wondering. It might be interesting to know those waters better."

"I'll bet Denny could tell you about that. He sailed out of Shanghai several times, an' out of Batavia an' Singapore, too. Maybe Pete could, I don't know."

"Denny's been around quite a bit, hasn't he?"

"You bet. I wished I was as smart as that guy! Shucks, I'd never go to sea anymore!"

"Do the men aft like him? I heard there might be some trouble."

"Most of them like him. Tex sure thinks he's okay. Mahoney hates him because Denny whipped his ears down, if that's what you're askin' about. Slug doesn't like him either. But those two stick together, Slug and Mahoney."

"You going to stay with this ship?" Harlan asked, turning to look at Shorty. "When we get back to 'Pedro?"

"I don't know. She's a good ship, except the food could be better. But maybe I just got the willies. I don't know, I guess it's all that naphtha tanker stuff; a guy can't forget it. Denny says it's the subconscious mind. He was going on the other day about those after tanks."

Harlan turned again, sharply. "What about it?"

"Well, nothing you don't know, I guess. But he was saying a tank that's not full like that was dangerous. It gives the gas a chance to gather. He said there could be enough gas in there to blow the whole stern off!"

Harlan nodded thoughtfully. "Yes, he's right about that. But it would take a spark or some flame to set it off, and the tanks are sealed at deck level and vented up above. The real trouble is if gas escapes belowdecks, then collects in a pocket somewhere else in the ship. But the *Lichenfield* is just out of dry dock. They even replaced quite a few rivets on one of those tanks you're talking about. If you ask me, I think we're as safe a ship as you'll find on the water."

"That's good to hear, Mr. Harlan. But you know what they say: When you get to the point where you're thinkin' about it too much, it's time to change ships."

As Shorty sounded eight bells, Borly Shannon came up the ladder to the bridge. "Anything in sight, John?" he asked. "I figured you might be running into the Jap fleet out here somewhere."

Harlan smiled. "What would you do if we did?"

"Nothin', I'm a peaceable guy. Still, if anybody starts trouble we can break out our Lyle gun an' let 'em have it! We could shoot 'em enough line to hang themselves with, anyway."

"War's something I don't want any part of," Harlan said, shaking his head. "It's a silly business for supposedly civilized people. And no one gains. I seriously doubt whether they'll ever finish another war."

"Yeah," Shannon said thoughtfully, "they'll fight till the novelty wears off and then they'll quit and come home. They'll quit in droves just like the Russians did, and like the French tried to do. And like I wanted to do." He grinned. "Killing people isn't my idea of fun. I like to do my fighting with my fists!"

Shorty Conrad put the wheel up a couple of spokes to bring her right on the course. Deek Hayes came in to take over, and winked. "There's a good poker game aft! Better cut yourself in—they need somebody with some money to lose!"

"Nuts t' you, Sailor!" Shorty said, and spun on his heel, leaving the wheelhouse.

The afternoon sun had taken a downward slant toward the horizon, but long after it was dark back there in America, it would still be light here. Back there in America where Doc Dunlap, Mrs. Haley, and Faustine were living. Or were they? Might they all not be dead now? Gone?

Shorty Conrad paused by the rail and stared back toward the eastern horizon. Dead. It gave him a sinking feeling inside, a feeling of such sadness as he had not known before. His mother was dead. His father, a good-for-nothing dreamer, was no doubt also dead. His sis—he found himself wishing suddenly that he hadn't come, that he had stayed ashore this trip, and put all his time to finding his sister. After all, someone in Hollywood might have heard of the family she went to live with. There were so many show people in town, and someone might know about the Mallochs or people in the British theater. He would have to ask Denny. He might know where to start asking around.

THE PRIVATE LOG OF
JOHN HARLAN, SECOND MATE

March 26th: Borly Shannon was in a talkative mood yesterday, and I stayed on the bridge with him for almost an hour. He is a big fellow, with broad shoulders, a thick chest, and big hands. Shannon is a cool, careful officer with a way of getting things done, and having seen him twice under the stress of an emergency, I can appreciate the way his mind works. Danger sharpens his wits and every iota of knowledge he has accumulated suddenly falls into the proper place.

He was in a reminiscent mood yesterday and was telling me a strange story of an experience he had some twenty years ago down in the South Pacific. He was an able-bodied seaman then, sailing out of Melbourne by way of South Africa and on to Liverpool with a cargo of grain. Heading for the cape, they struck a heavy blow and were taken far south of their course. The storm blew itself out after three days of frightful winds and terrific seas, and Shannon's description was vivid to say the least. In fact, with what came later, it was enough to make your hair stand on end.

It seems that somewhere (they weren't certain, as it was heavily clouded and they hadn't had a shot at the sun), probably in the vicinity of Latitude 57 degrees south and Longitude 123 degrees west, they sighted a sinking vessel. When they drew nearer they made it to be an ancient and very battered tops'l schooner with all the canvas blown away except for a jib. The mainm'st had crashed across the deck and left a tangle of rigging and broken spars. The decks were awash; it was a miracle the craft was afloat at all. They had lowered a boat and gone alongside, and there a strange spectacle presented itself. I wish I could write it here exactly as Borly Shannon told it, and will do my best, but his story was much better than I could possibly tell in any cut-and-dried narrative.

"You should have seen it, John. Sure'n a sight it was, like one of these here pirate yarns a fellow used to read when he was a mite of a lad. There was this man a-settin' in the stern sheets lashed to the bloody rail, and fair mad with shock or hurt. His hair was blown by the wind, his face was unshaven, and his lips were cracked, but a handsome man he was for all of that. There was a knife stuck inches deep in the railing just to the left of him, and you could see with half an eye it had been throwed by someone who knew the way of it. The man was holding a pistol and cursing a blue streak. In all me days at sea I've not heard the like; poetical, but cursing that would still turn your hair.

"We took a look around, and you could see there'd been a bit of hell aboard that schooner even before the blow struck. There was another man a-lying sprawled in the companionway. The cabin was breast-high with water, and we didn't go in, but there was two bodies a-floating in there that hadn't come by death in the natural way of it. On deck we found another one: big and with a shock of red hair. He had taken some killing, that one had. But he was dead too.

"We got to the man in the stern and shook loose his lashings, and after a bit of work got him aboard our own ship. We was just hoisting our boat aboard when one of the hands give a yell, and we looked up to see the old schooner dip her nose under a big one. When that wave had gone on, there was no more schooner. A body would've thought the old scow just stayed afloat a-purpose to give us time to get our man off and away."

"Did he recover? What was his story?" I asked.

"No, he did not recover. He'd been fetched an awful clout over the noggin with something, and when they peeled off his clothes they found he'd been shot through the belly, too.

"Guts, John. You'd never've thought it to look at him. A slim fellow he was, with pretty hands, and a body nicely made, but no great strength. You could see with half an eye he was not used to work. But he was a gutty lad, that one.

"We got his yarn, though, pieced it together from his ravin' and loose talk. Three of them had come to a lonely island near Cook Bay, not far west of the Horn. One of them, a lad by the name of Tracey, he had a map showing where a powerful lot've gold had been stashed. An old treasure it was; the Spanish from up north in Peru, they buried it there.

"Anyway, they found it. They hired the schooner and its crew and, by the luck of God, they found it. Then one of them lined up with the schooner crew and tried to take the gold. They had a fight, and killed Tracey, but our lad proved a stiffer sort than they figured on. Strange, but even as he was dying he was quoting poetry. I remembered it when I heard you reading *Hamlet* down there. He'd quote that stuff till you'd be blue in the face just from listening, and then he'd bloody well get to raving on this business aboard the schooner, mumbling something about the best role he ever had and not a bloody soul to see him!"

"An *actor*?"

"Aye, perhaps he was. Tracey, they figured, was the hard one. But this bleeding actor, he comes a-walking down there, playing it like there was an audience. Of course he would know what to do! He had played a hundred such scenes, but this one was kill or be killed . . . that was clear.

"And then the blow. That was the final touch. The old schooner battered and broken, slowly sinking in those cold, miserable seas, probably the last of them killed by the storm, for he'd been holding them at bay with an empty gun—those rats in the cabin thought he was just another man, they didn't know he was d'Artagnan, Monte Cristo, Cyrano, any of a hundred heroes."

And the man . . . the actor? I asked Shannon. I could tell this story appealed to his romantic nature.

"He died a day out of Punta Arenas."

So, to end the story, he died and they found only one thing that might identify him, a bit of a letter and an old book in his pocket. Shannon has the book now. It is a copy of *Macbeth*. The name, written on the flyleaf in a large flowing hand, was Raoul Carmody. The letter, he said, was evidently from the man's wife, but the postmark had been obliterated by the sea.

Today the sky is clouded, which, except for the warm temperatures, reminds me more of the North Atlantic than the Pacific. The low gray clouds seem scarcely above the ship's topm'sts, and there is a slight sea running. Twice there have been brief dashes of rain. Maybe we are about to pay for all our fine weather; ships to the west of us are reporting a series of storms and we are headed directly for them, or they for us.

I expect I had better get my gear together, for I have to take a shot of the sun at noon, and Mr. Wesley will, as usual, want to be relieved on the instant. A nice boy, Wesley, but I'm afraid there isn't much of a demand for his type. I have never seen a man so lacking in imagination. He is soon to be married, and I do not envy his wife.

Rain spattering against the glass of the port. It will be seaboots and oilskins today. I hear McGuire coming to call me now. I know his walk.

There, he is gone again, and just a few minutes now before eight bells, just long enough to add the last touch to the log for today. I told McGuire to get Shannon to tell him the story of the man they picked up in the South Pacific. I didn't give him the details, for Shannon will do that better than I. It's McGuire's sort of tale, full of mystery and adventure and perhaps made all the better by an added detail or two.

I opened the door and McGuire was standing there, his black oilskins glistening with rain, his dark curly hair sparkling with it. He almost never wears a sou'wester, no matter how rough and dirty the weather.

"Looks like it was wet up there," I said.

"Yeah, wet and rough," he said, smiling grimly. "Why, it's so wet we

were sailing upside down for half the watch before Mr. Wesley discovered it. He tried to take a bearing and got a fish in his eye."

"Come in," I suggested, "and we'll splice the main brace. Not," I
added, "that I approve of drinking on duty, but you're going off watch,
and from what you say I'll not be able to see anyway!"

He laughed, and waited while I poured a drink for each of us.
"Here's to a good cruise, and a short voyage home!" he said. When we
put down our glasses, I looked at him.

"McGuire," I said, "I'm not going back. This time I'm staying out
East."

He started to say something, and then smiled. "Why not?" he said
thoughtfully. "I might do the same thing myself, someday. There's
people who say there never was a Far East like Conrad and Kipling
wrote about, but Mr. Harlan, they're wrong. The gold and the glitter,
the bright-colored batik, the deep green of the trees; the beauty, the
crime, the death—you can find it all."

He started to leave, and then stopped, his hand on the door. "Yes,"
he said, "that is what you should do. You'll like it, Mr. Harlan. There's
still brown sails on blue water, and lots of sky and clouds and little
green islands."

He went out, and I turned back to the sideboard and put the bottle
away. Then I lifted my glass. "To Helen," I said, "with the best of
luck!"

GEORGE WESLEY

Third Mate

M r. George Wesley appraised himself in the mirror. His carefully combed hair pressed smoothly against his skull, and the small, neat face beneath it pleased him. He turned carefully, adjusting the set of the blue uniform coat across his shoulders. He did not smile.

Daisy said he was good-looking. Well, perhaps not as much as some, but neatness and efficiency had to count for something. Poise too. At least he wasn't like the second officer, John Harlan. Harlan allowed the men to think they were his equals. He had actually been back in the fo'c'stle talking to McGuire the other day. Wesley frowned into the mirror.

Even though the man was on his watch, Mr. Wesley disapproved of McGuire. He was too free and easy. A good seaman, he'd give him that. But wasn't that what he was supposed to be? At least McGuire never tried any of that casual stuff with him! As for Worden, well, Wesley knew that story of the *Rarotonga*, and had his doubts. Worden a hero? Why, the man was a thug, a perfect roughneck!

Mr. Wesley stepped out into the passage, closed the door carefully, and started aft. During the life boat drill four days earlier he had noted a sticking pulley, and last night the weather had been rough and

Sparks claimed that there was more to come. The pulley was the sort of minor malfunction that irritated him and he had it in mind to order either McGuire or Worden to fix it on the next watch. Safety was critical on a tanker and as third mate such things, especially when they related to the boats, were his responsibility.

The rain had cleared for the time being, and he passed several of the men playing cards. His lips compressed. They might at least stay inside or out of officer territory. It wasn't his place to say what the men should do or not do when off watch, but someday he would be master of his own ship and then he'd see there was no card-playing.

McGuire was sitting on a crate near them washing a pair of dungarees. He looked up, nodding. Mr. Wesley nodded in return and looked down at McGuire, but the handsome seaman had already gone back to his work. Wesley blinked; somehow it was as if he had missed the opportunity to speak. McGuire had a reputation as a bit of a celebrity, and Wesley found himself both resentful and curious. Maybe it hadn't been McGuire he'd seen in town. Still, it did look like him, and what right had a seaman knowing such people? A few questions before they got down to business would clear things up, they might even put the man in his place.

Mr. Wesley cleared his throat, and McGuire looked up. There was something disconcerting about the man. His eyes were so grave and yet there was always a glint of humor behind them somewhere. Mr. Wesley felt irritated. "Did you find work while we were in dry dock, McGuire?" he began.

"Me? I tried doing stunts in the moving pictures. Success has mostly eluded me, however."

"Mr. Harlan said something about you fighting, that you were a prizefighter, or something of the sort. Is that right?"

"Yes, I've fought some."

"You don't look like a fighter, McGuire," Mr. Wesley said, smiling a little. "Not exactly the type, are you?"

"What does a fighter look like?" McGuire asked, rubbing at a spot of paint on the dungarees.

"Well, I'd certainly say you don't resemble one! I don't imagine you fought very much, did you?"

"A great deal, as it happens," McGuire continued. "Have you known many fighters, Mr. Wesley?"

"I? Of course not! Why?"

"I supposed, of course, that you did, as you were saying I didn't resemble one. A man could hardly say that without knowing something about them, could he?"

Mr. Wesley was growing more irritated. He had left himself wide open, and felt it. "I don't think that makes any difference," he said. "The type is one I'm not interested in, but obviously it isn't a profession that would attract a gentleman. The fighters I have seen resembled thugs."

McGuire shifted a little on his seat and looked amused. "Well, Mr. Wesley, I guess I'll have to take your comment as a compliment, then. I do believe, however, that the matter of a fighter being a gentleman or a gentleman being a fighter is one that depends entirely on the individual. Some men play golf, some play chess, some play with business. As for me, Mr. Wesley, I was a boxer, and I'd like to believe that, under the right circumstances, I could be again. As for fighters resembling thugs, I scarcely imagine you've seen many. I might mention Jimmy McLarnin and Tod Morgan as a pair who looked like nice schoolboys even when they were champions."

"Well, maybe we'd better drop the subject. I think we scarcely agree."

Wesley looked aft, where Worden stood by the rail talking with Sam Harrell, an oiler. "You have a double, anyway, McGuire. I saw a fellow at Hollywood Bowl the other night that might have been your brother. With a young lady I was told was an actress."

"Double? No, I'm afraid that was me." McGuire looked up. "I was with Faustine Carmody. I'm afraid she doesn't share your prejudice against fighters, Mr. Wesley."

Mr. Wesley turned away. His face had scarcely changed, yet he was angry. Angry with McGuire for being such a colossal ass as to believe a girl like Faustine Carmody could possibly take him seriously, and angry with himself for even trying to talk to him. It wasn't fitting that a common seaman should know such people. He remembered how Daisy had eagerly pointed Faustine Carmody out, and how she had exclaimed over the good looks of the vaguely familiar young man with her.

Sometimes he found himself wishing Daisy were a little different. She showed too much interest in performers and people of that type. Given all the stories it seemed that very little could be said for their morals.

Well, as far as Daisy went, after they were married all that would change. Still, it pleased him to think that she enjoyed going to the Bowl. There was something eminently respectable about musical affairs, and Daisy took such an interest in everything cultural. He remembered that on the night he attended the concert he had seen Roger Grosset come in with his daughter. Grosset was the son of the founder, and a vice president, of the company that owned the *Lichenfield*. He would have to mention that concert if he ever met Mr. Grosset. Carefully, Mr. George Wesley had retained the program and had studied the names of the compositions.

Standing by the rail, Mr. Wesley let his thoughts drift back to his last days with Daisy. When he returned, they would be married. He had, with her assistance, managed to save five thousand dollars. It was a nice sum.

Stanley, the Negro who was the officers' messman, dumped a bucket of trash into the sea, standing for a moment to watch the gulls circle lower. Sometimes they would pick a piece of bread out of the air before it even touched the water. Now they dropped to the sea and began fighting over bits of food. Mr. Wesley watched them for a minute, and then turned back to his cabin.

Daisy's picture was on the wall, screwed into place to keep it from falling with the roll of the ship. She was a slender blond girl, her eyes wide and very blue. Not everybody could marry a girl as lovely as that. Or as thrifty. Not the type to be always wanting something, not the type to nag a husband.

Mr. Wesley smiled. Well, he wasn't a type to be nagged. Fortunately, it wouldn't be something to worry about. When this trip was over, they would marry, and then he'd find a place near Los Angeles and buy a home. Something small and neat that a man could own until he was big enough to have more.

It comforted him to think of having a home, of owning property. Property gave a man background, gave him something that divided him from the average seagoing man. It made him a man of responsi- bility, of worth. Mr. Wesley walked over and sat down on the settee. Carefully he took a book from under his pillow, glancing at the title, *The Psychology of Success.* He turned the pages to a marked place and began to read. The problem of the sticking pulley on number three lifeboat had been forgotten.

Outside, against the hull, the little waves ran swiftly aft with a sound like someone chuckling softly.

THE PRIVATE LOG OF
JOHN HARLAN, SECOND MATE

March 27th: Up at ten this morning, after six hours of quiet sleep. I rarely sleep more than five or six hours, but find that sufficient. Having the twelve-to-four watch as I have for so long, I find it best to turn in immediately when I reach my cabin. I awaken automatically at ten A.M., take a stroll about deck in the fresh air, read a bit, have my lunch, and am ready to go on watch again at noon. When I come off in the afternoon at four o'clock, my time is my own until midnight. It is not a bad day, and one very pleasing to me. I especially enjoy the night hours on watch, for at night, alone, one comes very close to himself. To live intelligently, to have a clear mind, one must be often by themselves.

The person who is uncomfortable when alone, and who must always be with others to find happiness or pleasure, is one who seeks in others what he lacks in himself. I like company, the company of intelligent, interested people, but in my profession one is much more solitary, or thrown among men who all too often have only their work in common. Among the officers on this ship we have two extreme types. Borly Shannon is a man always alive, a man with many facets and all of them interesting. He has a rich, salty humor, an interest in the world around him, and a fascination with solving problems in a practical, no-nonsense manner.

On the other hand, we have Wesley. A stiff, unimaginative sort, very self-righteous and secure behind an unshakably high opinion of himself. I think McGuire expressed him well: "Wesley? He is a man without humor, and there's nothing worse!"

Constantly, I am disturbed by the desire to write their stories. It would be something very fine and very interesting to capture these lives, to be able to know all that has happened, what has made them who they are. But I truly wonder if I could do it, though now, it seems, I will have the time, providing I can find a job with a new ship. The main challenge will be to find the right story to tell. It must be one that contains romance and wonder and yet retains that thread of realism that will ground it to the world around us.

A simple description of these men's lives would no doubt be little more than a directory to the bars and brothels of a hundred ports. The salacious stories, few of which would make it past the editor's pen, would be those of the drinking, brawling, cursing, working, and wenching of a seaman's life. At best all of it would be mingled with lusty good humor, the tang of salt air, and more than a little rough wit and wisdom. The sins of seamen, if they actually be sins, are more often than not red-blooded and earthy (and often exaggerated) and less often the private, and degenerate, sins of the overcivilized.

People with the reforming complex wouldn't like it, but to me it seems that those who are offended by the profane or obscene in literature are usually that way because of their own overconcentration on such things. I know that many times I have read books containing remarks not overly nice, and barely noticed them, or had them make much of an impression, until they were called to my attention by someone who was complaining of them and thus giving them value.

I somehow think an archetypical seaman might be Sam Harrell. He is a witty, droll, lecherous rascal. A man of some forty-two years with a son of twenty-one. Everyone seems to like him, for like my favorite risqué stories, Harrell has humor enough to disinfect him. Shakespeare would have enjoyed Harrell, for if anything could describe Harrell it would be to call him a lean Falstaff. He's an average-looking man with a pleasant manner, and appears at least ten years younger than his true age.

Worden was talking about Manila the other day, and about shipping out of Singapore and Batavia. It started me thinking. I have thought so little about myself of late, so little about my own plans. When I was home it was all for the kids, and trying to avoid any word of disagreement with Helen. Fortunately, I'd managed to save a little. I gave the place to Helen, and most of the money. I left a little money for Steve and Betty and made out my insurance for them. But living with Tom they will have no need of money, for he has more than I could ever have hoped for.

But through it all, I thought nothing of my own plans. Only that when I reached Manila I was going ashore. I will have a couple hundred dollars and must be careful of that until I can find a ship. Fortunately, I have my master's ticket, and there may be some rusty little inter-island steamer I can command. If not, I might find something in sail. It will seem strange to be adrift again. It has been so long since I was free.

Perhaps it is that feeling of impending change that makes me restless, the knowledge that my former life is a closed book, and that I am beginning anew. What will happen? Sometimes I am moved to wonder at the enormous calm with which we make plans. After all, "A man's Heart devises his way: but the Lord directs his steps."

SAM HARRELL

Oiler

Sam Harrell walked out on deck and stood in the warm sun rubbing his ear with a Turkish towel. He was naked to the waist, and his worn dungarees were greasy. He stopped rubbing and stared at the grime on the towel, then looked over at Denny, who was leaning casually against the rail. "You damned flying fish sailor! You ought to ship on the black gang once just to find out what work really is! You guys on deck just play around with a paintbrush half the time, or look for lights that aren't there."

Denny grinned. "Nuts! It's all of you on the black gang that are screwy. It must be the heat."

Tex joined them. "It ain't the heat. A guy's just got to be crazy before he'll ship below. Take O'Brien, for instance."

"You take him," Harrell said, leaning back against the deckhouse. "The third is so damned scared O'Brien will find something wrong that he works my tail off. You'd think O'Brien was chief engineer."

"Be glad you aren't on his watch," McGuire said. "At that, it's a wonder he isn't goofier still, working with Jacobs and Mahoney."

"You and Mahoney had a run-in, didn't you?" Sam asked.

"First day back," Tex offered. "Mahoney got tough, an' McGuire let him have it. He beat me to it by about ten seconds."

"Can he fight?"

"In a way," McGuire said. "Dirty stuff, in close. But I know a couple of things myself."

"I've known him a long time," Tex said. "He used to live down in Happy Valley, that shantytown back of Beacon Street in 'Pedro. He'd hole up for the winter with Russian Fred, the McFee brothers, an' a guy they called Pork Chops, all of them stew bums or worse. The guy who had the shack—squatted there or maybe he owned it, I don't know—is an old shipfitter named Fitzpatrick. If they're a gang of tinhorns, then he's the boss."

"Yeah," Denny agreed. "They'd look for a live wire who'd come ashore, anyone with dough. They'd take him around to some bar, get him half-swacked, and roll him for what he had. Some of them ship out occasionally, like Mahoney. Fitz, he just works over at the yards, if he's sober. He and I had a go-around too."

"What did young Wesley have on his mind?" Sam asked. "I didn't think he ever talked to anybody but himself and God."

"Him? Oh, he saw me at some shindig over in Hollywood with the girlfriend. He thinks seamen should stay along the waterfront, I guess."

" 'The girlfriend.' You should see this dame! Red-gold hair, the prettiest gal I ever saw!" Tex said. "He comes breezin' into that hearing in the commissioner's office with her an' Hazel Ryan!"

"How'd you rate, pal?" Sam demanded. "Who was she?"

"Faustine Carmody. Works in pictures. I've known her a couple of years. I met her in New York. Then we ran into each other in Hollywood when they hired me out of the Main Street Gym to double for some guy in a fight picture."

"You been in the *movies*? What the hell you want to go to sea for?"

Denny shrugged. "Being in a movie or two isn't being under contract. You can surely starve waiting for *that* ship to come in."

"Mahoney's got it in for the Dutchman, too," Tex interrupted. "You know what that's all about?"

"Nope," Denny said. "But Pete better watch his step. That mick will shove him over the side some dark night."

"Yeah," Sam said, "or Pete'll knock all his hinges loose!"

"Well, Mahoney's spoiling for trouble," Tex agreed. "So's Jacobs. You better keep your eyes open, McGuire. They both might jump *you*."

Denny turned and rested his elbow on the rail. The muscles on his shoulders were thick, and his body tapered sharply to a narrow waist and slim hips. He shrugged. "Let 'em come. Slug Jacobs has a streak as wide as his back. As for Mahoney? Well, he's tried it before."

"This is my last trip on this wagon," Sam said suddenly. "No more tanker runs for me."

"Scared?"

"No, but I'm not too damned comfortable! Every time a guy wants a smoke he has to go in the fo'c'stle. You forget and strike a match and the next thing you know somebody hands you a harp."

"Not you, Sam. It'll be a shovel."

"Maybe. Maybe I belong in the black gang anyway."

Tex Worden thoughtfully bit off a chew and slipped the plug back in his breast pocket. "You guys can have mine, too. I'm jumping ship in Manila."

"The hell you are!" Denny turned to face him. "What's the idea?"

"You ought to know. Want to go back there an' have that Winstead character hang a murder rap on me? I wouldn't have the chance of a snowball in hell."

"You'd have one good witness. Hazel Ryan should carry some weight. She's pretty enough to handle any jury. She'd make a monkey out of Price."

"Maybe," Tex spat. "But I don't want to trust my life to it. I did my job like I saw it. They ain't going to make me the goat. To the devil with them."

"I wouldn't go back either," Sam said. "They've got the money. What chance would a workin' stiff have in any case?"

"I'd hate to see you go, Tex. You've been a good watch mate. As far as that goes, this has been a decent ship. I like the crew, too." McGuire turned to look forward.

"How about Jacobs and Mahoney?"

"Sure. What the hell? They don't know any better. There's always a couple of screwy ones aboard."

"A couple? What about O'Brien? And old man Schumann?"

"What's wrong with them, after all? Schumann raises geraniums. If that's screwy, we could stand a few more. O'Brien is a little off his course, but we're all nuts about something, right?"

"Well," Harrell said, "I don't like it. It's a good boat. She's easy to work, light down below, no heavy lifting, an' damned near new. But I don't like it. She gives me the willies. O'Brien walks around looking like Dracula. Schumann talks to himself, Mahoney sits and stares at Pete like he could kill him . . . an' that Jacobs is just a big mean ape. I don't like it."

"It's the naphtha," Tex said. "For a couple of trips you don't mind it. Then you get uneasy. You get to watching hose connections. Ever' time you strike a match or hear a noise you hold your breath. I been on a couple of tankers carrying benzene an' high-test. Guys get screwy after a while. It gets on their nerves an' they get ugly, or strange."

"Yeah, I was wiper on a benzene tanker once," Sam said, "an' I had a buddy was on the *Pinthis* when she was rammed by the *Fairfax*."

"What happened?"

"The *Fairfax* cut her half in two, an' the gas that had spilled into the ocean from the busted tanks caught fire. It was hell. Both ships wrapped in flames from stem to stern. You could hear the screams miles away, those guys ran around on deck flaming like torches. Some of them jumped over into the sea, but it was all afire, too!"

"I'll take mine straight," Tex said. "None of these extra fixin's for me when I kick off."

"I wonder if what they say about a drowning man is true," Denny said thoughtfully. "That he remembers all his life as he's sinking?"

"If it is," Sam griped, "you're gonna remember that pie you gypped me out of with those phony dice of yours!"

"Why, Mr. Harrell!" Denny exclaimed in mock astonishment. "How could you suggest such a thing! Those dice are as straight as any I ever used!"

"I'd bet on that!" Sam agreed heartily. He got up. "You guys can stay here, I'm going below an' catch some shut-eye!"

It was hours later when he awakened. The sun had gone down but it was not yet dark. In the half-light of his bunk Sam watched the shadows change, resting before the call came to go on watch. He could tell by the movement of the ship that the sea was working up again, for the roll was longer and deeper.

Sam turned his head to look out the port. The sea was a deep green, shading into black with falling night. It looked sullen, angry. It would be rough tonight. The clouds were low, and the waves were beginning to crown themselves with white. He turned his eyes from the sea, and shifted uneasily, trying to get comfortable in the humid air. Strange, what McGuire was saying. What if all of a man's life did drift past his drowning eyes? There would be so much to remember, so many things that happened, and so many things that should have happened. Suddenly, Sam Harrell felt very old.

Forty-two. It wasn't old as ages go these days. But it was very old for him. So much had happened, and yet so little. So many years, so many ports, so many people. At forty-two most men were well along on a career. In a bank, or a business, or shipping as an engineer or mate. And at forty-two he was lying here in a bunk of steel gray pipe, just where he had been twenty years ago.

Twenty years. Twenty years gone—where? How different it had all seemed in the beginning! Back there before the war when he was in his late teens, just warming up to life and ready to dive into the fight. When he married, everything seemed bright and wonderful. There had been Mary, his home, and the baby. Then the war.

The war. Who would have guessed it would make so much difference? It had all been exciting to read about, thrilling to add up victories when one didn't think about the death, the stench of fallen men, the wounds. Then the draft got him, the flu took his daughter, his wife died in childbirth, and the war ended. He returned home to find a son he had never seen, the wife and child he had known gone. His job was gone, too, and he had no idea where to turn.

He shipped out the first time on a freighter bound for England.

He'd hated it; he'd been seasick for days, and Liverpool was just like France, all gray skies and gray stone and black river water. Coming back, there had been the fall.

It was the day before they made the coast. He'd been clinging to the outside of the bridge wing laying on a coat of white paint, loosely secured by leaning back against a length of rope. A gust of wind had caught him unawares, his feet slipped and he had crashed, first into the freshly painted steel and then off the rickety staging to the deck twenty feet below.

He was in a coma for five days. No doctor was called when they reached port, nor was he put ashore. They just laid him in a bunk and closed the door. Sam suspected that they were afraid he, the union, or a seamen's fraternal organization might call for an investigation. If he died they could just bury him at sea, and no one would be the wiser.

But he didn't die. When he awoke they were back at sea, bound for the Far East. He had broken an arm and the pupil of one eye was forevermore larger than the other. He stayed with that ship for another year. He was young and inclined to forgive and forget; . . . in fact, forgiving and forgetting became a way of life. "What chance would a workin' stiff have?" It had become a motto.

One trip drifted into another almost without interruption. Returning always meant going to the places where he had courted Mary. Visiting his aunt meant also seeing a son who was a stranger to him, and with whom he always felt ill at ease. Somehow the days became weeks, the weeks became years, and the years became twenty. And here he was: Sam Harrell, oiler on the eight-to-twelve watch.

Here he was, bound out for the Far East on a tanker as he might have been ten years before, or fifteen, or more. How was it that life had gotten away from him so? This life at sea wasn't the life for a mature man. Unless one was like John Harlan, the second mate. A quiet chap, Harlan, who enjoyed the life, the chance to study, and the opportunity to live comfortably and securely.

Sam Harrell's eyes sought the port again. Odd, that he, of all people, should follow the sea. He hated water, had always been deathly afraid of it. Like many merchant seamen, he couldn't swim a stroke. Not that it mattered out here, for even if one fell into the water, there was no place to go. Sometimes he awakened in the night thinking the sea was bursting in, that it was cascading through the side, a roaring Niagara, flooding the floor plates and mounting higher and higher about him.

But somehow he had made the sea his life, somehow he'd kept going. He had kept a job through the worst years of the financial crisis, but in the process his dreams had slipped away. It was hard to recall now, just what they had been. He had been around the world so many times, yet there was so little that he actually knew. He had been in Saigon, but had never even heard of Angkor Wat until McGuire had mentioned it. What had he seen in all his travels? A lot of ocean, ships, sailors, waterfront dives, docks, too many bottles, and women. The kind of women who wanted a man with money to spend, but the kind of man who would be gone in a week.

Sam felt lonely, depressed. It had been a long time since he'd felt that way. It had become a habit to drift along with the gang going ashore and have a good time. Down the avenue of his thoughts ran a shifting panorama of scenes. The American Bar on Lime Street in Liverpool, the Old Trafford Inn, and the Fox Inn at Manchester. Or was it Salford? The Maypole Bar in Singapore, the Dutch Club in Balikpapan. Malay Street in Singapore. Ah Shing's Café House on Avenue Edward VII in Shanghai. The Honkgew district, District Six in Cape Town, and the Kasbah in Algiers. They were places that he would like to tell his son about, but if he did, he'd have little to say except that he'd been stupid drunk in all of them.

Of all the crew, he had been aboard the *Lichenfield* the longest, longer even than the Old Man. It was a fact that embarrassed him, so he rarely mentioned it. He felt he was growing old right along with his ship. His hands were scarred and callused just like his ship was scarred and callused. They'd go to the breakers together if he wasn't careful, he thought.

He could remember when she'd hit the dock in Osaka, a subject of consternation to both the Nip authorities and their insurance company. They had also tangled with a dockside crane in Liverpool, the sort of accident that could spell the end of a tanker, and a fair bit of her crew if luck wasn't with you. As it happened the only damage was to the cabling around the stern mast, a bend in one of the vent pipes, and the new pump that had crashed to the deck courtesy of the crane operator's carelessness. Well, he could heal and the ship could be fixed. But just like his eye after that fall, and just like the vent pipe, which below the level of the deck was no longer straight, some things were never the same again.

He sat up, swinging his feet over the edge of the bunk. Across from him Fritz Schumann snored like a drowsy old tomcat. Old Fritz, who worked so quietly, and so surely, yet said so little.

Sam dropped to the deck and sat on a bench while he pulled on his shoes, the uncomfortable Romeos he always wore aboard ship. Then he slipped on his singlet and staggered into the mess room for coffee.

Worden was already there. "How is it?" he asked.

"Lousy!" Sam said, shrugging. "I don't know what's wrong with me. I've been all over the world an' haven't seen nothing! I gotta get off this tub."

Tex stirred sugar into his black coffee, and shrugged. "I don't guess a guy gets much out of this life but his three squares a day an' what he can drink in port."

"Ever tried going home?"

"Yeah, once. I went back to settle the estate. Mom was dead, an' ever'body I knew was gone or had grown older. I crawled on a bronc an' come damned near getting pitched on my head! You'd of thought I'd never had been in a saddle. I rode over to see Charlie Fry; I used to go to school with him. Hell, he was married, had three kids, an' a little two-by-twice ranch with a few cows. We sat there tryin' to talk to each other, but there wasn't a damn thing to say."

"Stay long?"

"Hell, no! I caught a train back to Galveston, an' didn't feel right until I got a whiff of salt air. Even that wasn't enough. I walked down along the waterfront an' a guy comes staggering out of a joint with breath you could cut with a knife. He bumped into me, an' I shoved him away. He yelled, 'Let go o' me, you miserable, deck-swabbin' scum!' An' boy, I could've kissed that guy! I felt so good to hear my own language again that I didn't even kick him once I floored him."

"I've got a boy older than Jones," Sam said. "He sent me a snapshot the other day with some swell-looking girl. Betty Deaton, her name was. I haven't seen the kid in years. 'Home.' Hell, I hardly know what the word means."

Davy Jones walked into the mess room and sat down on the bench. "Hello, Tex. Hi, Sam. She's certainly getting rough out there."

"You're tellin' me?" Tex exclaimed, and grabbed the mustard jar as it started sliding toward him. "I been spendin' half my time keepin' the grub on the table. I wish that fiddle was a bit higher."

"What fiddle?" Davy asked.

Tex grinned. "This thing, here. The fiddle is this frame around the table to keep the dish from slidin' off when the ship rolls. An inch high is okay, but it could be higher without hurtin' any."

"How you likin' it at sea, Davy?" Sam asked.

"Fine."

"You been puttin' on some muscle," Tex said. "You're a lot darker, too."

"Yes, I guess that's right. Maybe it's the salt air."

"Denny's been showing you the ropes, has he?"

"Yes. So's Pete. They've sure done a lot for me."

"How about Slug?" Tex asked keenly. "He been causin' you any trouble?"

"I can take it. I'm not gonna be fighting anyone again. Um, I mean, not ever, if I can help it! He's an animal and a bully, though."

"Who you callin' an animal?"

They looked up suddenly at the voice. Slug Jacobs was standing in the door of the mess room, stripped to the waist. He had just come from below to call the watch, and his body was streaming with perspiration and seawater. His flat, ugly face was almost dead white, his eyes small, and his lips thick.

Davy stood up, his face white. "You are," he said slowly. "You're bigger than me and you can push me around. But I won't fight you and I'll never be afraid of you, so get lost!"

"Get lost, huh?" Slug started forward, around the mess table. "I show you who's gonna get lost!"

Tex got between Slug and the boy, his eyes narrow. "You-all better stop right where you are," he said. "I don't want no truck with you, Slug."

"You shut up," Slug said, licking his lips, and staring at Tex. "I got nothing to do with you. I want him."

"No. Go call Schumann an' end your watch," Tex said quietly. "You get tough with me an' I'll cut off some of that beef, understand?" He picked up the knife they had used in cutting bread. "I'll cut you down an' stomp you. Now scram!"

"Say! Vhat happens here? You boys vait one minute!" Pete Brouwer stood in the doorway, as commanding a presence as the captain.

"I have been at sea for twenty year." He glared at them, his blue eyes cold as arctic ice. "T'is is vhat I know—vhen sailor, he fight . . . t'is is *bad luck*! Bad luck for t'e sailor men! Bad luck for t'e ship! If ve have problem, ve solve it on t'e dock, yes?"

Slug hesitated, breathing audibly. Then he backed slowly to the door. "You wait. You think you smart. I'll get you. I'll get Jones, too."

"Sure. Sure," Tex said. "Anytime you want to try."

Slug stepped past Pete, through the door into the passage, and Davy sat down suddenly. "Thanks Tex, Pete," he said.

Pete looked at Worden and shook his head, "He is trouble, t'is I know. But you should know better. One ship, she sink right under you. I vant to go home. Davy is a young man. Ve need no bad luck, okay?"

Pete turned and stalked off, leaving the occupants of the mess room staring at the floor.

"That Slug. I guess I am scared of him." Davy mumbled, "He doesn't look human."

"He ain't," Sam said. "He's only about half there. I heard the first tell the chief, Jacobs was no better than a moron. I think that was rank flattery myself. But as far as that goes, Davy, you stood right up to him."

"But I was scared," Davy admitted.

"Who wouldn't be?" Tex shrugged. "That guy weighs two-twenty if he weighs an ounce. I don't care what Pete says, you'd better be ready to defend yourself."

Davy Jones said nothing, but he didn't look all that healthy either.

Shorty Conrad walked in. "Hi, fellas! I see you're on your pin, Tex. Where's McGuire?"

"Who's that using my name in vain?" McGuire said, coming up behind him. He glanced around, and stopped, looking at Davy. "What's the matter, Jones? You look kind of pale around the gills!"

"It was Slug Jacobs," Tex said. "He came in an' got tough with the kid. I come damn near cuttin' the fool's heart out. I'd of tried it, too, if Pete hadn't stepped in."

"Maybe something will have to be done about that guy," Denny said. "I don't like that big lug, and I especially don't like the company he keeps."

"I wish you'd make it soon," Tex said, shaking his head. "Let's go for'rd. Where were you workin', half-pint?"

"*Mr.* Half-Pint to you, sailor!" Shorty said, reaching for a piece of bread and some cheese. "If you'll wiggle your tail up to the port bridge wing you'll find a scraper and a pot of red lead. After that, use your own judgment. In an hour it'll probably be too rough to bother."

Sam Harrell got up. For a minute he looked down at the table, and then he walked out to the deck, watching the sea rolling with white-caps and feeling the hot, damp wind buffeting his body. "I think," he muttered softly, "I think when this is over I'll go home an' see the kid. Yes," he said after a minute, "that's just what I'll do!"

When he had first gone to sea, that fall from the bridge wing had nearly killed him. Fighting aboard ship might or might not be bad luck, but the odds did build up. They hadn't gotten the best of him yet, but it might be the time to consider throwing in his hand.

THE PRIVATE LOG OF
JOHN HARLAN, SECOND MATE

March 28th: Six bells. I have closed the book I've been reading for the past hour and am now beginning my daily entry in this private log. Fortunately, I write with a fountain pen, for it would be impossible to keep an ink bottle from sliding off the table. However awkward writing is at times, I don't mind greatly, for I have long been familiar with the sea. At times the ship rises on a huge wave, the propeller is thrown clear of the water, and its violent threshing makes the ship tremble from stem to stern. I can feel sympathy for Augie Donato, the third engineer now on watch, for each time the ship rises he must ease the speed to cut the vibration. The unresisted whirling of the propeller is desperately hard on everything below.

All day we have been running into heavy seas, and the lookout has been using the flying bridge, for the decks are a crazy welter of angry water and even the catwalks over them are deluged. A man couldn't live ten minutes on the fo'c'stlehead. It will be something up there on the bridge tonight, watching those waves crash down on the foredeck, seeing them race aft, and hearing the scuppers gulp and gasp as the bow rises.

There will be no stars tonight, only the lowering black cloud and the glistening, metallic sea. I will stand on the bridge in sou'wester and oilskins, canting to the heavy roll, watching the hurrying white-caps, and keeping an eye open for other vessels. I often wonder on such nights as this how the Vikings ever managed in their tiny ships. It took courage to navigate in those days, when all was unknown, and so many of the ships were small, and many of them undecked.

The Phoenicians, too. The greatest seafaring race history has ever known—I wonder how much of the world they saw. Hanno rounded the Cape of Good Hope long before Dias and da Gama, and he completely circumnavigated Africa. That was a marvelous thing, and lends some credence to the stories of a Phoenician galley sunken in the mud of the Amazon. From the coast of Gambia and the Cape Verde Islands, it is not far across the Atlantic to Brazil.

The day will soon be gone, and my watch begins the new one. Eight bells, twelve o'clock. It is an end and a beginning. I have enjoyed my quiet watches in the night, and there are not many more awaiting me—Manila is but a few days off. I shall miss this ship, for it has been my home a long time now. And I shall miss the crew, but there have been many crews, and where have they gone? Like the snows of yesteryear of which Villon wrote, they have vanished. Perhaps I shall meet some of them again, walking the streets in Mombasa, Cape Town, Singapore, Nagasaki, Zamboango, or Makassar. Perhaps I shall meet one of them at Steamer Point, in Aden, or perhaps in Zunguldak or Zanzibar. Or someday possibly two of them may meet on the Skid Road in Seattle, or along Frisco's Embarcadero, and they may speak of me.

The ship moves on, and the seas break over her, and the water slides under the hull. We are our own world, a little cluster of lights in a world of utter blackness and angry sea. Green to starboard, red to port, and the tiny eyes of the white lights on the topm'sts. Under the ventilator in his accustomed seat, old Fritz will be sitting, dreaming behind his glasses of the days that are gone. Above at the wheel, Tex stands, quiet, inscrutable. In the dark at his left the chronometer steadily ticks, and outside Mr. George Wesley will be staring into the darkness and storm, annoyed that the privacy of his bridge should be invaded by the Man on Lookout. But Denny will be cool and respectful, having all the advantage possessed by a man with a sense of humor.

He should be coming along soon to give me a call. I never sleep at this hour, but the call is customary, and truth to tell I often need it as I begin reading and time fairly flies away from me.

There! A quick, sharp rap on the door. That will be Denny . . .

He's gone now. Tex Worden is going ashore in Manila. Denny told me that confidentially, knowing that I'm going too. I shall keep in touch with him. If I get a berth, I could probably ship him in some capacity. There are few better seamen, and I think Tex would make a top-notch ship's officer. He's an efficient sort. The account of his experiences after the *Rarotonga* sunk was typical of the man. He is a direct, matter-of-fact sort, and not the type to even consider himself until the job was done.

I answered the door, and Denny was standing there. "One bell, Mr. Harlan!" he said cheerfully. "And God have pity on the poor sailors on such a night as this!"

"Come in, Denny," I said, "and close the door. I'll get enough of that dampness in the next four hours. We might as well have our nightcap, hadn't we?"

"Sure thing," he said. He tasted the drink and then looked up. "Anything I can do for you in the States, Mr. Harlan? I get around a good bit, you know."

"No, I don't think so. I've got a couple of youngsters there, fine kids they are, but they have a better home now than I could give them."

"I'll tell you what, Mr. Harlan," he said, "you might get down into the Molukkens. If you do, I've got a girl down that way you can look up. At least, I say she's my girl, but anyway, we liked each other quite a bit. She's a fine person, interested in everything. She has a plantation and a good bit of money. I'll give you her name. If you look her up, give her my best."

I smiled at him. "Is this *the* romance, Denny? Or is it that girl back in the States? The one Wesley saw you with?"

He grinned. "I don't know. I haven't seen this woman in several years, but she stays with me. Maybe I've read too many books. We write, occasionally. Honestly, I doubt she's waiting for me ... but I think the one back in L.A. is."

"What's her name, the girl in Hollywood?"

"Carmody. Faustine Carmody."

"Name sounds familiar. Could I have seen her somewhere in a show?"

"Yes, maybe you have." He put his glass down. "Well, I've got a few minutes left on the bridge. See what you can do about getting rid of this storm. After all, a second mate should have some influence with the powers that be."

He walked out, and I returned to complete this page of my log. The ship is rolling worse than ever, and we are lucky to be in a modern tanker; liquid cargo has never been easy to transport by sea, but I'm guessing it was considerably worse twenty or thirty years ago.

And so another day ends, another begins. As we used to say: one more and one less.

SLUG JACOBS

Fireman

S lug Jacobs shuffled into the mess room and stared blankly at the night lunch. Cheese. Every night there was cheese. He picked up a slice of bread, buttered it thickly, and then turned over each piece of cheese until he found the largest and placed that carefully on the bread. He buttered another slice, and added another piece of cheese. Then he sat down at the table and began to eat.

Mahoney came in and joined him, drawing a cup of coffee, and drinking it in gulps. He looked up, staring at Slug. "What happened?"

"Huh?"

"I said, what happened? Yesterday."

"Nothin'."

"Yeah?" Mahoney was sarcastic. "I heard you near to got your guts cut out."

"Aw, nothin', nothin'. The Jones kid got smart. I tol' him off, an' I was goin' t' git him. Then Tex, he butt in. He had a knife."

"An' you was scared, huh? Whyn't you hit him with the catsup bottle? You're yella, that's what. A big guy like you. That Jones, he's McGuire's fair-haired boy. Now, you gots to be scared of McGuire—he's the tough guy in that crowd. He's the one that'll get you!"

"I ain't scared of him," Slug said defensively. "He ain't so big."

"He's going to get you, Slug. You better watch him. That guy'll kill you."

Mahoney stopped talking as Pete came in, followed by Shorty. The two newcomers didn't speak, but Mahoney glared at Pete. "Hi, Dutchie," he said. "What's the matter? Gettin' the high hat?"

"This is goot ship, Mahoney. I know you, ant I know him." Pete pointed at Jacobs. "I do not like fighting on ship. It is not right for shipmates to fight. Unt you look for troubles. You leaf me be, ya?"

They stared at each other for a minute, Pete very calm, very cool. There was no emotion on his face or in his eyes. Then he turned and walked out to the deck, buttoning on his oilskins.

"That's good advice, Mahoney," Shorty said. "The Dutchman is nobody to fool with."

"Yeah? I'll kill that bastard if he ever gets guts enough to fight!"

Shorty laughed. "Like you did with McGuire, huh?"

Mahoney got to his feet, his eyes gleaming. "Smart, huh? Everyone tellin' me what to do." He stepped past the table and came for Shorty.

Conrad crouched, his face white and tense. As Mahoney closed in, Conrad swung. The Irishman ducked low and kicked out. His foot caught Shorty in the groin, and the little seaman's face went white. He clinched desperately, and then Mahoney jerked free and hooked his right fist hard to Shorty's head.

Conrad gamely struggled to keep his feet. He tried a left that struck the Irishman's mouth. Mahoney took it staggering, but before Conrad could follow it up, Jacobs stepped up behind him and slugged him behind the ear. Shorty tumbled to the floor, and Mahoney kicked and kicked again. Then the two backed into the passage, Mahoney swearing, dabbing at the blood on his lip. "That'll show the bastards!" he muttered. "That'll show 'em."

John Harlan came up the ladder to the bridge, then walked into the chart room with Mr. Wesley. When they had finished estimating the ship's position, taking into account the weather and the time since their last fix, Wesley came out and went down the ladder. Harlan walked over to the wheel. "How's everything, Brouwer?"

"Ever't'ing okay by me," Pete said.

Harlan stepped out on the bridge, the wind striking him like a blow. Bending into the blast, he reached the canvas dodger. He looked over at Denny. Then he ran down the bridge wing as the ship tilted to port. "Where's Conrad?" he shouted.

Denny shrugged. "Can't imagine," he yelled. He leaned closer. "Thought I saw a light off to port, about three points on the bow."

For a tense minute they stared, but nothing revealed itself. Then Harlan turned and made his way into the wheelhouse. Pete looked up from the compass.

"Where's Conrad?" Harlan asked. "It's not like him to be late."

Pete shook his head. "Ve vuss toget'er in t'e mess room, unt—" He stopped, and his face stiffened. "Maybe t'ere is trouble—he vuss mit Mahoney unt Yacobs vhen I left."

John Harlan's eyes narrowed. He stepped to the door and blew his whistle. McGuire was unable to hear his voice with the wind blowing as it was, but the sound brought him down the bridge as it canted steeply. "Yes, sir?"

"Go below and have a look for Shorty," Harlan said. "Brouwer says he was in the mess room with Mahoney and Jacobs. They should be on now, but watch your step."

Denny wheeled swiftly and dropped down the ladder. Clinging to the rail of the catwalk, he hurried aft. Water boiled and seethed around the pipes beneath his feet. To let go even for a minute might mean being thrown into the turmoil of water on the main deck. He was almost running when he reached the passage to the mess room. Shorty was sitting up when he got to the door. "What the hell?" Denny demanded. "Who did this?"

Shorty tried to stand, his face bloody and drawn with pain. "Mahoney. Then Jacobs slugged me from behind."

Denny glanced back up the passage toward the entrance to the boiler room. "They go on watch?"

"Yeah," Shorty nodded. "I guess so."

"Then they got four hours," Denny said. "How you feeling? Can you stand your trick?"

"Uh-huh. Yeah, I think so. I was doing okay until Jacobs slugged me."

"Okay, you beat it for'rd."

When Shorty left, Denny sat down suddenly. Ever since they shipped it had been coming. Left alone, Jacobs was too dumb to be truly dangerous, but the stocky, hard-bitten Mahoney kept him stirred up. Well, tomorrow was another day, and sooner or later things were going to have to be worked out. Denny got up and turned toward the fo'c'stle.

Slug Jacobs scrubbed at a burner, an isolated figure in the bottom of the tall, dimly lit stokehole. Behind him the fires roared from the fans of the forced draft. Steam pressure from the boilers turned the giant turbine that powered the ship. The burners had to be clean or they would drip and build up uncombusted oil. Then they wouldn't work right and were even more of a mess to clean up. The second engineer didn't tolerate mess. He didn't tolerate uneven steam pressure either. Slug scrubbed harder. In a minute he'd have to check the fireboxes.

He set down the wire brush and opened and closed his fist. The scar on the back of his hand was no longer tight. He peered at it, dimly, then more clearly, remembering how it had happened . . .

He had come out of the woods at a shambling trot, stopping in a fringe of brush to stare at the road. He was wearing an old cracked leather jacket and khaki trousers, a battered felt hat on his head. He had slept outside the night before, and had traveled rapidly, keeping under the cover of darkness or brush most of the way.

Forty miles behind him, lying in a lonely farmhouse, was an old man. Slug had left him crumpled on the floor, his head crushed by the violence of a blow intended only to knock him out. For several minutes, Slug had stood staring dumbly at the slow red stream welling from the man's skull. He licked his dry lips, and his big hands opened and closed.

The old man had come home while Slug was ransacking the place, looking for money. He hadn't found any, and he couldn't bring himself to check the old man's pockets.

Turning, he fled. With animal cunning, he stayed off the highways after that first ride. The driver had carried him ten miles, and then Slug had taken to the woods, hiking southward just out of sight within the line of brush and trees.

A creek blocked his way. He climbed the steep grade to the hard-surfaced road and, seeing nothing, started walking swiftly. From time to time he looked back, feeling exposed. Somewhere behind him, he heard the whine of a distant car. Dropping swiftly over the edge of the grade, he sought shelter in a culvert, and remained there, hunched and tense, until the car passed. Then he crawled out and started on. Later, when the traffic grew heavier, he curled up in the brush and slept through the day.

At dusk, he awakened and started on. It was heavy going, over plowed fields and through gullies. From time to time there was a fence to climb through. And it was already dark when he saw the light.

He started toward it. There was no one in sight. A small house located a quarter of a mile back from the highway. For a time he crouched behind some rosebushes and watched the building. There was no car nearby and apparently no dog.

The door opened, throwing a sharp rectangle of light across the yard and silhouetting the pump under a flat roofed shelter. Then a girl came from the house carrying a bucket. When she bent to work the pump handle, her dress drew tight across her hips, and Slug shifted uneasily in the darkness. Then the girl straightened, took her bucket of water, and walked back to the house.

Careful to make no sound, Slug Jacobs started forward. The earth was soft and moist, the darkness wrapped around him like a cloak. He stopped before stepping onto the small platform at the back door, and peered through the dirty pane of glass. The girl was alone and setting the table. He stared, the thoughts of food competing with other, and

less understood, desires. Then he opened the door. He was just stepping inside when the girl looked up.

Her eyes widened and she straightened. Obviously, she was frightened. Slug stopped, in the bright light his small eyes blinked. Bits of
leaves and grass clung to his clothes, and on his sleeve there were
some flecks of blood from the old man's head.

"Who—who are you? What do you mean, coming in here like
that?" The girl's voice was surprisingly steady, and Slug stared, wet-
ting his lips.

"You're purty," Slug said. Then, not knowing how to go on from
there, "I'm hungry. Gi' me somethin' t' eat."

"You get out of here, and get out right now!"

"C'mere," he said.

He started for her, and she stepped back. He grabbed, and her
sleeve tore, ripping her dress over one white, rounded breast. He
lunged, but she jerked a drawer open, and before he guessed what was
happening, he found a gun pointed at him.

He stopped, surprised. "You put that down," he said. "You put that
down or I'll hurt you!"

Her hand was steady. "Get out," she said. "Get out of here and stay
out or I'll shoot!"

He started toward her. "No you won't," he said, grabbing at her
again. She swung around the table, and the little gun spat.

With a cry, he leaped back. Blood was running from the back of his
hand where the bullet had cut a groove across it. He stared, whimper-
ing like a hurt child.

"Now get out," the girl said. "Get out quick!"

Stumbling, he backed toward the door, and when he was safely outside in the darkness, he turned and ran. Twice, he stopped to stare
back at the house and to touch his wounded hand to his mouth. Then
he ran on into the darkness.

It was nearly dawn when the truck picked him up outside of Bakersfield. Slug had been riding half the night in an empty boxcar, and then
had walked a couple of miles. The big truck ground to a halt, and the

driver motioned him up. "Might as well ride," he said, grinning. "I need somebody to keep me awake. I been drivin' sixteen hours straight now. The name's Mike."

"T'anks. Gees, I sure am glad for the ride. I been hoofin' it too long."

"Here"—the driver fished an apple from a sack near him—"eat this."

"Yeah, t'anks. I sure am hungry. I ain't eat nothin' all day. No, two days."

"Come far?"

"Uh-huh." Slug bit off a big mouthful of apple, and nodded. "From Truckee."

Eventually, the outskirts of Bakersfield appeared, and they drove down the streets in the first light of morning. The sky was very clear, and the buildings stood stark in the morning air. A woman was buying some cabbages from a man with an old truck. A boy in a white apron was sweeping the walk in front of a café with a small neon sign.

"Listen," Mike said, "you want to make four bits? I ain't makin' much wit' this buggy, but if you want to help me unload I'll give you half a buck an' buy you breakfast."

"Sure t'ing. I'll help. Gees, four bits is a lot of dough when a guy's flat."

"Okay, then. Let's eat."

In a swirl of dust the truck drew to a stop in the lot beside the café and the two climbed down, stamping about to loosen their stiffened legs. The driver looked worn and tired. They walked inside.

"Give me a stack of wheats an' coffee," Mike said. "An' let me have the coffee right now." He turned to Slug. "What'll you have?"

"Okay, the same." Slug rubbed his face sleepily. His new friend gulped the scalding coffee and stared blankly at the deflated-looking frosted snails and bear claws in the chrome and glass display cabinet. A man in overalls was eating at the far end of the counter. He held a morning paper, half-propped against a catsup bottle.

He looked up at the cook. "Hey, Joe"—he pointed at the paper—"a murder up by Lodi. Somebody bashed an old man's skull in."

"Yeah? Rob him?"

"Hell, no! Just wanted to kiss him, I guess." The man took a swallow of coffee. "The guy didn't have nothin' anyway. It was some drifter, they think."

Slug turned his head on his thick neck and stared impassively at the man. The trucker was paying no attention. The man with the paper had a thin face and a long nose. He took a swallow of coffee. "Hit him with tremendous force, the paper says. What d' you think of that? A man ain't safe nowhere these days!"

Slug Jacobs drenched his hotcakes with syrup and cut off a healthy chunk. He ate silently, listening to the man reading the paper only in intervals. Finally, Mike nudged him. "Let's go," he said. "We got to take this stuff across town yet. We better get started."

The truck roared into life and pulled back into the street. "Hear what that guy was readin'?" Mike commented. "Some ol' guy got killed up near Lodi."

Slug said nothing for a moment, then, "I wonner—I wonner who done it."

"They don't know, I guess."

The truck backed up to a loading bay and stopped. The driver set the brake. "Here we go, pal. We got a lot of wheat to unload."

When the truck was opened Slug stepped inside and picked up a sack in each hand, carrying them by the loose fabric at the top. Mike stared. "Boy, you're sure husky. I wish I had you with me all the time!"

"Huh?" Slug looked puzzled. Then he looked down at the sacks. "Oh? Yeah, yeah." He walked on inside with the two sacks, and continued carrying two to the trucker's one until the big trailer was emptied. Then he stopped and wiped the sweat from his face with the back of his hand. He wasn't tired. He liked to work.

"Listen, pal." The truck driver tapped him on the shoulder. "Why not stick with me. I got a load for L.A."

"Me? Yeah, all right." He walked into the truck and kicked some old sacks together. "I want to sleep. When you're ready, holler."

Late that evening he left the truck in Los Angeles, and crept down the side streets until he reached Main. Mike had given him another dollar when they parted. The trucker had a load to drive to Long Beach, but that wasn't for two days and Slug wanted to keep moving. He ate in a grease joint, and then caught the Pacific Electric for San Pedro.

Beacon Street was bright with lights when he crossed from the PE station and started for the Shanghai Red Cafe. The Salvation Army was on the corner singing to a group of weather-beaten drifters and waterfront characters. Most of the seamen kept moving. Slug stopped for a few minutes, and then when a cop came along, he turned and wandered off. In the morning he would register at the Slave Market, and maybe he could pick up a ship. He'd only been ashore two months from his last trip. After he had a drink he would walk over to Happy Valley and find Fitzpatrick; he always had a plan to strong-arm some money out of someone.

Slug worked methodically, checking the fireboxes, breaking up masses of congealed oil with a long bar. His big body moved easily with the roll of the ship. The wound on his hand was healed now, and the old man in the lonely farmhouse near Lodi almost forgotten.

Mahoney came over at four bells. Slug looked up to see Mahoney's hard eyes watching him. Underneath it all, even while he believed Mahoney to be his friend, there was something about his short, blocky body and square jaw, blue with beard, that reminded him of someone who had once made him afraid.

"You better watch your step when you go up top," Mahoney told him. "McGuire'll get you. He's tellin' ever'body he'll kill you if he gets a chance. You better get him first."

"Aw"—Slug was worried, but doubtful—"he won't do nothin'. He ain't said nothin' to me. Maybe I shouldn't a hit Shorty. I don't know."

"You pigheaded fool! You goin' to let them run over you an' make fun of you all the time? Mr. Full-of-His-Self McGuire's sayin' you're stupid and useless. He's just waitin', that's all. He'll just wait until you come on top some night an' then dump you over the side. Don't be a sap all your life! A big, husky guy like you, afraid of him?"

"I ain't a-scared of him," Slug protested. "But he ain't done nothin' to me."

"Christ!" Mahoney turned away. "I didn't think you was so dumb! But you wait—you'll see!"

Slug stared after him, his brow furrowed. Maybe Mahoney was right. When there was a lull in his work and O'Brien was concentrating on adjusting their speed, he walked aft between the boilers and picked up a spanner, hefting it thoughtfully. At one bell he went up to call the watch with the spanner in his pocket. There was no sign of McGuire.

At four o'clock O'Brien came up the ladder and walked to the saloon. He was tired, for it had been a trying shift. Why, he wondered, with all its other modern equipment, didn't the *Lichenfield* have an automatic control to keep the propeller from racing when free of the water? In foul weather it was devilishly hard on an engineer to watch the engine revolutions for four hours at a stretch, to feel the movement of the ship and to predict, moments before the bow tipped downward, when to cut back the power. But the coffee was hot and strong, and he rested his elbows on the table and let his body relax. He was sitting like that when John Harlan came down from the bridge.

Harlan glanced at him. "Bad night up there," he remarked, drawing coffee. "No sign of a change either."

O'Brien looked up. "Um, yeah. B-Been—busy in the engine room, too. Maintaining the right revolutions, draining the separators, hard on my—the equipment."

Harlan nodded. "I'd imagine so." He sat down and sipped his coffee. "Notice anything between Mahoney and Jacobs tonight?"

"No . . ." O'Brien looked up, his forehead wrinkled. The thought of anything going wrong with the ship aroused him at once. "W-What happened?"

"They had some trouble with Conrad. Slugged him. This may be just the beginning. Worden and McGuire aren't the type to stand for much. All that's keeping them in line is Pete. There was some trouble back in 'Pedro."

"I know. McGuire h-had a fight with Mahoney."

"Do you know how that trouble started?"

"N-No." O'Brien looked up, and then away.

After a moment Harlan said, "You're a good engineer, Con. We're lucky to have you."

They shook hands, and then Harlan left. For a long moment Con O'Brien stood silent. Then he ran his fingers gently over the back of his head. It wasn't bothering him tonight, and the weather was bad, too.

In the shadows outside the fireman's fo'c'stle, Slug Jacobs hesitated. Then he turned, and staggering with the heavy roll of the ship, he crossed over to the door of the seaman's fo'c'stle. He stopped beside the door, eyes alert.

Only one dim light was burning. The bench had tipped over and was lying on its side, one end wedged beneath a bunk. The curtains before each bunk swayed gently with the roll of the ship. All was still; there was only the breathing of the sleeping men and the sound of the engine. Slug Jacobs hesitated, hefting the spanner. He licked his lips uneasily, and peered over his shoulder. Then he slipped through the door and carefully moved the length of the fo'c'stle until he was opposite Denny McGuire's bunk.

Gently, he lifted the curtain. McGuire was lying on his side, his dark hair rumpled against the hard pillow. He was smiling in his sleep.

Slug started to lift the spanner, then shuddered slightly and dropped the curtain. Turning, he was out of the fo'c'stle in three quick strides. When he reached the passage he stopped, his heart pounding. There was something in the silence of that fo'c'stle, something in the faint smile on the sleeping man's face . . .

Mahoney was asleep when he entered the fireman's fo'c'stle. Slug slipped off his shoes, put the spanner under his pillow, and stretched out on his bunk. After a few minutes he too drifted off.

———

Through the dark of night and the black, oily seas, the ship plowed its way. Great, towering waves crashed over her bows and ran wildly aft. She rolled heavily, and the running lights canted to port, then described a brief arc back to starboard. Water sucked and rushed around the pipes and valves of the main deck. On the bridge, sweating in oilskins and a sou'wester, Borly Shannon cursed the storm. He hunched his big shoulders against the wind, and bowed his face behind the canvas dodger to shield it from the driving spray that struck with the force of hailstones.

Phosphorus glowed in the water, and angry foam crowned the peaks of the seas. Down below, the saloon messman stirred in his sleep, dreaming about returning to his family in Malabang. In the silence of his cabin, Con O'Brien sat at his desk, head resting upon his crossed arms. Slow tears found their way down his scarred cheeks. A door in his heart was slowly opening.

In his bunk of gray pipe, Davy Jones turned restlessly and muttered in his sleep. Back behind him the moon shone gently upon the sleeping village of Morningside, where soon the people would be awake. The farmer that Davy had worked for would be crawling from his bed in the first chill of morning and lighting the airtight heater before going out under a cold, starlit sky to draw water from the well and feed his horses. David Jones stirred restlessly, longing for the life he left, and longing too for the life to which he was going.

Seen from a distance, the ship is a tiny, moving island of darkness starred by lights of green and red, scoring one more triumph of Man in his conquest of nature, Man who bends everything external to his will, but has not yet begun to conquer that which is inside. In the *Lichenfield*'s tanks lies the curse and the blessing of commerce and death, the sleeping cargo of naphtha that, surrounded by seas both warm and rough, is slowly turning to vapor. Vent lines whisk the gas away, releasing it into the atmosphere far above the decks. One pipe, however, contains a bend, the result of a collision with a dockside crane years ago in Liverpool. As the waves crash and the wind drives rain and spray, this angle slowly fills with water.

The warm seas; the flash point of the *Lichenfield*'s cargo; the storm transferring its motion to the naphtha in the tanks; evaporation turning liquid to gas—a gas which, with the vent line blocked, blindly gropes for another way out. In greater and greater volume it follows a path through which it has been creeping steadily ever since leaving San Pedro; a few feet of uncaulked rivets.

The storm weakens, the wind abates, and the clouds move on. Slowly in the east, a light grows, shoots a bright crimson arrow into the sky. Her engines muttering with the calm of a task too familiar, the ship moves on into tomorrow.

THE PRIVATE LOG OF
JOHN HARLAN, SECOND MATE

March 29th: The storm has passed, and yet it did not leave us unmarked. The No. 4 lifeboat was damaged, the coal-box atop the galley was wrecked, and about half the galley coal washed over into the Pacific, that most peaceful of oceans. More, it was marked by the trouble with Jacobs and Shorty Conrad. Or rather, when Mahoney and Jacobs did the job together. That, I'm afraid, will have more significant repercussions than any damage, for the strain already visible among the crew has been intensified. Right now, all seems calm, but it is only the calm that precedes another sort of storm.

The Old Man knows of it, and says nothing, which probably shows his wisdom. Sailors prefer to settle their own problems, and more often than not, settle them to the satisfaction of everyone concerned. That choice, of how tightly to hold the reins of power, is critical. I am not sure I would make the same decision but every ship and every crew is a different chemical mixture of personalities. I hope that soon I can be master of my own ship, with officers and crew that I can be proud of.

Those old tramp freighters of the Far Eastern waters have always seemed the essence of all that is romantic. Battered and scarred, their hulls marked with red lead, their stacks stained with grease and smoke, they trade in all the lonely, lost ports of those mysterious Pacific islands. They are the swashbuckling roughnecks of the sea, battered, and ugly.

Their engine rooms are a nightmare, their gear worn and old, their crews a hodgepodge of waste material from all the alleys and dives of the Far East, their cargoes a smelly, dirty collection of copra, pearl shell, oil-drilling machinery, rubber, goats, and hajji pilgrims.

I sometimes imagine having Tex Worden for my bo'sun, or if he wished to pass the tests, my chief mate. I'd like to have McGuire too, but I fear no ship could hold him for long, and perhaps no woman. I often wonder what will become of him. He may someday settle down ashore and be a godsend to the reporters during days when news is scarce, for he is the type who will always attract some sort of attention. Far more likely he will keep going to sea or wandering in the far places. Someday his foot will slip, and some barroom tough will slip a knife between his ribs, or through accident or misadventure, he will end his days drowning or dying of thirst on some waterless little island.

There are many ways out for him, but most of them I can picture are a thing of the moment, the nip and tuck, devil take the hindmost sort of adventuring somewhere. But probably I don't know McGuire better than any of the others, and he may be entirely different. That is the curse and the charm of living, observing this life, searching for the right story. We never know those around us well enough, and may overlook their most interesting aspects.

I'll admit McGuire fascinates me most of all those aboard. The man is so complex, so utterly different, and his personality is always cropping up in unexpected places, and showing some facet hitherto undreamed and unsuspected. I believe that he is somehow in the center of the situation aft, which is growing more tense as the days go by.

Troubled or not our ship moves on. But, can I say "our" ship? Does the ship belong to us, or we to the ship? One is moved to wonder, for like cogs in a number of wheels, we all serve the ship. We paint it, strip and replace the brick in its fireboxes, we minister to its ills, we guide it safely, and we watch its every symptom with utmost care. It now carries us above some of the deepest water in the world, riding as high over the surface of the planet as any aircraft.

Today, I have been reading Plato's *Timaeus*, in which he repeats Solon's tale of the lost continent of Atlantis. But, despite the fabulous nature of the story, and Plato's use of it merely to set forth certain ideas of his own, the account of Solon undoubtedly had some background. In so much legend there is certain to be some basis in fact. One account has it that the armies of Atlantis were away on a voyage of conquest when their homeland vanished in a gigantic earthquake and tidal wave. Could it happen again? Might it happen to the Japanese now as they invade China? Japan has volcanoes, and in the not-too-distant past has suffered violent quakes.

But I would not lose the beauty of Japan, for it is certainly one of the most lovely of all countries despite the mistaken psychology that has momentarily distracted the parties in power. Japan came on the historical stage too late. The phase they are trying to live now ended before they began to look beyond their shores. They have absorbed too much of the virus of the Western world and will go down with it.

Worden just came to call me to go on watch. I like the fellow. We talked about Manila, and I told him that unless he had other plans I'd like to keep him with me, and give him a chance to get a ticket. He was willing enough. Then I asked him about Mahoney.

"He's a bad one," he said. "So is Jacobs. But Mahoney is the trouble-maker, Denny thinks. Jacobs is the strongest man I ever saw. If he gets ahold of McGuire, it'll be bad."

"This can't get out of hand," I said. "If the officers have to get into it there'll be hell to pay for everyone."

"Well, Denny says if Slug does get hold of him he'll make him wish he hadn't." Tex grinned. "He's got that girl in L.A., but he's also like you and me. If the Old Man wants to fire him, he might be just as happy to stay in the Far East."

PATRICK MAHONEY

Oiler

In the short metallic cavern of the shaft alley, he looked like a troll. His massive head, deep-set eyes, and broken nose were accentuated by the dim lights. His thick-muscled shoulders and stubby, powerful arms added to the effect.

He moved quickly, noiseless as the ominous threat of the huge shadows beside and behind him. Once he hesitated, his head held slightly aside, listening. All that could be heard was the churning of the propeller outside and the rumble from the engine room. He cleared his throat, and echoing from the tunnel walls it sounded like a growl. He reached out and took the temperature of the stuffing box; all that kept the sea from filling the engine spaces was a few turns of flax padding. A trickle of seawater running away into the bilge kept it lubricated. Turning, he made his way swiftly out of the shaft alley and closed the tunnel door securely.

In the bright light of the engine room, the shadows receded into the being of the man himself. Mahoney walked up to the starting platform. O'Brien glanced down, his face impassive. Mahoney jerked his head toward the tunnel and spoke over the noise. "She's all right. I checked her."

O'Brien nodded, remembering what Harlan had asked him about Mahoney and Jacobs. "Just stand by, then," he said at last.

Mahoney turned and walked to where Jacobs was braced in the opening to the fire room. He stared at the hulking figure in the doorway. "What's the matter? You yella?"

Slug looked sullen. "What d' ya mean?"

"You know damn well what I mean! You had plenty of chance last night. Anything could happen on a night like that. For all they'd have known he'd have fallen off the bridge or been washed over-side."

Slug was silent, staring down at the floor plates.

"You better. He'll take you apart, that guy. He's a bad one. I'm lookin' out for you—who the hell else is gonna do that."

Mahoney walked away. Slug was a damn bone-headed fool. He could have fixed it all the night before. No matter how suspicious they got, nothing could be proved. Mahoney had more than one score to settle, but he had to be careful how he did it. He'd get that pretty-boy McGuire. Pete Brouwer too, just for getting on his nerves, just for keeping him in the doghouse worrying about being caught.

Of all the ships in the harbor, how in the world did the Dutchman end up on this one . . . showing up at the last minute like a bad penny? Luckily, the thick-skulled chump didn't remember him; he'd been too drunk. The oiler slipped two fingers in his trouser pocket and touched the watch. It was massive, old-fashioned. He had to carry it. Somebody might get into his locker and see it. He should have hocked the damn thing back in 'Pedro.

Pete had mentioned losing the watch several times since he'd been aboard. He'd told both Denny and Tex about being robbed, and described the watch. Shorty, of course, knew it by sight—he and Pete had shipped out together several times. Once, Mahoney had looked up suddenly and caught Pete Brouwer staring at him, brow furrowed. It had frightened him.

The four-to-eight oiler came down the ladder, rubbing his eyes sleepily. Mahoney looked toward Slug, who had turned the fire room over to his relief. Slug looked uneasy. "What's the matter?" Mahoney said sharply. "What's eatin' you?"

"Nothin'."

"Then what the hell you lookin' like a sick cow for?"

Slug mumbled something and shifted his big feet. He started toward the ladder, Mahoney following him and speaking in an undertone. "You better get that guy. You better get him. He'll hurt you."

"Uh-huh."

"Get close to him. Break him up. Don't try to slug him. You're stronger than anybody. Get hold of him an' it'll be easy."

"Uh-huh."

Alone on the poop deck, Denny McGuire stood by the taffrail watching the wake boil into white froth and vanish into the heaving sea. The days he had lived were like the wake of the ship: They had been here, left their momentary mark, and slipped away. What had been no longer was, and whether he was the better or worse for it did not seem to matter.

He was restless this trip. For the first time he was discontented with the journey and found himself wishing the ship were homeward-bound. Was it because of Faustine? What was the uneasiness that was with him so much this voyage? He had made this trip, and with this same cargo, several times before. He prided himself on knowing when to get out, knowing when a situation had gone from something that someday might make a good story to one that might get him killed. He had always been able to feel when to cut his losses and head for the border, and he was having those feelings right now. The difficulty was he didn't know what his instinct was telling him to avoid: the lovely girl who threatened his freedom, the violence that seemed to be brewing in the fo'c'stle, or the very ship beneath his feet.

Denny McGuire looked around him, at the windblown sea. It didn't matter what the trouble really was, he thought, because there was nowhere to go.

Down in the fireman's fo'c'stle, Mahoney sat and lit a cigarette. There had been no sign of McGuire on deck, and he had noticed Tex playing cards in the seaman's fo'c'stle with several others, including Shorty

Conrad. Mahoney placed the butt between his teeth and leaned back against the bulkhead, watching the door. Waiting made him uneasy. He was sure McGuire would not let their beating of Shorty pass unnoticed. Shifting on his seat, he watched the door, his thoughts drifting back to that kid on the dock, and to the fight with McGuire.

Mahoney had been off watch at the time and waiting for Tom McFee, who was bringing him a bottle. The boy had come walking down to the oil dock, his eyes bright and eager, yet he was hesitant, too. The man in the guard shack wasn't paying attention, and Mahoney watched with interest. Kids were not plentiful around the port, especially not schoolboys with a full-of-themselves attitude such as this one. He watched him walk past the ship until he could see the name on the bow, then he came back to the gangway where Mahoney was sitting.

"Sir," he began, "I wonder if you'd tell me where I can find Mr. O'Brien? He's second engineer."

Mahoney's eyes sharpened a little. "O'Brien? What d' you want with him?" he said. "He's crazy as a loon."

"He is not! He's my dad!"

Mahoney almost smiled. He'd been on O'Brien's watch for three voyages, and the man made every minute a living hell. Nothing was ever clean enough, never good enough, with his crazy eyes and that Frankenstein face.

"Crazy, boy. A barking lunatic who can barely keep his job."

"You're the one that's crazy! My dad is a good officer and a good engineer. And he drove the Indianapolis 500 three times! That's more than you'll ever do!"

"Think you're smart, do you?" Mahoney stood. "Too damn smart." His hand shot out, and he caught the boy by the shoulder. "You need some of that kicked out of you. All you little punks get too damn wise." He jerked the kid toward him and, desperately, the boy struck out with one small fist, a fist that smacked hard against Mahoney's mouth.

"Why, you dirty little—" Mahoney swung, but the boy stepped back. Mahoney started after him, stopping only when he heard McGuire's voice calling down the accommodation ladder.

"Hey! Let him alone!"

Mahoney turned, his face ugly. "You keep your damn nose out of this, pretty boy!" Mahoney grabbed at Connie, but suddenly a hand caught his shoulder and jerked him around. McGuire's face was emotionless. Out of the corner of his eye, Mahoney could see that the longshoremen had stopped work and were watching. With a sudden burst of fury, he swung, hard.

McGuire had gripped his arm, and when Mahoney's punch started, he merely turned him away, the fist whistling through empty air. One of the longshoremen laughed, and with a mumbled curse, Mahoney jerked free and leaped in punching with both hands.

Denny stabbed a stiff left to the mouth that stopped the oiler in his tracks, and then crossed a short, snapping right to the chin that made Mahoney's head bob. Before the oiler could recover his balance, McGuire stabbed three more lefts into his face so fast his fist was only a blur. "Jesus, would you look at that left!" somebody exclaimed.

Mahoney landed a hard right on McGuire's shoulder and piled in with a whirl of driving punches. He was a veteran of scores of waterfront brawls, but here his every blow was wasted. Some of them fanned empty air; some of them were carefully muffled and blocked. Then a short, wicked uppercut jerked his head back. A solid left hook jarred his chin, and the dock seemed to fly up and strike him in the back.

He turned over, and started to get up, a trickle of blood running from his lip, his head buzzing. Suddenly a hand caught his arm and lifted him to his feet. It was McGuire. Mahoney kicked out, striving for Denny's groin. McGuire turned sideways and the kick missed, and almost at the same instant, a stiff left shot out and split Mahoney's eye, sending a shower of blood down his face. Moving after him, Denny ripped a series of hard, driving hooks to the head that kept the shorter man backing up. Then another right spilled him on the dock, his face skidding against the hard, slivered boards.

For an instant, McGuire hesitated, looking down at the fallen man. Then he walked back to the boy, who was staring at him, fascinated. "Who was it you wanted to see, young fellow?"

"My dad. He's second engineer on this ship. His name is O'Brien."

Denny looked at him quickly. "O'Brien?" He was a little incredulous. "Well, sure thing. We'll go look him up."

They walked toward the gangway. The boy looked up, his eyes wide. "You sure can fight!" he said. "Do you know my dad?"

"The second? Yeah, sure, I know him." He stopped as they reached the deck. "Did he expect you?"

"I thought I'd surprise him. He will never let me come down to the ship, so I thought I'd come and make it a surprise. He tells me all about it—how the engines work, and about all the sailors. Gee, I'll bet they all like him! He's swell!"

"Like him pretty well, do you?"

"I'll say! I hope I can be like him when I grow up!"

Denny hesitated, his hand on the boy's shoulder. He was thinking of Con O'Brien. Just supposing this kid heard someone say what they really thought of O'Brien. He didn't even know how the man would react to his bringing the boy down there. Why, nobody had even guessed the fellow was married, let alone had a boy like this one. Denny grinned, remembering the punch the kid had taken at Mahoney. "What's your name, son?"

"Connor. After my dad. Ever'body calls me Connie, or else Junior."

"I'll call you Connie—how's that?" He leaned against the rail. "We better wait. I think your dad is busy right now. I was down below a little while ago, and they were taking a generator apart, and when your dad is busy, he's really busy."

"Do you have many fights?" Connie asked.

"Me? Yeah, every once in a while. I don't know why. Maybe it's because I look so peaceful."

"You sure licked that fellow."

"Shucks, Connie," Denny said, grinning. "It was that right hook of yours did the job! You set him right in my alley! All those guys might be thinking I did it, but it was you!"

Connie grinned. "Don't kid me, mister." He looked up at Denny. "What's your name?"

"I'm Denny McGuire, first, last, and always. I've been called other things, but not to my face." He turned to Connie, who was sitting on the rail. "Say, what did you hit Mahoney for?"

"He said my dad was crazy. Then he grabbed me and twisted my shoulder."

"He said your dad was crazy? Pay no attention to it—that guy's way off his course. You've got plenty of nerve to hit a man. That guy was supposed to be tough." He stood up. "Come on, Connie, let's look around."

They walked aft, slowly. Denny had taken the youngster from the bow to the stern, explaining all about the ship. Then they started for the engine room. "Now we'll go see your dad. But don't be surprised if he acts funny. He doesn't like to be disturbed. You know, lots of engineers get so wrapped up in their work they don't like to be bothered by anybody. And don't tell him about what happened out there. It might just cause more trouble."

Con O'Brien looked up as they reached the floor plates. He stopped, dead still, and his face turned white. But Denny walked toward him, and when Connie saw his father, he began to grin. "Hi, Pa! Gee, Mr. McGuire just showed me the whole ship. Everything but the engine room."

O'Brien's face was tense. "How'd you get here, Junior?"

"I delivered some packages for a man, and he gave me a dollar. So I thought I'd surprise you. Wasn't that all right?"

"Oh. Sure. Yes, of course, son."

Denny looked across the boy's head at O'Brien. "Yeah, I met him out on the dock. We've become regular pals." Denny leaned back against the engineer's desk. "But if it's okay with you, I'll wait around and walk him back up to Pacific Avenue."

It was twenty minutes before O'Brien came back with the boy. He looked cheerful but exhausted. "I never answered so many que—questions in my life!"

Denny smiled. "Oh, he had a few for me too!"

"That's right, Dad," the boy said. "He told me what a marlinspike was, an' a hickory fid, an' how they steer a ship, an' about the colored lights."

Denny and Connie climbed the ladder together, and it wasn't until they reached the dock that they stopped. Denny looked at something ahead of them and smiled.

It was Faustine. She had driven down to the end of the road in a neat gray convertible coupe, and was sitting behind the wheel watching him. She glanced from the boy to Denny and raised one eyebrow. "What's this? Something you've been holding out on me?"

Denny grinned. "No, not this one."

"I was wondering." She smiled at Connie. "At least he's darned good-looking."

"Thank the lady, Connie," Denny said. "She's quite a judge of attractive males. But," he added, "before you two pursue your acquaintance any further, I'd better introduce you. This, Miss Carmody, is Connor O'Brien, Esquire, and he is the eldest and only son of our extremely talented second engineer. This is his first visit to our ship, and he has just been seeing the sights with his father, and the amazingly intelligent and attractive Dennis McGuire, also Esquire. He now is being treated to the finest sight of all." He turned to Connie. "I leave it to you, pal. Isn't she a sight?"

"I think she's beautiful," Connie said.

"See?" Denny said. "Already the sea has begun to affect him! Just off the ship, and already he tries to flirt with the ladies!" He shrugged. "Anyway, Connie Esquire, this is Miss Faustine Carmody of Hollywood, and points east. She is one of the most lovely, talented, and stubborn girls in show business."

Denny pointed. "Listen, you—walk over to that box and sit down and watch the boats go by. I've got to talk with the lady."

Once Connie had gone, she looked up and asked, "When do you leave?"

"Four days."

"And when are you coming back?"

"In about three months, give or take." McGuire made a point of polishing his fingernails on his shirtfront. "Of course, the captain hasn't discussed the question with me yet."

"Will he?"

Denny shook his head. "Darling, you're naïve. The captain of a ship talks to no one but himself and God."

"But Denny, why do you go?" she protested. "There is so much for you here!"

"I often wonder myself," he said. "I like to drift. The sea, strange ports and places, odd people, narrow winding streets, temples, dancing girls, elephants, camel bells, sampans with eyes, the rose of a sunset breaking through a mist like fire through smoke. Maybe it's the Irish in me, or maybe the poet. My mother rode a merry-go-round just before I was born—ever since I've liked to travel."

"You're teasing me, though I used to think like that, too. But I want you to stay, Denny. I do, really!"

"It's tempting." He shrugged. "But I'm like a shark—if I stop I fear I'll drown. Also, I've got this job, and they are still damn hard to find."

"Why, Denny, you were successful in the ring! And you know what Nathan said—you could be in pictures."

"Honey, I'm tired of getting hit, and I could never stand all that waiting around and hoping for a job. I like to play pretend as much as the next boy . . . but this"—he gestured toward the ship—"is real."

"I've got to go, Denny. I don't want to, but I told Spence I'd meet him to sign that contract at four."

"*The* contract, isn't it?" he said. "Two grand a week. It's a lot of money!"

"No more than you could have, someday."

"Maybe." He smiled. "Still planning on Friday night?"

"Of course. The same place?"

"Sure. Say, before you go, how about giving the kid a lift? He's got to get back downtown. I'll trust you with him."

"Sure, I'll take him."

"Hey, Connie!" The boy hurried up. "Your girlfriend is driving you home. When you get there you can tell the neighbors you rode with a real flesh-and-blood movie actress, and a good one. Lots of luck, youngster!"

He stood watching as the car drove away, and then turned to go back to the dock. Mahoney was just coming down the gangway, dressed in his shore-going clothes. Denny grinned wryly at him. "Sorry, friend."

Mahoney did not reply. One eye was completely closed, there was a cut under the other, and his lips were puffed and swollen.

Out on Bay Street, Mahoney stopped to light a cigarette. He put it between his swollen lips. "The son-of-a-bitch," he said. He snapped the match into the dirt, and walked on.

Three men were in the shack when he entered. It was no more than 150 feet off the main drag. One turned up a shallow gully, passed a lone tree, and then walked between several tar paper and plywood cabins clinging to the hillside. The three men had finished eating, and there was a bottle among the dirty dishes.

They looked up when Mahoney walked in. "What the hell?" one of them exclaimed. "What happened t' you?"

"Shut up."

"Ain't he the nice one?" the man said. "Can't a guy ask a question even?"

"Forget it, Dynamite," Fitzpatrick said, sitting up and pouring a drink. "Here, Mahoney. Try this."

The oiler tossed off the rotgut liquor, and then dropped into a chair.

"Who was it?" the big man said.

"McGuire. That Denny McGuire."

Dynamite whistled and looked nervously at Fitzpatrick. It was no mystery that the big shipfitter had come out on the bad end of an altercation with McGuire in the Beacon Street Pool Room. Fitz had lost more than one shift at the yards because the beating had left him unable to work.

"Surprised you're showin' your mug around here, Mahoney." Fitz relaxed back into the chair. "You still owe me money . . . an' I know you took down that Dutchman off the *Johnson City*. I never got my piece o' that."

Mahoney's little eyes darted back and forth. "Okay, I got some— some of what I owe ya. An' maybe I heard somethin' that'll get you more payback. Payback on that S.O.B. McGuire!"

"Ought t' be plenty of chances wi' you shippin' out," Dynamite said. "He could always fall overboard some dark an' stormy night."

"Sure he could, but you're a fool. That gets us nothin', nothin' to put in our wallets!"

"What's this?" Fitzpatrick sat forward again.

Mahoney stood, dug into his pocket, and pulled out a roll of Pete Brouwer's bills. It was less than half the actual take, but who would ever know? Mahoney poured himself another drink and peeled off a portion of the wad.

"This guy McGuire," he said. "He's done some work in the movies. Some doll come to see him t'day. This afternoon. Dames like that don't pay no attention to a guy unless he's got dough. We're shipping out, and like as not he'll have all that movie cash on him for one last blow-out."

"When does he come ashore?" Fritz asked.

"I heard him say he was meetin' the doll Friday night."

"He'll catch the PE, huh?"

"I don't think so. I think she picks him up."

"How about her? She look like money?"

"She has more than him, I figger. An' t' top it off, she's got a sweet little convertible!"

McFee rubbed his jaw, and turned to Fitz. "Can we handle a car?"

Fitzpatrick's eyes gleamed, but he said nothing.

McFee grinned, looking from Mahoney to Fitz. "Why not?"

"Naw, forget it. It's too hot," Fitz said.

"Hell, Fitz . . ."

"Shut up, Tom. Forget it, I say!" He got up slowly. "That McGuire is too tough. An' a dame with money. Think of the police. It ain't like some waterfront skirt. Forget it."

Ten minutes later Mahoney was walking back to Beacon Street. It was all he could do to suppress a grin. Fitzpatrick came off all high and mighty, thinking he was some waterfront crime boss. Well, he wasn't up to matching wits with Mahoney, not at all.

He had pointed Fitzpatrick at McGuire like a pistol, and regardless of what he had said to McFee, Fitz had taken the bait . . . Mahoney knew it because Fitz had let him leave without demanding the rest of the money he owed him.

THE PRIVATE LOG OF
JOHN HARLAN, SECOND MATE

March 30th: The time is thirty minutes past four o'clock, and it is but a few minutes since I came off watch. The afternoon sun is hot, the air drowsy with springtime at sea. We have no green trees, growing grass, no wildflowers or blossoming fruit trees. Here spring is only in the air and in the hearts of the seamen. It is an intangible something that has descended upon us almost without warning. The men move lazily about the ship, and on the bridge, Borly Shannon, the chief officer, is standing on the starb'rd wing of the bridge, watching them, infected by the same feeling.

In my cabin the sunlight falls through the ports to trace a narrow path along the deck. As I watch, the light slowly withdraws itself with the roll of the ship to starb'rd, and then returns smoothly as the ship rolls back to port. The movement is very slight, the ship riding easily across warmer and warmer seas. The fan that is hinged to fit into my porthole turns lazily, moving its artificial breeze through my cabin and into the corridor.

Life at sea is usually monotonous. There are moments of adventure, it is true. There are times during storms when one works rapidly and desperately against the overwhelming power of the sea.

One night when only an able seaman, I was on the boat deck lashing down a spare ventilator when a towering wall of green water broke over two of us. I succeeded in getting hold of the galley skylight. It was a precarious hold, yet when the ship rose again, I was still there. I climbed to my feet, drenched to the skin, and found the man working with me gone! I started for the bridge to report him overside, but then saw him coming forward from the poop deck. He had been washed overboard amidships, and back aboard the ship at the stern with inches to spare. He had grabbed onto the rail, then climbed up and come forward. We went back to the boat deck and finished our job. There was nothing to report.

The expected difficulty between the crew aft has so far failed to materialize. I wonder if it will lead to bad feeling between the deck crew and the black gang. That seems unlikely, yet I tried to talk to Mr. Donato, our third engineer, however he made an excuse and walked hurriedly away. Still, I can't say that he has ever been very friendly. At least, not on this trip.

He came aboard the *Lichenfield* recently but was gone a good deal while we were in dry dock. There has been a death in the family, or so I have heard. He has not seemed his normal self, somehow. He is a slight man, Italian, and of the type some women would probably call romantic. Very dapper, neat, and good-looking in his way; his cabin is decorated with the pictures of attractive women, most of them blondes. Once, passing the door, I caught a glimpse of them.

Early next week we should sight the coast of Luzon, or one of the islands off the coast. And then—Manila. The end of the life I have lived thus far. I shall begin again, and this time I hope to do better. I doubt if I shall remain in Manila long. If something isn't immediately forthcoming I'll use some of my small supply of cash to send cables to shipping companies in Singapore, Batavia, and some of the larger ports.

Right in the middle of the above entry I was called away, and then spent the time before dinner wandering about the ship. Everything is quiet aft. I dropped in back there for a few minutes, and found

McGuire had packed his mattress to the top of the after house and was reading Plutarch. It always amuses me to find a seaman reading such books. Not that it is all that rare, but because so many would find it so. So many misfits somehow or other find the life at sea pleasing to them. Often they just can't buck the tougher competition, and prefer the shipboard life, where duties are well known and the lines of authority clear. The danger means very little. These men are more afraid of economic insecurity, afraid of being broke and jobless. Yet many are men who have ability, education, and talent.

In Manila, the *Lichenfield* will become a changed ship, for Worden and I shall leave, and perhaps even another man or two, one never knows. I have seen the entire atmosphere of a ship alter with the leave-taking of one man.

How soon it will be over! Helen, Steve, and Betty, Los Angeles, the drives to the mountains—all will be over. When I take my duffel ashore in Manila, that will be the end. What could I have done, back there along my yesterdays, that would have made it all different? Where in that track across the calendar of years did I make the first misstep? In what word, what move, what thing unsaid did the change come?

One is so helpless, for one can never know just when saying or doing something, usually a very simple, almost forgotten thing, may alter an entire future. Where, in the map of one's life, is the spot that one may say, "Here! This was it." There must be a turning point, but how is one to know?

It is like the history of a nation, for at some point the tide turns, and a people ceases to grow and begins to slip backward. What would happen, I wonder, if at that moment some man was strong enough to stay events, and by the grip of his hand, and the leadership of his spirit, turn the tide back to the best channel? But perhaps when a nation reaches such a place it no longer builds or breeds the men to perform such a feat.

Too often the truth that men fight for becomes debased in the mouths of later generations, used as an instrument to destroy all that their fathers sought. In my own country, Washington, Jefferson, Adams, that little group of brave souls, radical thinkers in their time, struggled for liberty of thought and speech. Now other men, in the name of progress or Americanism, would bring an end to just those things.

Enough for now. My time below is ended, and I must go up to the bridge and hold in my hands, for another four hours, the fate of this ship.

And so, until tomorrow . . .

AUGUSTO DONATO

Third Engineer

Augie Donato picked up a magazine and stretched himself full length on the settee. It had been a hard shift. All the shifts were hard when a guy like Con O'Brien followed a fellow. He was too damned particular. Not that he ever said anything, for he never did, or very rarely. He just mentioned it in those neat little notes he left behind. Mentioned having done the work, and just left it that way. But you always knew what he was thinking. The worst of it was, the chief and the first assistant were just as bothered by O'Brien as he was.

A life at sea was no life for a man, anyway. Why the hell couldn't he find a coastwise run, or something in port? Any man who was such a damned fool as to spend half his time at sea should be shot. *Half* his time? Forty days at sea for about seven or eight in port. And that's if he was lucky. Tankers could turn cargo around faster than a freighter, much faster.

And now he was in a spot. If a guy ever had bad luck, he did. How the hell was he to know the dame was Harlan's wife? A nice sort, too, blond and sweet. He had casually danced with her five or six times at the Cinderella Ballroom and The Majestic. Their meetings were accidental, two people who happened to be in the same place at the same time. Then he had suggested dinner. She seemed to enjoy going places, so he had started taking her around. She said nothing about being married. Then one night she sprung it on him. He'd known her over a year then, off and on.

Just before the ship returned and went into dry dock, his brother had died. Too bad, but it had left him a nice piece of money to spend. That was one thing he could say for Al: He left behind some dough. They never had gotten along, but they didn't have any other family, so the money naturally came to Augie. Hell, wouldn't Al be sore? But Al was always a fast driver. When anybody tried to slow him down he'd just laugh. Nothing ever happened to him!

Well, Al had gone over that hill doing at least seventy, and a truck loaded with pipe had been parked right there. What they buried was only part of Al. Hell, if they'd buried all of him they'd have had to bury his car, the rear end of the truck, and about fourteen lengths of pipe.

It was about then he gave Helen a necklace, and they went for a ride. They were on the way back when she told him to go easy calling for a while, that her husband was going to be home every day.

"Your what?" Augie was astonished.

"My husband."

"You got a husband? My God, why didn't you say something?"

"How did you suppose I got those kids?"

"I know how you got one of them."

"The less you say about that the better. Anyway, John's going to be around for a few weeks, days and nights, so you'd better not call or come around."

"Where's he been all this time? A hell of a husband! What's he do?"

"At sea. He's the second officer on a tanker. The *Lichenfield*."

Augie Donato suddenly felt sick. "Who? On the what?" His eyes widened. "Listen, sister, you sure pick 'em. That's my ship! I signed on last January."

"Your ship? You told me you were in the theater business!"

"I wish to God I was!" Augie looked disgusted. "What a break that is! So you're John Harlan's wife, are you? It's sure lucky I didn't do any popping off about you! Those cold, quiet guys, they're bad medicine."

"John's not cold. He wouldn't hurt you."

"Yeah, I know. I got over a fence about two jumps ahead of a charge of buckshot from one of those 'warmhearted' guys!"

That was the way it was. It wouldn't be so bad if a guy could figure what Harlan was thinking, but the fellow looked at you like he could see right through you. Had Helen said anything? It wasn't likely, but still, sometimes when a woman got sore they talked too darned much. If he only could figure just how much Harlan knew. There he was sitting across the table from the guy twice a day, even talking with him sometimes. Harlan was always pleasant, yet cool too.

Deep, that's what he was. You couldn't tell about guys like that. The worst of it was he might just be waiting. The sea was a poor place to have enemies. Like a mine. Too damned many things can happen.

It was getting so every time he stepped out on deck after dark he looked over his shoulder. Augie shook his head. That's what you got for fooling around with a married woman. But how was a guy to know? Half of them didn't wear rings, and there were widows of both the grass and sod variety around every corner. He'd supposed Helen was a widow, but hadn't asked any questions. It was getting so a guy should hand every girl he met a questionnaire before he dated her.

Maybe he was dumb. Probably he'd be a damned sight better off to take Wesley's advice and marry some nice girl. He might be wrong about Harlan. He seemed like a good guy, and sometimes he felt he could even like him. But you never knew what the guy was thinking. That poker face. Always something behind a face like that.

He hurled his magazine across the cabin. It was getting so he couldn't even sleep. And he couldn't walk out a door without being afraid Harlan would jump him. This ship was haywire anyway. To hell with it. After this trip he'd find something else. Damn tankers. Every time he lit a match he held his breath.

Augie paced back and forth across the deck, accommodating his stride to the slight roll of the ship. Now there was more trouble. The chief had called him in only a few minutes ago.

"Mr. Donato," he'd said in that precise, schoolteacher's voice of his, "what's this I hear about trouble among the men?"

"I don't know, sir," he'd answered. How the hell could he know about the men? He had his own problems. "I didn't know there was trouble."

"Well, there is. Something between Mahoney, Jacobs, and some of the sailors. That McGuire is in it. You make it your business to find out. The captain has been asking me, and something must be done. We can't have any trouble on this ship. It endangers us all!"

"Yes, sir," he said. "I'll see what I can do."

"Well, get busy, then!" The chief turned around and began filling his pipe just like he was already gone. To hell with it. He couldn't picture *any* officer trying to get any information out of that bunch. Why didn't they get Harlan to find out? He seemed to know everything that was going on.

Mr. Augie Donato put on his cap and stared into the mirror. Hell, he'd always thought he was a hell of a good-looking guy! But he looked just like any other wop, only with a touch of dyspepsia. He closed his door and took the passage aft.

The sea was smooth and the air was soft. The birds would be singing in the park today, and the cars on West Pico would spin past with that certain whine they only had in the spring. He could be home. There were other things he could do, he didn't have to go to sea.

Third assistant engineer Augie Donato slanted his cap on the side of his head and thrust both hands deep in his coat pockets. To hell with it. Even the food all tasted the same out here. It didn't make any difference what you ate, he could be blindfolded and know sea-cooked food at the first taste. What would his mother have said about that awful cold-storage chicken. The steward must have carried those birds in the icebox ever since it was installed. Every time he looked in there, it made him think of the morgue. Stewards on these ships were all a bunch of belly-robbing bastards anyway, pocketing whatever they could save.

He tramped along the catwalk and glared out at the water with angry eyes. Who the hell ever started this going to sea business, anyway? He used to like the sound of foreign names. And now the next port was Manila. Too hot, too brown, too much spoiled fruit, and everybody talking politics. Now they were worried about the Japs. My

God! Let the Japs have the place. You couldn't wish them any worse luck. Shannon had been saying something the other day about the islands, how green and beautiful they were. Let him have them!

Mr. Augie Donato reached the after house and took a deep breath. He felt mean enough to give somebody hell. He should have been a barber. Al had been a barber.

Sam Harrell was leaning on the rail staring across the water. "Sam!" he said sharply. "What's this I hear about some trouble between the men?"

"What men?" Sam looked innocent. "I don't know anything about any trouble, Mr. Donato."

"I mean Mahoney, Jacobs, and some of the sailors! The chief sent me back here to find out."

"Sorry. I don't know anything."

"Well, I can believe that!" Mr. Augie Donato snapped. He walked on. A hell of a ship!

He came around the after deck–house and stopped. Mahoney, Pete Brouwer, and Conrad were standing there, but he scarcely noticed them, for within six feet of him, his back turned, was Slug Jacobs. The big fireman was stripped to the waist, and the great muscles bulged in knots and bands across his shoulders. Denny McGuire was facing him. Then everything seemed to happen at once.

Later, called to the carpet and asked why he didn't stop it, Augie lost his temper. "Stop it? Stop what? One minute McGuire is standing there and the next thing Jacobs is blood from head to foot! Stop it how? I weigh one hundred and thirty pounds soaking wet, and together those guys weigh about five hundred!"

"You ought to know better, Slug," McGuire was saying. "Let Mahoney fight his own battles. Socking Shorty from behind was a dirty yellow stunt."

"Yeah?" Slug said. He was standing there, his big hands hanging loosely at his sides.

"Either you lay off—and I mean no trouble with anybody, okay?—or you take a beating."

"Boys, t'ink! You must not do this. Ve no fight on ship, do not make t'is mistake!" Pete glared at first one, then the other of them.

"Pete? Shut up! Just shut yer preachin' piehole," Mahoney barked.

Slug looked around sneering. "Who gonna give me the lickin', huh?"

"I will." McGuire stepped forward.

"You? You sonabitch. You—"

McGuire's left snapped against Slug's chin like the crack of a whip, but Slug took it, and swung one fist then the other. McGuire slid inside, and you could hear the thud as he struck the big man's body, then Denny stepped back and whipped up a driving right uppercut that jerked Slug's head back. Slug tried to clinch, but McGuire evaded him and snapped another left to the face.

Slug lunged, then pivoted and swung his heavy boot for McGuire's groin. Denny turned sideways and grinned. Then he shuffled backward, watching carefully. "Just stop," he said. "Quit while you're ahead!"

Jacobs, his face a smear of blood, crouched, trying to back McGuire into a corner. Denny shook his head, and deliberately backed into one. Then, as Slug charged, Denny kicked him in the solar plexus with his heel. The big fireman fell back against the rail, and before he could recover his balance, Denny stepped in and threw one, then the other fist to the chin. But Jacobs straightened, and legs spread, started swinging again. Denny stopped abruptly, and toe to toe, science thrown to the winds, they began to slug.

The ship rolled slightly on the light swell. Pete turned away from the sight, ashamed that trouble between his shipmates had come to this, ashamed he hadn't stopped it earlier, and afraid . . . afraid, because from all his years at sea he knew, knew in his heart, that fighting aboard ship was the worst luck. It was bad in itself, and it welcomed ill fate like whistling on deck or the sailor who'd shot the albatross.

McGuire swung until it seemed no human could stand such punishment and still keep fighting, but suddenly, Slug Jacobs started forward. Right into the fury of Denny's fists, he started, trying to clinch, to use his strength, his weight. Then Slug lunged, and Denny caught his wrist.

Turning swiftly, he jerked the big man over his back in a flying mare. Jacobs crashed to the steel deck. He lay there, his huge shoulders and torso a welter of blood, his breath coming in great gasps.

Then he gathered himself slowly and stood, numbed to everything but terrified to stop.

"Had enough?" Denny said. "You better quit."

Slug hesitated, swaying.

"The spanner, you damn fool!" Mahoney yelled. And almost as if Slug were acting with the thought, he desperately jerked the forgotten spanner from his pocket and threw it.

Denny's head jerked aside, and the spanner rang against the bulkhead. Then Denny stepped in, feinted swiftly, and crossed a right to the chin that struck with a thud. Slug staggered, and then fell on his face, out cold.

Battered but still menacing, McGuire turned toward Mahoney, and the shorter man took a step backward.

"This has been your doing. All of it."

For a moment Mahoney seemed to rally, to regain his defiance. Then his heel caught on a steam pipe serving the after winch, and he went down. The impact jolted something from his pocket. A watch. A large silver watch that hit the deck on its edge and fairly disintegrated, the front and back covers popping open and the guts, gears, and jewels scattering across the deck.

Mahoney looked up at the men surrounding him, dazed and foolish.

"Pete . . . ?" Shorty said. "Isn't that . . ."

". . . my vatch." Pete peered at the mechanical mess on the deck. "My fat'er's vatch!" He shook his head in puzzlement . . . and then with a speed and power that was breathtaking, even after the brawl they had all just witnessed, Pete grabbed Mahoney by the front of his overalls and, lifting, slammed him into the wall of the deckhouse!

"You robt me! It vas YOU!" Pete Brouwer stepped back and fired blow after blow into Mahoney's midsection as his shipmates looked on in shock. Pete, the man they respected beyond all others, the voice of calm and reason, was out of his mind with rage and grief. All the years of never going home: the years when he couldn't, the years when he simply *hadn't*, the loss, the futility, all became the energy behind those pile-driving fists.

"My fat'er! My brot'ers! I fall overboard, t'e vatch it still vork! Three. Times. Around t'e cape. *Still* it vork! My home! My home . . ."

The two men collapsed, Mahoney broken and unconscious, Pete gasping, weeping . . . as Shorty, his shipmate of many years, lifted him to his feet.

Mr. Augie Donato came to life suddenly. "Here now! What the devil do you think this is, anyway? A slaughterhouse?" He glared at Shorty Conrad and Sam, who were suddenly facing him. "There'll be no fighting aboard this ship!"

"Fighting?" Sam's eyes widened. "Why, Mr. Donato! Has there been a fight?"

For an instant, Mr. Augie Donato's mouth hung open, then, "Oh, get out of the way!" He started forward, his jaw set. By the Lord Harry they'd find out a thing or two! What the hell kind of ship was this anyway? Was everybody nuts?

Denny McGuire watched him go and turned back to Slug. The big fireman was stretched out on the deck, facedown. He didn't seem to have moved. Carefully, handling him as if he were a child, Denny picked the big man up under the arms and dragged him into the washroom. Tex emerged from the seaman's fo'c'sle rubbing his eyes. "What now? What's all the fuss?"

Denny put the big fireman on the floor. Carefully, dipping a towel in cold water, he began to bathe Slug's face.

"Well, I wish I'd seen the fight," Tex said. "But he's likely not to thank you, no matter what you do."

Slug opened his eyes, and seeing McGuire, started to get up. "Take it easy," Denny said. "Mahoney got you into this, now don't make a sap of yourself."

Mr. Augie Donato rapped on the chief's door. It opened abruptly. "Well, what do you want, mister?"

"About that trouble. There was a fight between McGuire, an AB on the eight-to-twelve watch, and Jacobs, the twelve-to-four fireman. Pete Brouwer, another AB, and that damn oiler Mahoney also got into it."

"A fight?" The chief barged out into the alleyway. "When?"

"Just now." Mr. Augie Donato was trying to keep cool. "It's over."

"Why didn't you stop it?" the chief shouted.

"Why didn't I stop it?" Mr. Augie Donato's face turned purple. "Why don't you go lay an egg? I shipped on here as an engineer, not a cop! You may be chief engineer on this packet, an' I may need my rating damned bad, but by the Lord Harry I'm not paid to go stopping any fights on this ship or any other ship. I think the whole bunch of you are crazy anyway!" He wheeled and walked away, his heels clicking on the steel deck, his shoulders stiff with anger.

The chief stared after him in startled amazement, and then went back in his room and closed the door. "The cocky little devil!" he exclaimed. "I didn't think the little squirt had it in him!"

THE PRIVATE LOG OF
JOHN HARLAN, SECOND MATE

March 31st: The sea rolls on. It boils up along rock-strewn coasts and rumbles and growls among the worn boulders. The silent sea, unlimited, unfathomable, unknown. There are barren wastes as large as the continent of Australia that have never known a ship. There are stories of the sea that no man can truly understand, of strange creatures and ghost ships that roam wintry, windswept coasts and vanish into the night and the storm.

Tonight, sitting alone in the soft glow of my reading lamp, I have been thinking of that strange ship Borly Shannon was telling me of, and of the man sitting alone in the stern, holding his empty gun, an actor having played his last and finest scene before an empty sky and barren sea.

And only tonight it has come to me. Only tonight have I realized that here in my hands I hold the threads of many lives, but of three in particular. Today I had a long talk with Pete Brouwer and some of the others about a subject I am officially supposed to know nothing about, the brawl on the afterdeck. To say the man is ashamed over his behavior is to understate the situation entirely. He feels like a Jonah and that he has let down the whole crew.

While he was talking, however, he mentioned to me that Shorty Conrad's real name was Carmody, and with that in my mind I returned here and fell asleep. When I awakened I realized I had my story. The story that I will tell as a work of fiction.

The Raoul Carmody of which Shannon told, the dying man in the stern of that wave and wind-battered schooner, was almost certainly Shorty's father. More than that, Shorty is likely the brother of Faustine, Denny's girlfriend in Hollywood. How easily it all fits when one gathers the threads together and weaves them into a little pattern of life.

Soon Shorty will be coming on watch, and I shall tell him. And I shall tell Denny when he comes to call me tonight. I feel strange now, as though some mysterious power had opened those lives to me. Knowing something of Shorty's story, I can understand better than ever the motives in the heart of Raoul Carmody when he made his grand gesture, and took his chance at winning financial security once and for all, for his family and for himself. He didn't abandon his wife and children, not in the end.

When I am settled on a new ship, this is the first story that I will attempt to write and to publish. It is something that I can do in the free hours of my day, a way of reaching out to the world, of telling whoever will read it about the connection between these lives, these men I have known who are connected, by blood or friendship or enmity . . . or simply by the ships and the cargoes they carry, to us all.

Outside the sea whispers against the hull, whispers of lives like my own, so far unknown, unchronicled. I sit here and run them over in my mind, these men I have met: Pete Brouwer, Tex Worden, Shorty Conrad, Fritz Schumann, Jacobs, Mahoney, Harrell, and all the rest, each going on, remote from his neighbor. Lonely yet still so near.

Come what may, I shall be glad that I have gone to sea, glad that I have known and worked with men, glad that I have touched their lives, and they have touched mine. I have heard their profanity when it was like a prayer, and their drunken rambling when it was like poetry. I've seen them at their best and their worst and, in the end, I'd not like to have missed either. How can, in a world such as this, any man condemn another? Who can say what circumstances of birth or breeding, of work or strife brought him to what he is? Understanding and tolerance, I think, come first. For myself, I only want to understand; for others I shall have no stones to cast, for I myself am not without faults. The laws of nature were old before man in his arrogance began to legislate and regulate the world, but the laws of man are feeble and can mean nothing to the dark tides that flow through humanity. The laws of men can only punish and never prevent, and they can only punish the sins they create themselves.

At this moment, all over the planet ten thousand ships follow an invisible network of tiny lines upon tiny charts, each one moving out to bring home the wealth of the world in its hull. We carry food and explosives, medicine and soldiers, life and death, the materials of exultation and sadness. We connect the stories of everyone on the globe, and so we are the story of everyone, from the lowliest Burmese fisherman to the captains of industry in London or New York. Where do these lines of fate begin and end? The sea alone could make reply, but it does not answer.

McGuire has come and gone, signaling my turn on watch. "All set, Mr. Harlan?" he asked. "It's a grand night! A night for poetry, or for almost anything but being trapped on a tanker where there aren't any girls about."

I poured us each a drink, just a touch to put the taste in our mouths.

"Heard you got in a little trouble today. Sparks said he had to spend some time patching up Jacobs and Mahoney. I'm hoping that's the last we hear of it."

"Mr. Harlan, I apologize. But it had to be done. It was Mahoney's fault. Jacobs is a brute. He's not a problem if left alone, although he does things on impulse, and seems to have absolutely no sense of right and wrong. Maybe none of us do."

"Luckily, he's not my problem," I said. "You might check up on Pete, however. There's something about this whole affair that seems to have damaged his morale."

I added soda to the glasses, and we stood there by my little table looking at each other. "Well," he said, "let's just make it the crew, the ship, and tomorrow!"

We drank. Then he put his glass down. "And now for the lookout again. I feel lonely tonight. Maybe somebody is walking over my grave, or my girl is thinking of me."

I turned. "That reminds me, Denny. Do you know Shorty Conrad's real name?"

"Why, no. I don't." He looked up curiously. "What about it?"

"His real name is Conrad Carmody, and he tells me he has a sister somewhere. She was raised in England by a family in the theater."

He stood there staring at me. "Well, I'll be damned!" he said finally. "Shorty, and Faustine? Who would ever have thought it?"

"And that's not all. I know what happened to her father. Did you ever hear Borly Shannon tell that story about his experience off the Horn?"

"No."

"It'll keep for tomorrow. We'll all get together then. I'm sure Shorty would like to hear it, too."

"All right, tomorrow it is!"

He left me, and I walked to the port for a glance at the sea. Then I sat down here to complete this entry before I collect my sextant and some papers to go aloft.

I have realized that I have been feeling sorry for myself these days, and fatalistic too. I will continue on with my plans, but I have decided to send this and my other journals to my children. They must know me in my absence. I may find another ship, I may remain in the South Seas or Asia, but I will return whenever I have the opportunity. I cannot allow my hurt feelings or fatalism to keep us apart.

I poured another drink; it seemed fitting somehow, to make another toast.

I lifted my glass, and stood there in the darkness, my feet canted to the roll. "To my children," I said, "and my wife!"

DENNIS MCGUIRE

Able Seaman

He walked out on the deck, and turned forward, a soft wind stirring about his face. When he reached the bow he leaned on the rail, staring down into the water. To think of it: Shorty was Faustine's brother! One had enjoyed every advantage that money and shrewd dramatic training could give her, the other had drifted alone across the world; and now, through the merest chance, they were to be united again.

The day in the shipping commissioner's office returned to him vividly. Shorty had been looking on from the back of the room when he and Faustine had come in with Hazel Ryan. For about thirty minutes the long-lost brother and sister had sat within a dozen feet of each other!

Denny turned and looked toward the bridge, then back at the sea. It was pleasant here, in the last few minutes of his watch, to remember Faustine, to recall their last night together. Sometimes, however, it had all felt like a trap. He couldn't figure it out, couldn't come to any conclusions.

His whole life he had been a mover, part of a rootless family that followed the harvests. When people in a small town called you a "mover" they meant you weren't one of them . . . and you weren't ever going to be. And if that's how they were going to treat you, well, Denny McGuire would make it a word to live by. He didn't just drift from town to town but from continent to continent, going places and seeing things the little people from those little towns could never imagine.

And he moved from woman to woman. He had told himself that in a way he was doing them a favor by forever moving on. They would have a romantic memory that would never sour because they had seen him one too many times, bleary and unshaven in the morning. In their minds he would remain young and perfect in a way that future husbands could not. He told himself it was almost like a gift.

But it was all beginning to sound like the tired rumblings of his own ego. A boy never needed to care if he'd amount to anything—a man, a *real* man, had to be different. He thought of himself as a boxer, and he had been very good, but his brief career was barely enough to justify the term. He'd had no good reason for leaving Los Angeles—he had some money, he had a girl. He didn't want to be an actor, but the two movies he had worked on after the talent scout discovered him at the Main Street Gym had introduced him to the business of the stuntman. It was a careful balance of intellect and risk. There just might be a career in that . . . a career that wouldn't make him feel like he was sponging off of Faustine; the working-class boyfriend she would soon be tired of.

He had his memories. The first sight of that old dhow on the beach near Aden, the camels in the desert coming up to Taudeni, the volcanic loneliness of the Tibesti. There had been the excitement of seeing the lights along the Bund in Shanghai for the first time, and the sound of far-off thunder in the misty mountains of Java. He would also remember the soul-crushing effort of walking through the night along the UP tracks, walking farther than he thought humanly possible and of boxing twenty-six rounds in the sweltering heat of a Borneo oil camp for just enough money to eat for two more days.

He would carry the fear with him too. The unrelenting heat and flies of those three days behind the sandbag parapet before the attack finally broke and a few of them, Spanish soldiers and foolish sailors,

limped their bloody way back to the Mediterranean coast and freedom. His future wouldn't be the life, the adventuring life he had lived,
but it wouldn't include the ugly compromises, the moments that returned to you in the middle of a sleepless night. It wouldn't include
bleeding to death in some filthy, freezing alley surrounded by people
whose language you couldn't understand.

And it wouldn't include the women . . . but how many had really
cared for him at all? How many wouldn't have turned their backs if it
was Dennis McGuire who needed something.

Why had he left Los Angeles? Habit? A pattern so old he couldn't
break it? He was a mover. The shark who, if he stopped swimming,
would drown. He'd had a sense of something wrong, an impending
loss of . . . freedom? He didn't know.

Denny walked across to the starb'rd rail and let his eyes search the
sea. His mind wandered content with its own thoughts, while his eyes
remained alert. After a while one became attuned to anything wrong
about the picture, and noticed the slightest glimmer in the darkness.
But there were no ships in sight, and the sea was deep here, very, very
deep.

Faustine, that last night, had been different . . . or maybe it was he
who was different. Something had changed between them. And that
something was going to require a change in him. Was that it? Well, a
reminder of one's mortality could change any number of things.

It had been dark when he came down the gangway clad in his shore-
going clothes. Dark and still. There was a light at the bottom of the
ramp, and the man on watch loafing contentedly. When he stopped on
the dock he could see a faint glow from a fo'c'stle port, and could hear
the low gulp and gurgle around the piles under the wharf. He had
turned away, walking slowly up to the gate, where he let himself out.

The tank farm crowded down close to the waterfront, throwing
long shadows across the narrow street. Farther up were some warehouses, and a material yard. Denny had taken no more than a half
dozen steps when something moved in the shadows ahead. His eyes
held on the spot as he walked toward it. There was only one reason

why a man would be waiting there. Would he have a gun? Denny decided it was unlikely, and walked on. Probably a strong-arm job. Not a bad spot for it either. Still, he didn't have much time. His eyes, accustomed to the dim light of the street, glimpsed something in the road. Two more steps and he dropped his handkerchief. When he picked it up he also held a good-sized rock. Easing it into the center of the silk square, he gathered the ends together. He was going to have to make this good.

There was no further movement as he stepped abreast of the spot. Nothing happened. Denny walked on, frowning. This wasn't right. It had been a well-chosen place for a mugging—the guy should have tried whatever he had in mind when Denny passed him. Denny checked his watch, and took the opportunity to glance backward. A man was following him.

He walked faster and had made two blocks when he looked again. The man was a big fellow, heavyset, and now considerably closer. Denny turned the corner by the old power station just as Faustine's car pulled to a stop. He walked rapidly up to the car, hearing the gravel crunch behind him. Then he put his left hand on the door and turned sideways, swinging the rock backhand as he turned. The movement caught the man entirely by surprise and the rock thudded against his jawbone with terrific force.

The man staggered, blood streaming down the side of his face. The rock had slipped from the handkerchief, so Denny followed his momentary advantage by hooking both hands, one and then the other, to the man's chin. He went down in a heap. Denny caught him by the collar and jerked him to his knees. It was Fitzpatrick, the bully from the pool hall. The man who'd picked a fight with him weeks ago.

"Denny! What's going on?" Faustine had turned half around in her seat.

"Put the car in gear, honey. We're going to need to get out of here."

McGuire looked around. All he could see was empty streets and mist. He could hear the horn from the navigation light at Angel's Gate, the rumble of the car, and nothing more. The man was still conscious, but the side of his face carried a fearful cut from the rock, and there was a swelling over one eye where Denny's fist had landed.

Denny slugged him again, and then dropped him, stooping to pick up the weapon the man had carried. Denny got into the car. "Let's go," he said.

He sized up the weapon. It was six inches of inch-and-one-half gas-pipe plugged in both ends, and filled with sand. The plug in one end was long and had been whittled to form a handle. Altogether it was enough to fell an ox if properly used.

"What happened?" She was looking at him wide-eyed. "Who was that?"

"One of our choicest of waterfront bullies. He must have known about you, because I saw him down there in the dark and he passed up a good chance at me. Maybe he planned on killing two birds with one stone. I beg your pardon—I mean gas-pipe."

"You don't seem very excited."

Denny laughed. "How could I be excited about a man merely trying to kill me when you're here? I'm only excited by you." He had always been able to turn a rush of adrenaline into banter. He tossed Fitzpatrick's makeshift weapon out of the car.

She glanced at him out of the corner of her eye as she took the road to Los Angeles. "So now what?"

"Let's just make it food at some quiet spot." He didn't want to go and meet up with her crowd, not any longer. ". . . The quieter, the better."

"I have food at the bungalow."

"Well then, it'll be just like home."

"Am I to take that as a proposal?"

"Me? An AB at seventy-two fifty a month proposing to a lady now netting two grand?"

She shook her head. "You must remember I knew you when you were making several times what I was, and I know you could again, if you'd just stop reading travel magazines and looking at maps."

He laughed, amused by the conversation but concerned at the direction it was taking. She was right—they had known each other before, in New York when he was boxing and she was a starving actress. But he had gone off adventuring again, left that career as he had left the possibility of several others. Now he was older, likely too old for a comeback, and there were still places he hadn't seen, things he hadn't done. He might be getting too old for some of that too: too old for begging for money on the streets of Cairo, or for dysentery or malaria . . . too old for a bullet in the brain; let's not forget there had been *that* possibility.

The fog wrapped tightly around them, letting go only as they skirted the lights of Hollywood and began to wind their way into the hills.

Faustine turned the car in to her driveway, ratcheting the emergency brake. He took the key, went up the stairs, and opened the door. He snapped on the light and stepped back for her to go in ahead of him. "All right," he said. "Let's see whether all that dough has spoiled you for making coffee."

While she was lighting the gas and getting the percolator out, he leaned back in a chair and began riffling the pages of a movie magazine. "Seems like old times, doesn't it?" he said. "Remember when you and the Burple sisters or whatever their name was had that two-by-four flat in the Bronx?"

"And you went to Jersey City and fought that heavyweight? You hadn't trained a day."

He laughed. "I paid for that!"

"We used nearly all the money we had getting you back to the Bronx in a taxi."

"Was that how I got back? I'd often wondered." He grinned. "But I won. The record books say so!"

"You got up so many times the referee must have counted to five thousand without ever getting to ten. They may have let you win out of sheer boredom."

"I can see you have a great admiration for my fighting ability."

She came over and sat down on his lap, rumpling his hair with her free hand.

"Listen," he said, after a few minutes, "I think I'll wash it out after this trip."

"You mean quit chasing around?" She sat up, looking at him. "Oh, Denny, I wish you would!"

"Leaving this time isn't going to be so hot, not after meeting up with you again." He meant that part, he was certain of it.

Her body was warm, unresisting. Their lips met, and he held her close. Faustine tilted her head back a little. "Honey, that coffee's going to perk itself completely away."

"Skip it. Listen, if you'll move your body I'll fix that gas, and then—"

"Then what?"

"Well, there isn't a reason in the world why I should be back on that ship before eight o'clock. That leaves us a lot of time."

He turned the fire out, and started back. Faustine had slipped off her shoes and was sitting on the edge of the bed. He snapped out the light, then came in and sat down. They kissed, and he drew her gently down beside him. "Denny, what did that man mean? That watchman on the dock where your ship is? The other day I started to light a cigarette, and I thought he was throwing a fit. He made me put it out."

"Yes, I'll bet he did. You see, they were loading the tanker with naphtha, and it's explosive. That is, the vapor will explode. Worse than gasoline."

"Is that what your ship carries? Denny, don't go. Oh, please! Stay here with me."

"Next time, honey. I've got to make this trip. After that—well, I'll figure something out."

Her body was warm and soft and moved closer, tense with longing. Outside a car passed, crawling up the hill, headlights leaving leaf-shadowed streaks of light on the ceiling, then just a faint trail of sound that washed up against the shores of the night.

Denny McGuire straightened and walked across the deck to the port-side. He was a fool to have left. There were so many girls, but not so many like her. And they had known each other a long time now, in different circumstances and in different towns. So many things could happen on such a ship as this. Even in that situation with Jacobs. Even the best of fighters can make a mistake.

It seemed so long now that all he had known was going, moving, finding the next thing. Part of the time at sea, then fighting, then Arabia and North Africa, and always returning to the sea again. There was something about it that got in the blood. Maybe it was the salt air, or the smell of tar and paint, or the careless comradeship of the men. Anyway, he liked it. There was too little about life these days that a man could sink his teeth into.

Well, it was time to stop. Denny straightened and stared off toward the Matson liner he didn't know was there, miles away steaming its own course through the darkness.

He prided himself on knowing when it was time to leave; it had kept him moving, kept him safe, even saved his life a time or two. In the sands of the Sahara he had been the one to decide it was safer to go than to stay. Three sailors come to see a war on a lark, and he had led them out along with five Spanish Legionnaires, two of them wounded. If Denny McGuire knew anything, it was when the party was over. On his final morning in Los Angeles, in that little house surrounded by eucalyptus and chaparral, he had wondered if he was feeling that way about Faustine, but now he realized he was wrong. It was something else: It was time to come home from the sea, to find a new life.

The heat of the tropical night lay about the ship. All was very still. A vessel of dreams and memories, men whose bodies were present but whose minds defied time and distance: Pete Brouwer, a box bearing the delicate pieces of a once-fine pocket watch at his side, knuckles scraped raw in a fight for which he could not forgive himself, dozed at the galley table. He was one day closer to his home in Holland. And Fritz Schumann, with his geraniums, and his slow, old memories of a beautiful girl, and the sons he had left behind. He was dreaming of going back, of returning again to the shores of that warm island where they waited for him. In his bunk, Davy Jones stirred restlessly, trying to keep from remembering, remembering the looks from people back in Morningside, the debts his mother's illness had caused, debts he could never begin to repay . . . remembering how he had never really wanted to leave home at all.

Out of all of them, it is not surprising that it was Con O'Brien who sensed something wrong. He prowled the passages, the pump room, the engineer's stores. His ship was in danger, and he was searching for the cause. He knew it instantly by the odor. A potato vine of aromatics, a tendril of hydrocarbons. At times the deck of the ship had its chemical smells, but they were wiped clean by the sea breeze. His engine room had its scent of dusty oil and grease. But this was different, a smell that, after loading, after cleansing waves and weeks at sea, should only be found high up the masts at the head of the vent pipes.

He could not find the source of the smell, but it didn't matter. His skin crawled along his burn scars, and he could feel it again, the roar of mechanical death and the lick of flames. Second Engineer O'Brien started for the bridge. He must see the captain; there were procedures that must be started at once.

In the dim light, Mahoney lurked in the locker room forward of the fireman's fo'c'sle. It was hot and close but he didn't want to see anyone, didn't want to talk. Outside the sea-scummed porthole the wake of the ship began, boiling away into the night. Revenge was on his mind—he had his enemies, he had a list . . . oh yes, he had a list.

Mahoney tapped a cigarette against the pack to tamp the tobacco. It was his first smoke since the beating that ruined his lips and broke his nose. He was aching for it, the tobacco. He'd rather have a whiskey, but this would do. He put the smoke between his lips. He struck a match . . .

The narrow space was just inside the open-flame line, but from the portside wing tank, Port Wing Tank Number Seven, that potato vine of fumes leaked, snaking its way into a pocket atop the bunker of fuel beneath his feet. And from there . . .

The explosion tore the fireman's fo'c'sle apart and breached the deck above, a stunning detonation that ripped metal and took the breath from the lungs of Con O'Brien, who was just mounting the ladder to the bridge.

Con turned to look in horror, blinking and nearly blind from the light briefly reflected off the bulkhead in front of him. There was a moment of silence, a diminishing of flame, and then a second huge explosion blossomed from the portside wing tanks. Con was thrown against the ladder by the concussion, but as he started to fall, his hand grasped the rail . . . the instinct to hang on that was ingrained in every seaman. He swung there for a moment, then his feet found the ladder and he turned.

Dropping down the ladder, O'Brien raced toward the towering blaze. His fire station was in the engine room. His ship would not live without pumps to fight the fire or to empty the seawater should it come pouring in. There was no need to warn the captain any longer— his ship needed him.

John Harlan found himself on his knees on the floor in front of his settee. At first he thought the ship had struck something, but then a second shock sent him crashing into the frame of his cabin door, and he knew. He knew what had happened. The one thing that tankermen feared beyond all else.

He plunged into the passage. The alarm bell was ringing, and as he scrambled up the ladder to the captain's deck, the bell stopped and the ship's siren began to wail—fire!

The radio operator's cabin door was locked or jammed. Harlan pounded on it, then as the siren died and the bells began again he backed off and kicked it in. He wanted to shout the man's name to verify that he had made it to the radio room before going automatically to the next item on the list that had been drilled into his brain. But through the porthole a tower of fire illuminated the cabin. The little man lay on the floor, fragments of the shattered port, both glass and the brass frame, embedded in his face and neck. Sparks must have gotten up to see what the trouble was, and now he was on the floor in a widening pool of blood.

Above him, Harlan could hear the shout of commands and knew that Shannon and the Old Man had the bridge. He saw the wash of flame shift and knew they were maneuvering to let the wind carry the fire and heat off to port rather than across the deck. Good God, it hadn't been half a minute since the alarm and already they were reacting. He felt a surge of pride to be serving with such officers. Harlan dove past the fallen man and into the radio room: The SOS was now his responsibility.

Dennis McGuire charged aft along the catwalk above the forward tanks. He crashed through the bridge superstructure and out into the blinding Hades that was the after deck. It seemed crazy to be rushing toward such devastation, but training had taken the place of any source of common sense. A huge hole had appeared in the deck, serrated edges and glowing red tongues of flame licking upward, higher than the derrick masts. That flame was driven forward by the wind as the ship came about and Denny saw the vent pipes begin to flare off. For the moment fireproof gauze protected the tanks but he knew that, as the heat grew, that couldn't last.

He slowed, and a crazy shadow, the running figure of Seaman Jones, appeared, slamming pell-mell into him and carrying them both to the grate of the aft catwalk. The ship's siren and bell were going again. A new message: seven short and one long.

"Abandon Ship."

McGuire jerked the younger man to his feet. "Come on!"

They had lifeboat stations. They were trained for this, but Denny knew—knew as he had never known anything in his life—there was no time for that. His whole existence had been rehearsal for this moment. He had always known when the party was over, when the price of life or freedom was a speedy departure.

They staggered off the catwalk and tumbled along the deck. McGuire dragged Davy to port and, half-blind from the heat and the smoke and the glare, they crashed into the bulwark.

"Jump!" McGuire commanded.

Jones looked at him, uncomprehending.

"Jump and swim! Get as far from the ship as you can—when she goes down she'll suck everything near her under!" He ripped off his singlet and kicked off his shoes. The boy was just starting to do the same when he clambered to the top of the rail and dove.

———

Sam Harrell knew he was going to die. Shell plating was sprung and leaking all along the portside. The pipes for the steam smothering system were broken, pressure streaming away to somewhere. The shaft alley was full of water, and the ship had a heavy, out-of-balance feeling that was even apparent on the grating above the engine. As the *Lichenfield* maneuvered, metal screamed and tore; she was broken in some manner he could barely fathom. A race of burning fuel slithered along the floor plates, Schumann chasing it with a Foamite hose, a nearly useless gesture.

He struggled upward but the hatchway at the top of the boiler room stairs was a wall of flame. O'Brien had crashed through a moment earlier, his hair charred and his eyes wild, but now "Abandon Ship" was sounding and there was no way out. Sam turned, tried to yell to Schumann to get out, to try the ladder in the engine room. He couldn't. He couldn't even get a breath. The rail was scalding, his hand was blistered, and it seemed as if all the air around him was being sucked upward.

Then, through the flame that blocked the hatch, in a searing blast of steam, a blackened gargoyle loomed. Jacobs. Slug Jacobs, hunched over a brass nozzle spewing water. Beating fire back from the passageway, roaring incoherently, he lumbered forward. Behind him on the hose was Shorty Conrad, the water around their feet boiling.

"Come on, Sam!" Shorty yelled through the hatch. Then he urged Slug onward, "Fight it, buddy, beat it back. Let's get these guys outta there!" trying to give confidence to the only man who seemed big enough to attack this inferno. Harrell ducked his head and hurled himself through the door.

Below him in the engine room, O'Brien closed valves and flipped switches with the speed and dexterity of a dancer. The ship was an extension of his body and that body knew what to do in the midst of flame and trauma—slow the ship. Fuel from the starboard tanks would keep the boilers going. Power to the pumps, power to the electrics for the radio and lights. Every minute the ship survived would save lives. He looked around; he was alone. Alone with his engines.

John Harlan sat at the key, trembling. Around him were the gray metal cases of the wireless gear. He had to force his mind to think about the order of switches, the position of dials. Mr. Wesley stopped in the doorway, standing almost at attention. He leaned into the radio office and slapped a piece of paper on the desk. The looping hand of the Old Man was immediately identifiable.

"Our course and approx—approximate position, Mr. Harlan!"

"Very good. Man the boats." Wesley saluted like a soldier and disappeared. Harlan took a breath and bent to his task. His Morse was slow and hesitant . . . and he knew this was it, the end. A captain might or might not be the last man off a sinking ship, but the radio officer stayed until the bitter end, the only hope to bring help. He had struggled so hard to write, to communicate, if only with his children. But now *this* was his job: one last message, one last call into the darkness . . .

Off the starboard side, McGuire plummeted down through the sea. The velvety water closed over him, a cool gloom in which he stretched his powerful muscles, and came to the surface, swimming strongly.

Behind him there was confusion: a hoarse shout, Wesley trying to lower his boat, a jammed pulley causing it to upend and dangle, sending a cascade of men and supplies into the water, a gout of liquid fire rushing and swirling around the plumbing on the deck. Then the night was ripped apart by a terrific, rending blast, a sound so powerful that it was no sound, a deafening, stunning shock wave that crushed and lifted and collapsed.

The sea flamed with the glare of a million suns; a rending, mounting tower of light shooting into the heavens that roared with unholy power and unbelievable grandeur. McGuire dove and swam deep.

When he came up, he glanced back. The sea burned; the ship a groaning monster; dying, twisting, diving. Then the tanker was gone. Only a shadow of something dark beneath the water, only a little turmoil, a bubbling up of debris, the spread of burning oil.

No bobbing heads—no sign of Davy—nothing. Time passed; he had no idea how much. All too soon there was only the starlight and the sea, tranquil and still.

He treaded water. He called out, got a mouthful of brine, and coughed. Would help be coming? Had there been time to get off a message, their location? There hadn't been much time, that was for sure. He was strong, but he was only so strong, and he couldn't tread water forever. He had to make a choice . . . do *something*.

Dennis McGuire took a deep breath and swam. This was what he did—he moved on. He knew how to keep going; keep swimming, keep moving.

A long time later the gray dawn began to turn the sky pale green, and the sea slate gray. His movements were dull and mechanical now. He must be growing tired.

He had never told Shorty about Faustine.

The infinite arch of the sky took on pastel shades, slowly growing brighter and more glorious. In all the vast sweep of sea there was nothing, nothing but his head inches above the water.

In the east the sun lifted its fiery brows and threw a brilliant glare into his eyes. The dull gray escaped mysteriously, and the sea was scattered with cascades of glowing, lambent light. It lifted higher and higher, and the waves licked at his naked shoulders like blazing swords. East. That way was home.

His arms moved queerly now, like those of an automaton. He seemed no longer physical, but some strange entity without soul or consciousness. He seemed to be floating above his swimming body. He swam through the molten metal of the sea into the opening rose of the sun, swimming . . . swimming . . . swimming.

Somewhere off to the south, the radio officer of the Matson liner had noted the time and written in a small book: "Received a fragment of a message. Possibly an SOS but did not have time to get a bearing."

Above him, the third mate walked the bridge, yawning. He had heard a dull, distant boom before sunrise, but the flare that lighted the sky for an instant had come when his back was turned, walking the other way.

Concerned, Jerry, the radio man, clutched the phones to his ears, but there were no further sounds other than the buzz and hum of the universe and the interference of the ship's own electrics. He began tapping away as the night turned to dawn, raising other ships, asking if anyone was in distress . . . but there was nothing.

As he waited for a response, he began to dream, dozing at the key, head on his desk. He would be leaving the Radio Service in a few weeks, headed home to Raiatea, where the surf made a mist above the reefs and palm trees rustled in the breeze above white sand beaches.

They would be waiting for him, as they had waited so long for his father. He had seen the world, but now the good island people would welcome him home.

Eventually, he signed off: "Dot, dot, dot. Dash, dot, dash."

SK

End of contact.

Silent Key.

AFTERWORD

Reconstructing this book has been much like the work of an archaeologist excavating, then rebuilding the ruins of an ancient city. The truth was well preserved, but scattered and deeply buried. I had considered working on it several times since Dad passed away, but it was not until just recently that I felt I knew enough about my father's life and had enough control over my own abilities to really do it justice.

The only existing manuscript of *No Traveller Returns* seemed to consist of several attempts that had been roughly patched together. This was not surprising: Louis mentioned a number of times that he had stopped and started, and on other occasions that he was trying to rewrite it. After I'd considered the manuscript over many years, the intent of the entire piece and the detailed trajectory of the different characters finally became clear to me.

As always, I have attempted to apply as light a hand as possible while still delivering a manuscript that is professionally polished and contains some important elements that were implied by, but not specifically contained in, the original text. That said, what I have done here is considerably more than an editing job. Reading between the lines, I have struggled to discover what this story was trying to become, and the goals that Dad had in mind when he first created it. Completing and enhancing those elements without straying too far afield from his original manuscript was the most significant challenge.

In a few minor cases that meant leaving certain details, which I know to be incorrect, alone—they were my father's memories of other types of ships or earlier days in port. Those problematic elements were important pieces of Louis's life, and so I felt they should remain. However, I have attempted to make all of the other aspects of shipboard and portside life in the 1930s as accurate as possible. Of course, one can always do better, so if you notice a mistake it is probably mine.

"Write what you know" is an oft-repeated axiom about the business of being an author. It may be interpreted by beginners as "Only write what you already know," whereas the more mature approach might be "Educate yourself and get to know the subject you are going to write about." Luckily, there are as many ways to tell stories as there are writers to tell them.

Educating himself was the route Dad took as he created the Westerns and many other research-inspired stories that made up the bulk of his career. But *No Traveller Returns* is about a world Louis L'Amour knew from firsthand experience . . . and it is certainly his most personal novel.

Following that bit of advice about getting to know your subject, I have gone to great lengths to learn about my father, the times he lived in, and the jobs he worked. It's very likely that I know more about his early days than he would have been entirely comfortable with, but there is no question that I now have a pretty good sense of what his life was like before I came along.

In the few years he spent at sea, Louis *did* serve on a tanker, though not one as large or modern as the fictional SS *Lichenfield*. And he did experience a chemical fire on board a ship: at a dock in Salford, England, where part of a two-thousand-ton cargo of sulfur went ablaze. Though it seems to have been rapidly controlled, both the fire and the fumes could have been extremely dangerous. He also went to sea on at least one ship where the deck crew and the black gang were divided into rival factions, and disputes were settled with fists and improvised weapons. One such dispute, in this case between members of the engine crew, was severe enough to end with a man being slapped in irons and crew members, including Louis, being taken before the U.S. Consul in Singapore.

Dad's ship at Balikpapan, N.E.I., about two weeks before the trouble broke out.

In San Pedro, the Port of Los Angeles, Louis did spend time living hand to mouth in a manner sailors termed "on the beach." He applied for work at the Marine Services Bureau, or what the union men called the "Slave Market" or "Fink Hall." He slept at the Seamen's Church Institute when he had the money, and in gaps in the lumber piles on the E.K. Dock when he didn't. He rented one of the squatter's shacks for a time and went mano a mano with several of the rougher denizens of Happy Valley. He also "bucked rivets" in a shipyard.

However, it is the people, the characters of *No Traveller Returns*, that have the most interesting intersection with my father's life. Throughout the rest of his career, it was very rare for Louis to use anyone he personally knew as a character in one of his stories, or to even model a character after a person he had known. But in this novel,

many of the characters are either closely associated with or specifically intended to portray men that he had lived and worked with in
the 1920s and early 1930s.

The inspirations for the drunkards and thieves of Happy Valley—
Fitzpatrick, "Russian Fred," Dynamite, and "Frisco" Grady—are all
mentioned multiple times in Louis's journals or notes. Louis claims to
have known the real-life model for "Tex" Worden, though I am not
sure when they went to sea together.

The real versions of Shorty Conrad and Pete Brouwer accompa-
nied Dad on his first trip to sea and are reported to have been much
as they are portrayed in this story. Pete was truly the sailor who, as in
Eugene O'Neill's *The Long Voyage Home*, was forever going home, and
Shorty did have a past in Australia, as well as a facility with musical
instruments. Together they visited the American Bar in Liverpool
and the Old Trafford Inn in Manchester. Other bars that Louis visited
which are mentioned in *No Traveller Returns* are the Maypole Bar in
Singapore and the Dutch Club in Balikpapan; however, that was with
another ship and another crew.

The American Bar in Liverpool circa 2004

The most mysterious characters in this story, however, are the ones that I believe Louis modeled on himself. While Davy Jones is very much the way I imagine Dad to have been when he first set out on his own, he might not have admitted to Davy's level of naiveté and vulnerability. And John Harlan is like Louis in many ways, but much more mature than my father was even at the time this book was written; he is almost like a fictional model for the man Louis L'Amour would eventually become. Strangest of all is Dennis McGuire, who seems to be some sort of idealized image that Louis had of himself . . . or a romantic version of how he would like to have been seen by others.

Adventurer, storyteller, boxer, ladies' man—all of these were actual aspects of Louis's character. They may be somewhat exaggerated in McGuire, yet they directly reflect the way in which Louis was attempting to sell himself to the public at the time he was writing *No Traveller Returns*. He had not yet become the modest and thoughtful John Harlan.

To take things in a stranger direction, the original manuscript (prior to my revisions) contained many references to how much the other characters liked, approved of, respected, or were impressed by Dennis McGuire. He was described in glowing terms by the third-person narrator, too. I'm not sure exactly what was going on with all of this adulation. Perhaps it was ego or insecurity. Perhaps Dad was trying to discover some version of himself that the public would accept. Whatever it was and however ill-advised it may have been, it was a learning experience for later in life, when he more confidently and humbly assumed the role of a celebrity.

Additionally, the inspirations for a good deal of Louis's later fiction run all through this first novel. Most obvious is the inclusion, nearly verbatim, of the short story "Survival," which chronicles Tex Worden's struggle in the wake of the sinking of the *Rarotonga*. The story of Fritz Schumann's voyage to Raiatea and his besting of Captain Wallace Benson is remarkably like Louis's "The Dancing Kate," and Raoul Carmody's fatal adventure on the Chilean coast echoes Louis's yet-unpublished novel *Sky Ring Water* . . . which was not even written until 1960 or so.

There is also the inclusion of what later became my favorite line from the novel *Conagher.* When Duck Stevens, a crewman from the *Johnson City,* notices Shorty Conrad's black eye, he asks: "Who gave you the black eye?" To which Shorty replies, "Nobody *gave* it to me! I fought for it!" In reality that was a line my father heard while hanging around the bunkhouse at the Katherine Mine in Arizona.

However, for me, the oddest story in *No Traveller Returns* is the description of the death of Engineer Augie Donato's brother:

> Al had gone over that hill going at least seventy, and a truck loaded with pipe had been parked right there. What they buried was only part of Al. Hell, if they'd buried him all they'd have had to bury his car, the rear end of the truck, and about fourteen lengths of pipe.

That was almost exactly the story that Louis used to tell about the death of his adopted brother, Jack. Jack was a lively little guy, similar to the character of Shorty Conrad. He lived life to the fullest, and according to my father (who didn't drive at all) tended to drive too fast.

John Otto Lamoore, known to my father as "Jack", not long before his death in 1946

It wasn't until I reached out to Jack's family, many years after my father's death, that I learned for certain that he did indeed die from being decapitated in a collision with a pipe truck, though not in a dramatic, high-speed accident like the one described above. His death was caused by a slowly reversing semi in the parking lot of a baseball stadium, the driver of which had no idea, until it was too late, that he had backed into the car in which Jack was a passenger.

The truly weird thing is that Jack died six to eight years *after* this book was written . . . yet, for the rest of his life, whenever Louis told the story of his adopted brother's death, he told the version from this, his unpublished novel.

That's a pretty good example of just how confusing it can be to live with a fiction writer!

I'm sure that there will be some discussion of the language, morality, sense of history, politics, and philosophy contained in *No Traveller Returns*, since they are somewhat different from what is regularly found in many of Louis L'Amour's Westerns. Although I have done quite a bit of revision on this novel, I have left untouched as many of the elements of Louis's writing style from the late 1930s as I could. Specifically, I have not significantly added to or subtracted from any of the items mentioned above, nor did I alter any of Louis's 1930s-era commentary on climate change or Japanese intentions in the Pacific . . . both of which might be considered mildly prophetic.

The *Yondering* stories (though Louis didn't think of calling them that at the time) were written for a completely different sort of audience than his Westerns. In the 1930s, Louis was quite proud to be writing material that would have been considered "realistic," or even risqué. Nor did he shy away from such characterizations later, near the end of his career, presenting the material in the collection *Yondering* without revision.

All in all, Louis was much more of a man of the world than the Western genre would often allow. He loved writing of Arizona and Colorado, the wide-open prairies and the far, blue mountains, but his real life also played itself out in remote parts of the Indies and the Middle East, the bustle of New York and Shanghai, on the waterfronts of Liverpool and San Pedro. Those were different worlds with different rules.

No Traveller Returns may have been Dad's nostalgic farewell to those days and those people. When the war took him away from working on this manuscript in 1942, Louis was trying to pull strings to get a commission in the Navy, difficult if not impossible to wrangle because he hadn't gone to college. Later, before he was shipped to Europe, he was briefly made an Army cargo-control officer in the port of Oakland, California, and he expected to be placed in a similar position somewhere in the Pacific. It would have been a near-perfect use of his abilities, since he knew the world of longshoremen and merchant sailors.

That situation was not in the stars, however. Orders put him on a train that gathered officers from all across the country. No one knew it at the time, but they were bound for England and the Normandy invasion. When he boarded the freighter that traveled in convoy from New York to his old stomping grounds in Liverpool, it would be the last time he would ever sail on a merchant ship . . . and the pages of this novel remained in a binder in Choctaw, Oklahoma, a binder that was rarely opened until after his death.

A last note: The novel takes its title from the famed "To Be or Not to Be" soliloquy in Shakespeare's *Hamlet:* "The undiscovered country, from whose bourn no traveller returns." Though the "undiscovered country" to which the Bard refers is the land of the dead (certainly the destination of the crewmen of the steamship *Lichenfield*), the quote had an additional meaning for my father. As John Harlan suggests in this work and as Louis wrote in the text of his 1979 novel *Bendigo Shafter,* "no traveller returns" refers, in Louis's alternate interpretation, to the process of maturing as a person. As our lives are changed by travel or experience, our bodies may return to the same places we have long known, but in our hearts we are no longer the same. So it was with this book. Given all its resonances with other aspects of Louis's life, and even though it has remained unpublished for three-quarters of a century, it is obvious that writing it was a journey that changed Louis substantially. *No Traveller Returns* is a well from which much else was drawn.

I sincerely hope you have enjoyed it.

Beau L'Amour
November 2018

GLOSSARY

ABAFT THE FORM'ST—behind the foremast or first mast.

ADEN—a British possession or protectorate (now part of Yemen) and an important refueling station for merchant and naval shipping.

AFT—the rear of the ship.

AFTER HOUSE—the structure in a ship's stern.

AIR HAMMER—an automatic hammer or chisel powered by compressed air, used to cut or shape metal.

BARK/BARQUE—a square-rigged sailing ship with three or more masts, the aftmost of which is rigged with fore and aft sails. An elegant compromise of speed and maneuverability.

BEACON STREET—a street just off the waterfront in San Pedro, California. The central four blocks of Beacon Street housed a large number of bars and bordellos, and was known for many years as one of the toughest neighborhoods in the world. While the street itself still exists, the majority of its infamous businesses were removed by bulldozer and wrecking ball in the early 1970s.

BITTS—pairs of heavy metal posts used to secure the mooring lines of a ship.

Black gang—the crew of a ship's engineering department, so called because in the old days coal dust and soot stained their clothes and skin.

Black Maria—a "paddy wagon" (a police van or truck for transporting prisoners).

Blackfella—Australian slang for an Indigenous Australian or Aborigine.

Blackjack—a short club, usually with a core of dense material to increase its weight and connected to a handle to make it easier to hold on to.

Boat deck—the deck where the ship's lifeboats are stored, often above the main deck.

Boat station—the lifeboat that a crewman is assigned to in an emergency.

Bridge—the centrally located room containing a ship's navigational controls. Sometimes the entire multifloor central deckhouse on a ship is referred to as "the bridge," and in that case the command center might be known as the navigation bridge or the wheelhouse.

Bridge wing—the thin strip of decking that stretches from the enclosed bridge area to the sides of the ship. From the bridge wing it is often easier to look forward and aft and to see how close the ship is to a dock or other obstacle.

Bull Durham sack—a small cloth sack of loose-leaf tobacco.

Bull of Barney—a fierce wind, blowing like an angry bull. Probably a reference to John Masefield's "Sing a Song o' Shipwreck."

The Bund—the riverfront area that housed the mercantile exchanges and banks of the International Settlement, or "Treaty Port," of Shanghai, China.

The Bunk—nonsense.

Burner—the system in the firebox that spreads burning oil beneath the boiler. Burners had to be regularly cleaned because of the heavy impure fuel many ships burned.

"Call the watch"—Just before the end of a ship's four-hour watch, one member of that shift goes around and reminds the next group that it's nearly time to go to work.

Canned heat—jellied alcohol used for heating food. When squeezed through a cloth filter, the resulting "sock wine" can be consumed as a cheap, though quite poisonous, alternative to liquor.

CANVAS DODGER—a strip of cloth set up in foul weather to protect a seaman from spray.

CAPE STIFF—sailor's slang for Cape Horn, at the southernmost tip of South America. The wind and waves of Cape Horn made it some of the roughest sailing in the world.

CATWALK—For stability reasons, tankers were built to sit as low in the water as possible. The catwalk allowed sailors access to the forward and aft "islands" of the ship without having to descend to the often wave-swept maze of pipes and valves on the main deck.

CELEBES—an island in Indonesia now known as Sulawesi.

CHART ROOM—Usually situated behind the wheelhouse, the chart room holds the ship's library of charts and the instruments used to plot courses and navigate.

CHIPPING RUST—On a ship, surface rust or blistering is scraped or chipped away and then the area is repainted.

CHISEL BUM—a mildly derogatory term for sailors often used by the engine crew. It refers to the chiseling away of rust and then re-painting that is the constant job of a seaman from the deck crew.

CHRONOMETER—a ship's clock. Marine chronometers are specifically built to remain accurate despite the motion of the ship and changes of humidity and air pressure. They are used alongside astronomical sightings to determine the ship's longitude.

CLEW—the lower corner or connecting point of a sail. On board the *Lichenfield* it might refer to a metal loop attached to the corner of a canvas awning, or "dodger."

COAL-BOX ATOP THE GALLEY—a receptacle for holding the fuel for the galley's stove.

COASTWISE RUN—a predictable shipping route that serves ports in the same general locality. A coastal service job would allow for a known schedule and the ability to spend regular time at home.

COMPANIONWAY—usually a passage leading up or down; other times just a passage.

COMPASS BINNACLE—the magnetically compensated console that holds a ship's compass.

COOK BAY—the western approach to the Beagle Channel on the Chilean side of Tierra del Fuego. It is to the northwest of Cape Horn.

COPRA—coconut meat.

CORK FENDER—a net or bag of rope containing cork. Fenders keep a ship from hitting its hull against the dock.

CUT PLUG—tobacco. A plug is a condensed mass of tobacco rather than loose leaves. Pieces can be cut or bitten off as needed.

DAVY JONES'S LOCKER—Davy Jones is a seaman's version of the devil, so his "locker" is a bit like hell. "Davy Jones's locker" is the bottom of the sea.

DEVIL'S ISLAND—A section of a larger system of prisons situated in French Guiana that specifically dealt with political prisoners. "Devil's Island" may refer to any of the Guiana prisons, because conditions in all of them were very harsh. Few who were transported to Guiana ever returned to France.

DHOW—Typically an Arab or Indian sailing ship sporting one or more lateen sails; large triangular fore and aft sails hung from a long angled yardarm.

DOCKMAN—a longshoreman. One of the crew of laborers who loads and unloads ships.

EUROPA—a highly advanced German passenger liner built in 1928.

FIDDLE—the edge or lip around a table or stovetop that keeps plates from sliding off in rough weather.

FIDDLER'S GREEN—the afterlife for sailors. A place full of music and dance. The opposite of Davy Jones's locker.

FIDDLY—the trunk or shaft above the boilers or engines, used for ventilation and servicing the heaviest mechanical elements. At its top is a skylight that can be propped open in good weather. The Fiddly often contains an access ladder or stairway, and in the days of steamships, crewmen would commonly string a clothesline across it to use the heat of the boilers to dry their clothes.

FIREBOXES—Situated under the boilers, these provide the heat which generates steam to drive the ship's turbine.

FLOPHOUSE—a hotel offering the most minimal of accommodations, intended for transients or hoboes. A small step up from the crudest of homeless shelters.

FLYING BRIDGE—an exposed control station situated on the roof of a ship's wheelhouse with reasonably unobstructed views in all directions.

FO'C'SLE OR FO'C'STLE—contractions of "forecastle," originally meaning the deckhouse in the forward part of a ship where the crew's quarters are situated. Eventually the term came to refer to the crew's bunkroom, wherever it was situated. On the *Lichenfield*, it was housed in the aft part of the ship, with quarters split in two: the "Firemen," or engineering crew, on one side and the "Seamen" on the other.

FO'C'STLEHEAD or FORECASTLE HEAD—the triangular deck atop the forecastle in the bow of a ship. This is usually the spot where the anchor winches are situated; it is common for a sailor on lookout to be stationed there in good weather.

FORCED DRAFT—the mechanical air supply for the fireboxes.

FORESTAY—the cable stretching from the ship's foremast to the bow. Though most steamships do not carry sails, the "masts" are used as part of the cargo loading equipment, to support antennas, lights, signal flags; on tankers, they also serve as a trunk for the pipes that vent the cargo tanks.

FOR'RD BULKHEAD—forward bulkhead. A bulkhead on a ship is a lateral dividing wall, often reinforced and watertight in case of accident.

GAFF TOPSAIL or GAFF TOPS'L—the triangular sail that stretches between the topmast and gaff (the spar along the top of the mainsail) on a fore and aft rigged ship.

GALLEY SKYLIGHT—the skylight over a ship's kitchen. Ships never let their stoves get cold, so a vented skylight was necessary to allow the hot air to escape.

GANDY DANCERS—railroad track workers. A "gandy" is a tool for aligning the rails, but it is not certain whether Gandy Dancers got their name from it or if it got its name from them.

GANGWAY—also known as an accommodation ladder. It is a hinged ramp or stairway attached to the side of a ship that allows access to a wharf or landing stage.

GAOL—A synonym for jail, the term was more commonly used in the British Empire before WWI.

GEAR—the winches and derricks and lines used to load and unload cargo. A tanker might use its gear to manage heavy hoses.

GENERATOR—a device used to generate electricity for the ship's lights and electric apparatus.

HAJJI—the title of respect given to a Muslim who has completed the pilgrimage to Mecca. It is also a term, usually used by Westerners, for Muslims on their way to Mecca.

HALF-SWACKED—mostly drunk.

HAPPY VALLEY—a poor shantytown in a narrow draw behind San Pedro's Beacon Street.

HATCH COVERS—wooden planks fitted inside the metal frame of a ship's cargo hatches. Several layers of canvas are stretched over them and then tightened around the hatch frames with wedges.

HEAD—the name for a ship's toilet.

HEIDELBERG UNIVERSITY—one of the most prestigious schools in Germany. Its student organizations were once known for a particular style of fencing which, while not specifically intended to cause significant injury, often left distinctive scars. "Heidelberg scars" were a mark of pride among upper-class German men.

JACKSTAFF—a short flagpole in the bow of a ship.

JONAH—a sailor's term for a person who is believed to be a jinx or bad luck.

LADDER—a term used on ships for both stairways and typical vertical ladders. Many stairways on ships are steeply angled to save space.

THE LINE—the equator.

LOOSE THE FALLS—prepare to lower something with pulleys, in this case a lifeboat.

LUCKENBACH BOAT—a ship belonging to the Luckenbach Steamship Co., a very successful American shipping line started in 1850.

LYLE GUN—a small cannon used for shooting a rope to another vessel, intended for use in rescue operations.

MAINM'ST—mainmast.

MANIFEST FREIGHT TRAIN—a train with a mixture of cars: boxcars, tank cars, flatcars, and so on. These are often slow-moving, low-priority trains, that are reshuffled at many rail yards along a route, and it takes a "manifest," or list, of what is on the train to be sure that all the cars get to their intended destinations.

MARLINSPIKE—a tool used for working with rope or cable. Similar in many ways to a hickory fid.

MINDANOU—another spelling for Mindanao, the southernmost island in the Philippines.

NAPHTHA—a name for various highly volatile petroleum products.

ON YOUR PIN—on your watch or shift.

OPEN-FLAME LINE—According to one of the sources for this book, some (or maybe all) tankers had the safe areas for exposed flame marked on the deck. Inside these safety lines, the engine room and galley were situated; it was also a place where a crewman could smoke, if he hadn't already taken up chewing tobacco.

PACIFIC ELECTRIC or PE—a light rail system that connected the outlying communities with Los Angeles. It also operated regular streetcars and buses, and lasted from 1903 until 1961.

PEARL SHELL—Mother-of-pearl, from the inside of oyster shells, was a valuable product until synthetic materials came into widespread use. Before cultured pearls, the pearls used in jewelry were so rare that it was not worth looking for them. Prior to WWII, any moderately sized pearl of good shape and color was extremely valuable.

PILOTHOUSE—another name for a ship's wheelhouse.

PLIMSOLL MARKS—markings on a ship's side that indicate the maximum load it can carry in different densities of water.

POOP DECK—the raised deck in the stern of some ships.

PUMP ROOM—the space that houses a tanker ship's pumps and cargo plumbing, and a critical spot in terms of safety.

PUNTA ARENAS—the southernmost city of significant size in Chile.

RAT GUARDS—cones which when fitted around the mooring lines of a ship prevent rats from climbing aboard.

RATING—rank.

RED BALL FREIGHT—a train with priority routing along the tracks; a "fast" freight.

RED-LEAD—lead oxide paint primer.

Rigging—the system of ropes used to control a sailing ship's sails and to stabilize its masts.

Rigging the booms—unlimbering the cargo derricks from the manner in which they are secured at sea and preparing them to handle cargo.

A roll—a roll of money; a lot of money.

Rolled him—robbed him.

Romeos—low slip-on boots.

Royal yard—one of the horizontal spars (from which a sail is hung) closest to the top of the masts on a large square-rigged sailing ship.

Running lights—As a way of signaling their position and heading to one another, ships always display a red light on their port, or left, side and a green light on their starboard, or right, side. When ships cross paths, the ship on the starboard side has the right-of-way.

Saloon—the dining and reception area used by a ship's senior officers.

San Pedro—the Port of the City of Los Angeles. Due south of Los Angeles proper, it has been at times one of the busiest ports in the world.

Schooner—a sailing ship with two or more masts, the lower sails of which are fore- and aft-rigged and on which the foremast is smaller than the mainmast.

Scuppers—the holes or gaps that allow water to drain from a deck.

Sea boots and oilskins—a sailor's foul-weather gear. Sea boots are very much like a waterproof "Wellington" boot, and oilskins were so named because they were often made of canvas coated with linseed oil to help them shed water.

Seas—Besides what you'd expect, this is also a term for individual waves, usually large ones.

Set of tops—slang for dice. The term was based on a type of dice with a pin through their centers that could be spun like a child's top. Crooked "tops" had a weight inside that could be adjusted to make the dice fall a certain way.

Shacks—slang for a train's brakeman. In the late nineteenth and early twentieth century, the brakeman's job evolved from the delicate business of braking a train without automatic air brakes to being a multipurpose member of a train's crew.

SHIPFITTER—a worker in a ship repair or construction facility, often a steelworker.

SHOT OF THE SUN—At noon a ship's officers, each using his own sextant (a device for measuring angles), takes an independent measurement of the height of the sun compared with the horizon. These are compared to discover the ship's latitude, and in conjunction with the ship's clocks and other celestial sightings a ship's position is determined. The "noon sight" is the foundation of marine navigation.

SIGN THE ARTICLES—sign onto a ship. The "Articles of Shipping" are the contract between the ship and its crew.

SILENT KEY—SK in Morse code. SK stands for "end of transmission," but a "silent key" is also a term for an operator (or station, or call sign) that has died.

SING SING—a notorious prison in Ossining, New York.

SINGLET—a sleeveless shirt like a tank top.

SLAVE MARKET—San Pedro's Marine Services Bureau was one of a number of nonunion employment agencies for sailors. Union and nonunion men alike called these operations "Fink Hall" or the "Slave Market."

SLUM—slang for terrible food, usually the sort of greasy stew served to large groups like construction workers or ship crews, or at soup kitchens.

SOOGEY RAG—a cleaning rag. "Soogey" was a term for various cleaning solutions, often soda and water.

THE SORBONNE—Located in Paris, it is one of the oldest universities in the world.

SOU'WESTER—an oilskin rain hat with a long back to keep water from running down a sailor's collar.

SPANNER—a wrench. Some wrenches used on ships are very large and heavy.

SPARS—the horizontal or diagonal poles that sails hang from.

SPLICE THE MAIN BRACE—to have a drink. Named for a difficult, often emergency, operation used to repair sailing ship rigging; afterward, you need a drink to celebrate or to calm your nerves.

STACK OF WHEATS—pancakes.

STARB'RD HALF DOOR—an access point (in this case on the right side) in the hull of some ships used for loading cargo into the lower decks.

STEAM STEERING GEAR—the "power steering" system for a steamship. Instead of the rudder being controlled by direct muscle power from the wheel on the bridge, the wheel activates a steam-powered set of gears.

STEERING BY DEGREES—using a more sophisticated, 360-degree compass rather than the older 32-point compass.

STEERING BY POINTS—The basic points on a compass rose are north, south, east, and west, but they are split and split again into elements like north-north-west until a full thirty-two points are reached. "Boxing the Compass" is an exercise in which a seaman names all thirty-two points.

STERN SHEETS—the rearward, or after part, of a ship or boat.

STEW BUM—a drunk or a drunken vagrant.

STOKEHOLE—the area, often straddling the width of the ship, where the fireboxes and boilers are serviced. In the days when ships burned coal, "stokers" would shovel coal into the fireboxes. On oil-burning ships, it is where the firemen would adjust and maintain the firebox systems and monitor the water for the boilers. This area is also known as the boiler room or the fire room.

STOPPER KNOT—a knot that prevents a rope from paying out or slipping back through a device by establishing a usable length out of a longer piece of rope.

STOVE IN—broken, collapsed.

STROP—Stropping a straight razor along a piece of canvas or leather straightens (and thereby "sharpens") the nearly invisible edge of the blade.

TAFFRAIL—the railing around a ship's stern.

TAILOR-MADES—mass-produced or prerolled cigarettes.

TANK FARM—a cluster of tanks used to store or load oil or chemicals.

TAUDENI—a salt mine in modern-day Mali. Before World War II it was reputed to be the site of a secretive French penal colony, considered a more horrible prison than Devil's Island.

TERMINAL ISLAND—the island that forms the south or seaward side of the San Pedro ship channel.

THREE SHEETS TO THE WIND—slang for intoxicated. The reference is to a sailing ship with poorly set sails that is at or nearing the point of being out of control.

TIBESTI—an area of northern Chad.

TINHORN—a braggart, or a person pretending to be important, possibly named after the cup that is used to shake dice.

TURBINE—Ships like the SS *Lichenfield* get their power from steam turbines like the ones used in municipal power stations. Steam pressure from boilers turns the turbines, which, after going through a series of gears, turn the propeller.

UP TRACKS—the Union Pacific Railroad.

VENT PIPES—pipes that release the vapor from a tanker's cargo tanks. They end high above the deck to allow the wind to carry away any dangerous fumes.

VENTILATORS—occasionally known as wind scoops, the large hornlike tubes that are seen on ships' decks. They allow wind or the forward motion of the ship to funnel air into the cargo holds and engine spaces.

WAKE—the trail of disturbed water behind a ship.

WASTE—leftover or otherwise useless cloth used for janitorial duties.

WATCH STANDING AND BELLS—Seamen's traditional watches are four hours long. They stand the same watch both A.M. and P.M., so a man on the eight-to-twelve watch will work from eight in the morning until noon and then from eight in the evening until midnight. Watches are divided into eight thirty-minute sections, each of them marked by a bell. Thus, when a sailor hears eight bells, his watch is over.

WHEELHOUSE—the cabin on the navigating bridge that contains the ship's wheel.

WINCH—a motorized or steam-powered mechanism for winding up or letting out cable. Winches are used in conjunction with the ship's derrick arms to hoist and move cargo.

WINDJAMMER—a sailing ship.

WING TANK—Tanker ships carry liquid products in a number of individual tanks to prevent liquid from shifting or sloshing too much in heavy seas. The wing tanks are on the sides, as opposed to the tanks placed along the centerline of the vessel.

WIRELESS—early radio equipment. Before it was practical to communicate over long distances by voice, shipboard communications were transmitted and received by radio using Morse code. The ship's radioman, or "Sparks," would often be an employee of a radio service, which supplied not only the operator but the equipment itself. One of the best known was Marconi's Wireless Telegraph Company.

ACKNOWLEDGMENTS

Obviously, none of this work would exist without my father, but in addition to the original manuscript I was lucky to have access to his thoughts on both going to sea and life in San Pedro. I not only got to record interviews with him, but he also left behind journals, short stories, and notes about those long-ago days. I'd also like to note the work of Howard Pease, a writer of my father's era whom I read in my early teens. That material taught me things about the life of a merchant seaman my father could not and inspired me to revisit this story time and time again. Additionally, my great friend Michael Pizzuto was good enough to lend me his apartment in San Pedro so that I could more easily visit the archives there and get a feel for the location.

Over the years Paul O'Dell, Jeanne Brown, and Charles Van Eman have helped me find and organize thousands of pages of material on my dad, and Marleene Boyd from the Bill Laxon Maritime Library at the New Zealand Maritime Museum was a valued resource. Liz Ruth-Abramian from the Los Angeles Maritime Museum and Anne Hansford of the San Pedro Bay Historical Society were very generous with their time, knowledge, and copious archives. Janna Jones was gracious enough to both read this manuscript in its developmental stages and offer many thoughtful comments. I would also be truly remiss if I didn't thank my lovely mother, who has continually cheered me on in my quest to discover more about my father and her husband. I couldn't have done it without her—heck, I wouldn't even be me without her! Thanks, Mom!

ABOUT THE AUTHORS

Our foremost storyteller of the American West, Louis L'Amour has also thrilled readers with his work in the adventure, crime, and science fiction genres. He wrote ninety-one novels, a book of poetry, and over two hundred short stories. There are more than three hundred million copies of his books in print around the world.

Beau L'Amour is an author, art director, and editor. He has also worked in the film, television, magazine, and recording industries. Since 1988 he has been the manager of the estate of his father, Louis L'Amour.

louislamour.com
louislamourslosttreasures.com

ABOUT THE TYPE

This book was set in a Monotype face called Bell. The Englishman John Bell (1745–1831) was responsible for the original cutting of this design. The vocations of Bell were many—bookseller, printer, publisher, typefounder, and journalist, among others. His types were considerably influenced by the delicacy and beauty of the French copperplate engravers. Monotype Bell might also be classified as a delicate and refined rendering of Scotch Roman.